OVATIONS FOR
THE FAITH ABBEY MYSTERY SERIES

A Matter of Roses

" . . . an intriguing and shapely mystery."
–Chicago Tribune

"This promising first installment in the Faith Abbey mystery series introduces a contemporary, monastic sleuth in the tradition of Brother Cadfael. . . . Well-developed characters, an authentic eastern Massachusetts location (shades of Jane Langton's mysteries) and a complex plot make this a gripping read."
–Publishers Weekly

"*A Matter of Roses* is a page-turner that keeps the reader guessing till the end. It also provides engaging subplots. . . ."
–Cape Cod Guide

A Matter of Diamonds

"Tense and enthralling."
–The Detroit Free Press

"Filled with likable characters who struggle with their lives and callings whether secular or sacred, this is not just Brother Cadfael updated, but a thoroughly thought-out observation about the sacred and the profane in our contemporary world, and the importance of determining one's role in that world."
–Kates's Mystery Books Newsletter

"Manuel's characters are refreshingly complex for a mystery novel, making this not so much a 'whodunit' as a 'whydunit.' The cliffhanger ending will pique readers' interest in the next installment of Bartholomew's adventures."
–Publishers Weekly

"I cared about the way in which Manuel made an idea into a diamond; he holds it up to the light and lets it glimmer in all its prismatic glory and invites you to open your thoughts to different perspectives. This is a mystery that, for all its frantic activity, is punctuated with quiet thoughts and refreshing perspectives."
–The Mystery Review

A Matter of Time

" . . . a tight, complex plot and a varied cast of characters, *A Matter of Time* is a multi-faceted page-turner."
–The Cape Codder

A MATTER
of PRINCIPLE

a faith abbey mystery

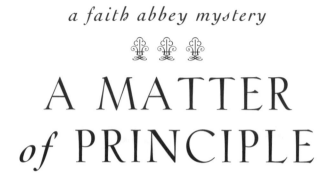

A MATTER
of PRINCIPLE

DAVID MANUEL

PARACLETE PRESS
BREWSTER, MASSACHUSETTS

Library of Congress Cataloging-in-Publication Data

Manuel, David.
    A matter of principle : a Faith Abbey mystery / David Manuel.
       p.   cm.
    ISBN 1-55725-346-3
    1. Bartholomew, Brother (Fictitious character)–Fiction. 2.
Americans–Spain–Fiction. 3. Pamplona (Spain)–Fiction.
4. Pyrennes–Fiction. 5. Monks–Fiction. I. Title.
    PS3563.A5747M377 2003
    813' .54–dc21

                                 2003015248

This book is a work of fiction. Names, characters, and incidents are either products of the author's imagination or are used fictitiously. Any resemblance to actual events, or persons, living or dead, is coincidental

10 9 8 7 6 5 4 3 2 1

ISBN 1-55725-346-3

Published by Paraclete Press
Brewster, Massachusetts
www.paracletepress.com

Printed in the United States of America.

For
two good friends
who know the meaning
of tough love

editor/publisher
Lillian Miao
whose intuition
is priceless

and

master of the mysterious
Barbara Peters
who taught me
what a caper was

acknowledgments

It seems that no matter how meticulously one fine-tooths a manuscript or galleys or page proofs, invariably a typo—or a misspelling or a grammatically infelicitous usage—will find its way into print. Paraclete Press's master copyeditor Robert J. Edmonson catches nearly everything, and my brother Bill and his wife Christy nab the bits that elude Bob. Even so, one or two manage to evade detection.

A MATTER
of PRINCIPLE

1 | night visitor

As spring pried loose winter's iron grip on the southern Pyrenees, night fog was not uncommon. This evening it was impenetrable. The light from the balcony window of the mayor's office on the second floor barely reached the fountain in the center of the square.

The chandelier above the mayor's desk flickered but did not go out. Electricity had only recently come to Pamplona. The mayor's office was its first recipient, and the portly, prosperous magistrate was taking full advantage of it, working on the speech he would read from the balcony to launch their fiesta.

He glanced at the bullfight poster on the wall. Come July, the two most popular matadors of 1917 would be fighting bulls in their *corrida*. Pamplona might be a poor town, a farmers' town, but once a year it rivaled the grandest cities of Spain. Their *Fiesta de San Fermín* was second to none.

Taking a final drag on his cigar before adding what was left of it to the butts overflowing the cut-glass ashtray, he balled up the page he'd been working on and started again. It had been a long night.

Beyond the open door a floorboard creaked. Craning around to see his visitor, he forced a smile. "A little late, is it not, Dom Esteban? Should you not be up the hill, observing Grand Silence?"

The cowled, gray-robed figure entered. He did not return the smile. "I've come for San Fermín and Santa Benedicta," he announced.

"The statues? We loaded them on the train last week. You know that."

"Get them back."

"Impossible." Still smiling, the mayor waved the old monk to a chair. "As long as you're here, join me in a Calvados." He nodded to the bottle on a tray on the desk, surrounded by dusty little glasses. "A gift. From the American museum agent."

The monk did not move. "They must come back."

The mayor's smile vanished. "Business is business. The two statues in exchange for access to the aqueduct being built to carry water from my family's estate down to the town. You were doing your monastery a favor, remember? For centuries it had depended on two wells—which were utterly undependable. Your words, Dom, not mine."

"I was wrong."

"Well, what's done is done."

"It must be undone."

"Look," said the mayor, exasperated. "Even if I wanted to, I could not get them back. They've gone to the coast. For all I know, they're already aboard a ship to America."

The old monk shook his head. "I was hoping you would not say that." From the folds of his habit he produced a pistol, one of the new automatics.

The mayor stared at it. "Where did you get that?"

"A gift," replied the monk with a wry smile. "From a German pilgrim who spent a night with us on his way to Santiago de Compostela. After he realized that on the Camino he should be depending on God to protect him, not a Luger."

The mayor's eyes narrowed. "I've already told you, I can't get your statues back, so—"

"You and I are going on a journey."

"Where?"

"To the falls. Your falls, which feed the aqueduct."

"*Now?* In the middle of the night?"

"Now." With the barrel of the automatic, the monk gestured for the mayor to get to his feet. When the latter made no move, the monk drew back the Luger's slide and let it shoot forward, chambering a round and leaving it cocked, ready to fire.

The fat man got to his feet and frowned at the monk. "You don't expect me to *walk* up there, do you?"

"How else?"

"We'll go in my automobile."

The monk shrugged and waved the barrel toward the door. At the bottom of the stairs he retrieved the lantern he had brought with him.

The mayor, proud of his new yellow Hispano-Suiza with its white-walled tires, had parked it in the square for all to admire. At the first turn of the crank it sprang to life, and he lit the headlamps as the motor warmed up. The two men motored out of town and into the hills—slowly, for the fog was thick and the unpaved road steep, with frequent switchbacks.

They heard the falls before they saw them.

"Stop here," directed the monk, and the mayor brought his yellow charger to a halt, leaving it in gear and carefully engaging the handbrake.

"Light the lantern," the monk instructed, and the mayor did so, using a match from the small box he carried for his cigars.

"Now give me the matches, and hold the lantern up. Walk where I tell you."

They were about to leave the road when the monk called, "Halt." He went over to the motorcar and released the hand-brake. It did not move. Reaching in further, he pulled the gearshift lever into neutral. The car began to roll backwards.

"What are you doing?" cried the mayor, rushing to the Hispano-Suiza.

"Leave it alone!" commanded the monk. When the latter ignored him, desperately trying to reset the handbrake, the monk raised the Luger, took aim, and fired, shattering the windscreen and narrowly missing the mayor's head.

"Have you lost your mind?" screamed the fat man.

"Perhaps," replied Dom Esteban, smiling calmly.

The two men watched the elegant motorcar gather momentum until it plunged off the road and down the rocky mountainside, noisily breaking into smaller and smaller pieces.

Silence returned.

"You must be mad!" gasped the mayor. "You have just destroyed thirty thousand pesetas worth of machinery!"

The old monk looked at him. "So *that's* where the money went."

Waving the automatic, he indicated they should now head into the brush toward the falls. Holding the lantern high, the fat man led the way.

"Now where?" he asked when they'd reached the falls.

"Go through them."

"What?"

"Don't worry; you'll only get a little wet."

The fat man hesitated, until he felt the muzzle of the Luger in his lower back.

As soon as the water hit it, the lantern hissed and went out, but at the monk's direction the mayor soon had it going again.

They stood in a hollowed-out space behind the falls. At the back was a large hole at ground level, big enough for a man to crawl into. An equally large boulder resided next to it.

"I didn't know this was here," muttered the mayor.

"No one does. I found it when I was a boy. We're going in, so put the lantern on the ground in front of you and move it forward as you crawl."

With a little prodding, the fat man got down on his hands and knees and entered the hole, his mass brushing both sides of the opening. Behind him, the monk removed a small stone from under the boulder, freeing it to roll into the entrance, sealing them in.

2 | return to darkness

For a long time they crawled, past passages leading to the left and right, before coming to an open space with three possible exits. "The middle one," the monk said.

"How do you know?"

"See those?" He pointed to two faint scratches over the middle one. "I put them there when I was a boy. As long as we have light, we won't get lost."

They crawled for another long stretch, until as they rounded a bend the monk suddenly declared, "Stop!"

Ahead of them loomed a drop-off. It appeared to be slight, but when the monk flipped a stone over the edge, five seconds passed before they heard it land.

"That was close!" exhaled the mayor, shaking.

"This is as far as we go."

"Good! I've ruined this suit anyway, and I'm tired."

"You'll have time to rest," murmured the monk. "All you need."

They sat in silence, the lantern between them.

The mayor shivered. "It's cold in here."

The monk nodded. "If someone got lost in here, they'd die of the cold, long before they died from lack of water. But I understand it's a merciful death. The blood withdraws to the heart to keep it warm, so you fall asleep—and don't wake up."

The mayor shuddered, not from the cold. Then he asked, "Why?"

"The monastery has always had to depend on God for its water. Like the Israelites. The Egyptians could get all they needed from the Nile. But up in the rocky hills, the Israelites had to be right with God, or He would withhold the rain."

The mayor said nothing.

"The water level in our two wells was a direct reflection of the level of Living Water in our souls. As long as we were grateful to God, were quick to forgive and help others in need, we never had to worry about having enough water."

The mayor frowned. "You're supposed to be men of God—vowed, surrendered, all that nonsense."

"We're no more perfect than anyone else. We can be just as proud or selfish, just as jealous or vengeful or mean-spirited." He stared at the lantern flame. "Up in our hills, when such feelings harden in enough of us, when God ceases to be at the center of our hearts, the wells run dry. Then the Abbot calls for a day of fasting, humiliation, and prayer." He paused. "Sometimes—it takes longer."

He lifted his gaze to the mayor. "When you came, we'd gone three *weeks* without water, the worst drought we'd ever had. Our new crops had failed. Our two horses were exhausted from hauling our drinking and cooking water up from town."

"Your fasting and prayer didn't work?"

"Oh, they worked," replied the monk with a rueful smile. "Before the end of the first day, I knew exactly what lay buried in my heart. Others may not have known what their sins were, crusted over and calcified," he nodded in the direction of a slow drip from above them that had formed a limestone spire, "but I knew mine."

"Then why not—"

"Just confess it? I should have; I'm the abbot. It was for me to lead the way. But—I could not bring myself to."

The mayor waited.

"So the drought wore on. One week. Two. One of the horses died, and the younger monks had to help the other horse pull the wagon with its water up to us."

He stared into the dark abyss. "I grew angry at God." Then, glancing up, he cried, "Drive me into the ground like a tent peg, and the last thing you'll see of me is my upraised, clenched fist!"

The mayor was taken aback.

"At the beginning of the fourth week, Palm Sunday, you came. So solicitous! You'd heard of our plight and offered us access to the new aqueduct. Of course, the price was beyond anything we could pay. But we *did* have something you wanted. Actually, something the American museum agent wanted. In Madrid he had heard of our cloister's statues—exactly what he'd been scouring Europe for. He went to your office, to see if there might be a way to break the Church's in-perpetuity ownership. And when you heard how much he was prepared to pay—you informed him there might be."

The mayor's eyes flared in the lantern light. "That was *your* signature on the agreement!"

"You came when I was so angry at God I would have signed anything! Enough of dry wells, broken horses, sullen monks!" he shouted, the words echoing in the darkness that yawned in front of them. "Enough begging His forgiveness, humiliating ourselves by exposing our sins to one another! Now we would have water whenever we wanted it, simply by turning a spigot! And if that meant selling family members, so be it!"

"Family members?"

"Those twelve saints had been hearing monks' prayers for eight centuries. Of course they're family!"

"I still don't see what this has to do with me."

"You," exclaimed the monk, pointing at him, "were the agent's agent! And you were both agents from hell. The devil

knew the monks would never part with them! But he also knew
that I, acting alone, might."

He lowered his voice. "The seed you planted in our private
talk on my terrace grew quickly. In two days I was ready. We
worked out the best time: Good Friday. All the monks would
be down at the Cathedral for the Three-Hour Vigil."

The old monk rubbed his eyes, seeing again the events of
that afternoon. "You came with the American and a truck and
three Christ-hating workmen."

"Christ-hating?"

"Their families were in church," Dom Esteban snapped.
"Why weren't they with them?" He resumed his narrative.
"They had a wooden scaffolding and ropes, and were skilled
at their work."

He looked at the mayor. "Can you imagine how I felt,
watching them lift San Fermín off the place where he'd stood
for so long, and lower him to the ground? My God! I was
witnessing my own Pietà! I was the devil's centurion, overseeing
the same work that had been done on Golgotha at that very
hour!"

He shuddered, squeezing his eyes shut, then forced himself to continue. "When the others returned, they were in
shock. Enraged! But soon," he shook his head in wonder,
"*repenting*. They blamed *themselves!* The loss of the statues
accomplished what the drought could not. Hearts that had
been hard for months, softened. They poured out their con-
fessions to me and to one another. Monks who'd not spoken
to each other in ages fell on each other's shoulders, weeping!"

"Dom!" cried the mayor, "This is not my problem!"

The monk over-shouted him. "*This must be told!*"

The fat man fell silent.

"That evening after Compline, Father Juan—we'd been
novices together—started praying for the return of the statues.
And the next morning before Matins. Kneeling in front of the
empty pedestal—Fermín's in the evening, Benedicta's in the
morning—he begged God to return them. After Easter, some of
the older monks joined him, more each time. And then even

some of the younger ones. There's talk now of organizing a permanent vigil."

The mayor glared at him. "What do you want, Dom?" he asked, his voice redolent with sarcasm. "Absolution?"

The monk held up his hand. "You haven't heard the worst. Last Christmas we had the eight-year election of our superior. I knew God did not want me to continue. He wanted Juan, who was far closer to Him than I was. And He wanted me to tell the others. But—I enjoyed making all the decisions. Dining with the Bishop. So—" his voice dropped to a whisper. "I started to speak against Juan. Not overtly. Just poisoning the well, as it were. A drop in this ear, a drop in that one. . . ."

He looked over at the limestone stalagmite. "By the time of the election, enough men had second thoughts about Juan's suitability that they reelected me. They were not happy with the choice, but better me than what I'd led them to expect from him."

The mayor slowly nodded, his lips pursed. "I can see why you did not want to reveal this."

"Not to a living soul—until now." He looked up at the roof with a wry smile. "And you know what? God has forgiven the others. They repented. And now," he ended with a bitter laugh, "the wells are full again!"

"Then why are we here? Why did you force me to come?"

"Force you?"

The mayor nodded toward the automatic pistol, which the monk had forgotten was in his hand. Surprised, the old man flung it away from him, as if it were a serpent. When it landed, it fired, the report echoing and re-echoing.

For the first time since they'd left his office, the mayor relaxed. "Well," he said with a wry smile, "now that you've made your confession, should we not—"

"Go back? I can't. I'm doomed. And now," he threw the matches and then the lantern into the darkness, "we both are."

"What have you done?" screamed the mayor.

"Made sure you never consign another soul to hell for thirty pieces of silver."

Far below, the lantern burst on impact, its remaining fuel igniting and briefly illuminating the vast cavern beneath them.

"When Iscariot realized what he'd done," said the monk softly, "he hanged himself. This will have to do." And with that, he launched himself out into the cavern.

As the last of the light died away, the darkness was so complete it made no difference whether the mayor's eyes were open or shut.

3 | a measure of comfort

The only problem with giving your heart to a pet, thought Brother Bartholomew, unplugging his cell phone from its charger and gazing down at his old friend asleep on the foot of his bunk, is that sooner or later they die.

Reaching down, he ran a finger lightly over the Maine Coon cat's forehead. Slowly Pangur Ban opened his eyes. With difficulty he raised his head to give the monk's hand a lick, then fell back asleep. He had not eaten in five days.

Bartholomew rubbed his eyes; this was going to be harder than he thought. He looked out the window. Beyond the friary driveway, cars were waiting patiently to get into the Eastport harbor parking lot. It was a good thing they were patient; it *was* the Fourth of July, and the lot was overflowing.

He was grateful—they all were—for the big back lawn of one of the abbey families, the Caulfields. The abbey could have its picnic there in semiprivacy, with the beach and sand flats just across the little boardwalk over the dune. And though a cloudbank was moving in from the west, it looked like the sun might prevail.

Glancing at his watch—noon—he went to his bureau where he'd taped a tide chart. Two hours till dead low. Four till enough water returned to make the harbor navigable again. He smiled; the tide would be out, exposing the flats for the duration of the picnic.

He had started to turn away when his eye was caught by the small, two-photo leather album, propped in front of the beer mug with the green D on it that now served as a holder for pens and other writing implements. The photo on the left was of four Marine corpsmen. Jocko was an EMT now, up in Hyannis. Dan and Teddy never made it.

He shuddered to recall the night they died. But it wasn't the horror and death of Viet Nam that had turned him to God over there. It was learning of the death of his father, a commercial fisherman, when his boat went down out over the Grand Banks. Everyone had loved Buck Doane, and no one more than his son. He had vowed that if he survived 'Nam, the first thing he was going to do was get to know his father.

Never happened.

When he got the news, everything in him shut down. So numb he was nearly catatonic. He'd wandered off into the bush. It was a miracle he wasn't killed—a *real* miracle, as the chaplain later led him to understand.

Dartmouth was his mother's idea—her dream, really. Which he'd semi-spoiled by majoring in forestry instead of English. English was her love; she'd taught it at Nauset High till they made her retire. Now she ran Norma's Café uptown, and she served the best coffee in Eastport—an opinion shared by most of the town's beanheads. Not that *he* was addicted; he'd kicked caffeine—twice.

After Dartmouth he'd joined the National Park Service and gotten himself assigned right here, a ranger at the Cape Cod National Seashore, complete with a Smokey-the-Bear hat. Then he fell in love with the local librarian. And nearly married her. And then God called him up higher, into the local monastery. His mother stopped speaking to him. That beautiful, expensive education thrown away (in her eyes), and no grandchildren.

The other photo made him smile. Of a tall, blue-eyed, grinning man in his first habit, holding a big, brown, ring-tailed cat. They'd arrived about the same time, twenty years ago. Pangur Ban had been not much more than a kitten then, and the close-cropped hair of the newly-vowed friar was blond. It was gray now, the weathered face showing every one of his fifty-one years.

Turning back to the dozing Pangur Ban, he remembered the morning the cat had arrived—scruffy and abandoned but still proud. He'd sauntered up to the friary and announced to one and all that he'd decided to adopt the Brothers. He then presented a list of demands that no other novice would dare contemplate: He was to be excused from all services, indeed from any scheduled activity he chose not to attend. Nor would he be required to eat when the others did, and if he felt like sleeping in, he was not to be disturbed.

In exchange, he would keep the mouse population down, watch the night from the library window seat, and bring a measure of solace to whoever needed it. It was eerie how Pangur Ban seemed to know which of the twenty-four monks needed a leg rub as he passed. Moreover, he was a blatant respecter of persons. The only lap he would deign to grace was that of the Senior Brother.

When he'd completed night watch, Pangur Ban would move silently through the sleeping friary and retire on the foot of Brother Bartholomew's bunk, where he was now.

"Bart! You coming?" It was Clement, one of his two roommates, summoning him to the abbey picnic. "The under-forties have forgotten again."

"Forgotten what?"

"What we have to remind them of, every Fourth. Volleyball is a game of finesse, at which we are the undisputed masters."

Chuckling, Bartholomew joined him.

There were thirty-six privately owned homes in the abbey, one of which was the Caulfields'. With an acre of lawn right on the bay, it was ideal. Out on the sand a volleyball match was already being contested by half the abbey convent's seventy Sisters. The Brothers' turn would be next.

Meanwhile, over a smaller net on the grass, a shuttlecock was fleeing from battledore to battledore, while Frisbees were achieving flights of impossible duration and older children were lofting a colorful array of kites. On a well-manicured pitch in the far corner of the yard, some of the middle-aged civilians (i.e., neither Sisters nor Brothers), uniformly attired in immaculate whites, even to white bucks and sun parasols, were playing croquet with a set of antique mallets, balls, and wickets.

The most important activity—cooking the hamburgers and hotdogs on the plethora of charcoal grills loaned by various households—was the responsibility of the older men, while in the shade of a clump of locust trees beside the house the Abbess, Mother Michaela, was talking with a circle of the older women.

Completing the picture was Mac Charles, the abbey's resident naturalist. He had a gift for making tiny sand creatures exciting to the under-four-feet-tall. And now, far out on the flats, he was leading a band of them from sandbar to sandbar like a modern Pied Piper. Renoir would have loved it.

Something for everyone, thought Bartholomew with a sad smile. All 350 of us. Except at the moment he did not feel like being with any of them. It was an hour till lunch, an hour and a half before what remained of his spiking skill at the net would be required on the field of honor. He decided to go for a walk on the flats. Alone.

As he crossed the footbridge leading to the beach, the sun slipped behind a cloud. He looked up; a light overcast was gathering—not enough to spoil the picnic, just enough to keep everyone from being parboiled.

Out on the flats he drifted west, trying not to think about Pangur Ban—yet incapable of thinking about anything else.

Father, he thought, looking up at the overcast, I know he was your gift. To all of us. We've loved him all these years, and I guess he's loved us, though with cats you can't always be sure. But must you now taketh away what you gaveth?

Let him go, my son, he seemed to hear in his heart. *Don't pray him back, as you did last winter. He's completed his assignment.*

I'm going to miss him. I didn't realize how much.

He will be here waiting for you, when you come home. This is his home, too.

Why is this so hard?

Because you have a giving heart.

That was too Zen for him. He turned and started back toward the distant happy throng. He thought about the time he'd so resented the heavy lump on the foot of his bunk, he'd booted the cat off—a bunch of times. Well, he'd soon have all the foot room he needed.

He swallowed. I can't go back there like this.

Do not try to avoid the pain or shorten the grieving process. It will come in waves. When it does, turn to me.

Okay, how about now? He walked on, but nothing changed. Well, so much for answered prayer.

The cell phone in his pocket started playing *Fur Elise.* Wishing he'd left it back on his bureau, he fumbled it out of his pocket.

"Brother Bart? Dan. I'm out at Nauset, fishing, if you want to come over."

"I would, but we've got our annual Fourth of July picnic going."

There was a pause. "I, uh, need to talk to you about something." Pause. "But if this isn't a good time—"

Dan Burke, Eastport's Chief of Police, had been a friend since they'd played soccer together as boys. They still got together for coffee, still went surfcasting when they could. And occasionally Brother Bartholomew would lend him some aid if he had a particularly thorny crime to solve. But when his friend needed to talk—like now—it was never casual.

"Okay," he said, trying to sound upbeat. "And if it's not okay, I'll call you back." He would check with Anselm, the Senior Brother, but the abbey's policy was for him to assist Chief Burke whenever he was asked.

"Usual place?"

"Yup."

"Look for me in about twenty minutes."

4 | the threat

The thickening overcast had driven away all but the heartiest beachgoers, who were not about to abandon their prime real estate just because the sun was taking a time out. Besides, the miniature golf courses would have waiting lines, the stores were closed, and they could go to the Cineplex at home.

Brother Bartholomew found Chief Burke at his favorite fishing locale. "They biting?"

The Chief threw him a look of disgust, *"Moogers!"* he muttered, employing one of the milder epithets in his lexicon of substitute swear words. "I've been out here ever since the parade ended two hours ago. Nothing."

"Glad I didn't bring a rod."

Far down the beach a young water nymph, all skinny angles in a blue bathing suit, darted in and out with the sliding foam, her blond hair flying.

The monk waited while his friend reeled in and selected a different plug from his tackle box. Finally he said, "Were you cleared for SECRET in Viet Nam?"

"Briefly. When we had to go into Cambodia."

"Well, consider yourself cleared again." He flung the new plug out over the breakers.

The monk's curiosity was piqued now. But Dan would tell it in his own time, his own way.

"Did you wonder why the National Threat Level just went back up to orange?"

"Yeah, I did. The news was pretty vague. I figured it had to do with the Fourth."

"It does. But it's not going to be over today. It'll be ongoing."

Bartholomew resisted the urge to prod him along.

"I started to tell Peg what I could of it—I *had* to tell someone—but it was too heavy. She suggested I call you."

"Well," said the monk, smiling, "here I am."

"The FBI has finally gotten a bomb-maker to talk."

"You're kidding! Al Qaeda?"

"No, Russian. A nuclear physicist. One of the ones who designed the suitcase bombs."

"You mean, there really are such things?"

"Their government denies it, but now one of their scientists has defected and is talking. The bombs were about seventy or eighty pounds, small enough to fit into a large backpack. But they could do a lot of damage, about a kiloton's worth."

"Is that a lot?"

"The Hiroshima bomb was fifteen kilotons. We're told it would have a total-destruct radius of half a mile."

The monk frowned. "And they're worried that some of these may have gotten into the U.S.?"

The Chief shook his head. "Not 'may have'—have."

He hesitated before going further, then shrugged. "They've left it to our discretion whom we tell. They just don't want rumor wildfires, with the media picking them up. If the terrorists can panic the populace, they'll have achieved their objective without having to set off a single bomb. Like FDR said, the only thing we have to fear is fear itself."

The monk nodded. "Okay, what's said on the beach, stays on the beach." He smiled. "Not that I was about to call CNN."

Dan glanced around to make certain no one was within earshot. "The FBI has made some key phone intercepts of the person they suspect is running all the Al Qaeda sleeper cells in New England. Basically, it's a wake-up call. Some of these sleeper cells have nuclear devices, obtained a long time ago from the Chechens. They're poised to do a coordinated assault on all of our nuclear power plants. And Homeland Security says we've got to assume that if it's getting ready to happen here, it's going to happen other places, too."

Bartholomew winced. "Their own version of 'Shock and Awe.' I feel like I'm going to be sick."

"So did Peg."

"How does this affect you?"

"Their plan is to get close to every nuclear plant they can. And since security on land around the plants is tighter than it's ever been, those plants near water are going to be approached by boat."

Bartholomew groaned. "I don't like the sound of this."

"How do you think *I* feel? Now you see why I called you." He looked around them again and lowered his voice further. "Police chiefs of New England ports and harbors have been asked to investigate any boats that don't belong there, any unusual activity, no matter how innocent."

He looked at Bartholomew. "The rest of the country may be at Threat Level Orange. But we've been told, confidentially, to consider ourselves at Level Red. This *is* going to happen. We just don't know when."

"Whew," exhaled Bartholomew. "Thanks for making this a Fourth to remember!" They both chuckled, though neither saw any humor in it.

"What does it mean for us, exactly?"

Dan reeled in and again cast the plug far out over the breakers. "What it means is this: New Hampshire's got Seabrook to worry about. Connecticut's got Millstone; we've got Pilgrim. In Plymouth, directly across the bay."

The monk closed his eyes. "Worst-case scenario?"

"Casualties: fifty-six thousand. Damage: eighty-two billion dollars. And parts of Plymouth would never be inhabitable again." He paused. "But the absolute worst would be if the wind is from the south, which it often is. . . ."

"Then what?"

"Boston gets it."

ॐ

For a long time neither of them spoke. Then Bartholomew said softly, "We have teams of prayer warriors at the abbey. Old hands who've prayed away hurricanes, prayed down healings, that sort of thing. One team's praying for the President and his family, nonstop. Another's praying for our military wherever they're in harm's way. And then there's the Rees Howells Brigade, praying specifically against terrorist plots and activity. With your permission, I'd like to get them praying."

"Can you do it without being at all specific?"

"Yup."

"Will they be discreet?"

"Yup."

"Who's Rees Howells?"

"A Welsh miner who got caught up in their Revival. A lot of people believe that the Miracle of Dunkirk—getting the British Expeditionary Force out of France intact at the beginning of the Second World War—was due to the prayers of the group he led. Also, the outcome of the Battle of Britain. And Hitler turning east instead of invading."

The Chief scowled. "I don't mean to sound ungrateful, but I don't put much stock in it." Then he shrugged and smiled. "But—I guess it's like chicken soup for a cold; it can't hurt."

Suddenly the rod in his hand bent and almost pulled out of his grasp. Out beyond the breaker line, a bass—a big one—broke surface. For the next six minutes Dan Burke, using all his skill, fought and successfully landed the largest bass he had ever caught.

As Brother Bartholomew bid his friend a hearty appetite and strolled away, smiling, he realized that since Dan's call, he'd not had one thought of Pangur Ban, lingering at the edge of this world.

5 | sleepers wake

Three other men were looking out to sea that Fourth of July afternoon. On a rocky promontory overlooking White Horse Beach south of Plymouth, a father and two sons sat in a black pickup. Beyond the beach a beige concrete cube loomed against the gray overcast—the main reactor of the Pilgrim Nuclear Power Station.

The father was fully bearded; the sons wore moustaches. He had brought them here, to this site where a Coast Guard Rescue Station had once maintained surfboats ready to react to a maritime disaster, to contemplate a disaster of a different sort. Every few months for the past several years they visited this place, in what had become a ritual of preparation and purification.

"We will come from there," said the father, Abou-Ali, quietly, pointing to the eastern horizon where a lone charter fishing boat was cruising. "Why?"

The elder son, Ahmed, responded, as he had so often. "The station has one weakness. On land the perimeter of the Protected Area extends inland a third of a mile. Beyond the

Exclusionary Zone they depend on the State Police, the National Guard, the Coast Guard, and local law enforcement. The station is completely surrounded by a wired fence topped with razor wire, with electronic surveillance that includes infrared sensors and motion detectors. All of its input goes to the command and control bunker, from which random patrols augment security."

The younger son, Khalid, picked up the familiar narrative. "To enter the inner Protected Area requires the highest security clearance. Anyone seeking entry has a coded card that must correspond with the electronically-scanned hand print of that person."

But his older brother went further. "Forcible entry is impossible. There are concrete barriers at the main entrance, with a National Guard unit there in combat readiness." He paused. "We must assume there is a SWAT team ready at all times, including a light armored assault vehicle out of sight, armed with cannon and missles. Anyone trying to ram through the main gate would not get a hundred meters."

The younger brother nodded. "Any attempt to infiltrate by land would encounter the plant's private security force, former elite military personnel, armed with weaponry so modern that when they upgrade, they give their old weapons to local police departments, as it is far superior to anything they have."

The father smiled, pleased at their command of the situation. "There is, however, a weakness."

Ahmed answered before his brother could. "The station's condenser is water-cooled. It depends on seawater—315,000 gallons of it a minute. It takes that water from the bay, specifically from that entry canal on the other side of that stone jetty."

Khalid quickly added, "The Coast Guard has extended the restricted area out five hundred meters from shore and marked it off with eighteen warning buoys—big white cans with orange diamonds on them. But that canal would allow a boat to reach within a hundred meters of the reactor."

Abou-Ali rubbed his beard. "What about the reactor's protection?"

His younger son quickly described it. "The outer containment shell is steel-reinforced concrete. The inner shell is also concrete, four feet thick. The reactor itself is encased in steel, five inches thick. Nothing but an atomic bomb would crack that nut."

The father chuckled. "Which is exactly what we will be bringing. How will we bring it?"

"By charter fishing boat," Ahmed replied. "Cannon and missiles are ready there, too, but the infidels are American. They like to believe they are civilized. They would not shoot without warning. They would give several warnings, in fact."

The father turned to his younger son. "Why several, Khalid?"

"Because the repercussions of blowing a pleasure boat out of the water, whose captain may simply have had too much to drink, would be disastrous for Pilgrim Station—and for the whole nuclear power industry."

The father smiled, deeply pleased. His sons had learned well. "So," he mused, saving the best part for himself, "as we approach, we will maneuver erratically. Not in straight segments, as fisherman might. But turning this way and that for no apparent reason. Clearly the captain and all on board are intoxicated. That will be the deduction of the security officer manning the radar scope. His supervisor will alert the Coast Guard. They will sound the warning horn and use the loud hailer to command us to turn around."

He was being selfish, and stopped, to let his cubs enjoy the kill.

Ahmed said, "They might even dispatch their patrol boat to warn us off. But they will be extremely reluctant to start shooting, until they are absolutely certain of our intent."

Khalid said, "So, once inside the restricted area, we still meander, drawing closer, bit by bit. After the final warning, we go at full speed into the canal. Even if we don't reach it, the blast will break open the reactor, contaminate the sea, and spread its radioactive poison all the way to Boston."

The father reached out and touched one, then the other, on the back of the neck. "I am pleased with you. Allah is pleased with you. Now all we must do is wait."

He turned to his elder son and looked him in the eye. "Are you ready to die for him?"

"I am, Father," answered Ahmed solemnly.

"And you, Khalid?"

"I, too, Father." But there was the slightest hesitation before his reply.

6 | bombs bursting

In the parking lot behind a big hardware store, not far from the last stop on the MBTA's Red Line serving the northwest suburbs of Boston, an old moving van was parked. And since it was the Fourth of July, and everything was closed, it was the only vehicle in the lot, other than the old Volvo wagon parked next to it. A moving van? A little odd, but not too odd—except that one of the van's rear doors was slightly ajar.

Inside the back of the van, illuminated by a flashlight suspended from the roof as well as the daylight coming in from the cracked rear door, three figures moved silently and deliberately. They were donning nuns' apparel—the traditional black, ankle-length habits that had gone largely out of fashion after Vatican II and were seldom seen in the twenty-first century.

Black cowls bordered white wimples that covered the edges of each face, making each resemble the others. Even their sunburns, set off by the snow-white damask, drew attention, causing one not to notice their distinguishing features.

The first to complete the robing process was short, heavy, and broad, with a clipboard in her hand. On it was a list of items whose presence she was in the process of visually confirming—two dollies, collapsible crane with winch assembly, eight lengths of nylon line, two crowbars, four containers of gelignite, one plastic fishing tackle box. . . . She opened it and checked its contents—ether, handkerchiefs, timer, fuses, detailed map of downtown Boston.

As she neared the end of her inventory, the middle one—medium height, medium build—kept a watch out the back of the truck for any unwanted visitors, while the third one, tall and graceful, put the finishing touches on her attire. Then they carefully checked one another's appearance.

"Time to go," declared the broad one, gruffly.

The middle one took a final, careful scan of the parking lot. "All clear."

Eschewing the hydraulic lift on the back of the van, the three exited adroitly, went forward, and got into the cab with a minimum of wasted movement—as if they had practiced the maneuver. Which they had. Behind the wheel, the broad one started the engine and headed for downtown Boston—three nuns in an old moving van.

෴

Along the south bank of the Charles River every inch of grass in the park known as the Esplanade was covered with picnic blankets, lawn chairs, and coolers. Children played while their parents chatted and waited for the sun to go down. The best seats, the ones directly in front of the bandshell, had been taken since the park opened in the morning, with family members taking turns holding on to their space.

As the afternoon wore on, more and more people arrived (a third from out-of-state), till there were more than half a million. It had been a gorgeous day—in the lingo of the Blue Angels now performing a fly-over, CAVU—Ceiling Absolute, Visibility Unlimited. A day for visiting Quincy Market or Old Ironsides, or walking the historic Freedom Trail. And now everyone was a little sun-drunk and looking forward to the perfect end of a perfect Fourth—the Boston Pops' traditional open-air concert on the Esplanade that, thanks to CBS, had become an event the whole nation looked forward to.

It was the last hour of sunlight, when everything was bathed in soft-focus golden hues. A bearded young man threw a Frisbee for an amazingly quick Irish border collie. In front of the shell, where musicians were already warming up, a street mime played to the greatest audience of his life, teaching a gaggle of little children how to peer out through spread fingers. At river's edge a silver-haired gentleman in a blue blazer, white ducks, and a white yachting cap was guiding a remote-controlled model of a wooden Chris-Craft, while out on the river a brace of oarsmen glided past in sleek Thomas Eakins sculls. The scene was Seurat-like in its pastel tranquility.

The only hard edge was created by the National Guard troops. They were everywhere, their presence required by the threat level. The picnickers were unmindful of their presence. In previous years the Guard's sole function had been to fire off the four howitzers lined up along the Charles at the climax of the Esplanade Orchestra's signature piece, Tchaikovsky's "1812 Overture." This year there were no cannon—not as a security precaution but because the town fathers had been persuaded to liven up the familiar event by having the Guard heli-lift their field pieces to the tops of tall buildings in old Boston.

Promptly at eight the downbeat came, and the audience greeted the patriotic medley with thunderous cheers, singing along wherever possible. John Philip Sousa's "Stars and Stripes Forever" brought everyone to their feet, as fireworks danced in the heavens.

And then came the 1812, the piece everyone had been anticipating.

The Esplanade Orchestra did Pyotr Ilyich proud. Synchronized with the building excitement of his overture was the building excitement of the fireworks finale. At its peak, as Mother Russia triumphed over the Emperor Napoleon, the

heavens went berserk! Bombs bursting in air were joined by
the deep baritone of the field guns, their salutes rebounding
off the walls of the concrete canyons of downtown Boston.

It was the perfect end of a perfect concert—and no one
noticed the *ka-boom* that blew out the back of the Isabel
Langford Eldredge Museum.

7 | the incoming tide

The following morning most of the seats in the friary's refectory were already taken when Brother Bartholomew arrived. Taking a tray for breakfast, he had no trouble seeing why. Waffles with fresh blueberries or strawberries and real maple syrup would quicken the step of anyone leaving the basilica after Mass. As he added a second scoop of strawberries and a second ladle of syrup, he promised himself he would skip lunch. Yeah, right.

Looking around, he noted a place next to Dominic, but he could not face a rehash of yesterday's All-Star game or an impassioned argument about why this could yet be the year the Red Sox finally rid themselves of the Curse of the Bambino. Not this morning.

At the small table occupied by the Senior Brother, Novice Nicholas, a big smile on his face, was just getting up. Bartholomew took his place, grateful for the chance to talk to Anselm.

"Koli looks happy," he observed, nodding towards the departing novice. "Happier than he did at Lauds."

"Pre-vow jitters," said his old friend, smiling. "I told him to invite his mother to the vows ceremony, in spite of her abusive attitude."

Bartholomew nodded. "That ought to do it. It certainly did with my mother, twenty years ago."

Anselm looked at him, startled. "Has it been that long?"

"Time flies when you're having fun."

"*Are* you having fun?" The Senior Brother was smiling, but the question was serious.

"Don't worry," replied Bartholomew with a wry chuckle, "you're not going to have to send me back to Bermuda."

"That turned out better than you expected."

Bartholomew laughed. "I felt like I'd been banished to Devil's Island!" His smile faded. "It *was* a turning point. The most important since I became a Brother."

"And you even did some forensics." Anselm looked at him, head tilted. "You still dialoguing with Him?"

Bartholomew nodded. "My favorite thing. Too favorite. The other morning He had to tell me, *A little more Martha, a little less Mary.*"

They both laughed.

"How's the Chief?" Anselm asked, referring to Bartholomew's meeting the previous afternoon.

"Not good."

"Can you tell me?"

Bartholomew hesitated. "A little. There's a terrorist alert— not public yet, but right in our own backyard."

Anselm looked at him, pensive. Then he said, "Pilgrim One."

Bartholomew stared at his old friend. "You said that, not me."

"You've told the Howells group?"

"What I could. They'll pray without knowing any specifics."

Just then, Ambrose came in from the library. "You two might want to see this." He nodded toward the television set behind him. They got up, cleared their trays, and followed him. "I was trying to get the weather. Big robbery up in Boston last night. Too late to make the papers. The Isabel Langford Eldredge Museum was knocked over."

New England News had a camera crew on the scene. Yellow police tape kept them and everyone else well back from the rear of the building, where a huge hole gaped. A female reporter was in mid-comment: "Police estimate the explosion must have occurred around ten o'clock, timed to coincide with the cannon and star-shells going off at the end of the concert and fireworks display. Two statues were taken. One of the two security guards on duty at the time of the blast is in a coma and listed as critical. . . ."

With a sinking feeling in the pit of his stomach, Bartholomew left and walked down to the harbor. The parking lot was full, though not overflowing like yesterday. He walked out to the end of the stone breakwater and sat down on the last boulder. He was starting to remember something—and try-ing to stop the memory from returning was like trying to stop the incoming tide.

8 | dr. d

With a sigh he got up and went back to the friary, to the library where the TV was now turned off. He turned it back on to the New England News channel. Sure enough, they were covering the robbery, interviewing a local art expert—whom he recognized. Sean Padraig Doyle. Professor Doyle. History of Art, Dartmouth, twenty-four years ago. His favorite professor, who had awakened such a love of art in young Andrew Doane that he nearly shifted his major from forestry. The only thing that had stopped him was wondering what he would do with a degree in history of art—teach it?

Dr. D had also introduced him to Irish ballads and Irish whiskey. They had spent many a pleasant evening in the professor's study, sipping Bushmills and listening to Richard Dyer-Bennett. And then, when he returned for his senior year, Professor Doyle was nowhere to be seen.

Rumor had it he'd become involved with the wife of the head of his department. Bartholomew, né Andrew, had not wanted to believe it, though there was no question the good doctor gave new definition to "charming Irish rogue."

At the moment, he was giving some cub reporter his assessment of the robbery. "I'd have to respectfully disagree with the police inspector who was just on. I seriously doubt the statues are being held for ransom. There's not much market, black or otherwise, for twelfth-century stone statues carved by an unknown hand."

"What can you tell us about the statues?"

"Not much, I'm afraid," replied Doyle with a smile, his brogue thickening. Bartholomew smiled too. One of Dr. D's degrees was from Oxford. He could easily have lost the brogue. Instead, he flaunted it like a green silk neckerchief.

"Sure'n they're from France or Italy or possibly Spain. The museum acquired them in 1917 to stand on either side of the entrance of their new Pre-Reformation wing. Where they've stood for all these years—until last night."

"Where were they acquired?" asked the young man with the microphone.

"Ah," replied Doyle with a conspiratorial wink. "Now *there's* a mystery! Three years after they arrived, the building next door to the museum had a fire. The firemen were able to keep it from spreading to the museum itself, but all the museum's records were in that building. The museum staff who were alive then are all dead now. So," he smiled and shrugged, "no one knows. Which makes their theft the more intriguing."

"Fascinating," mused the reporter, so absorbed he forgot he was running an interview.

In his earpiece, the director must have reminded him. Now he almost shouted, "So you think ransom is ruled out as a motive."

"If it *were* the motive, they'd have taken the two Van Goghs, the Rembrandt, and the Breugel, which together are worth millions."

"You mean, like the art theft at the Isabella Stewart Gardner Museum?"

"Exactly. Thirteen canvases, cut out of their frames. It happened in 1990, and despite a reward of fifty million dollars, they still haven't surfaced."

The young reporter's eyes widened at the amount, as he tried to think of the next intelligent question. Doyle helped him. "No, this is something else. This is a collector. Someone who knew exactly what he wanted and hired black-bag specialists to get them for him."

Grateful for the rescue, the reporter was still at a loss. Doyle helped again. "That's one place where the inspector and I are in agreement. It *was* the work of professionals. Skilled professionals, disguised as nuns. Brilliant!"

The reporter was dying to ask why but did not want to appear a doofus. So Doyle answered it. "Look how the security guard described them. He couldn't!"

The reporter nodded. "All he could say was there were three of them—short, medium, and tall. And they were sunburned."

"Indeed they were! Which went perfectly with their cover story. When they rang the night bell, they told the guard that one of them had gotten too much sun, and could he possibly bring them some water? I mean, who's going to refuse a sunstroked nun?"

"I see what you mean. They must have gassed him."

"Chloroform, more likely. But when the police pressed him, he couldn't be sure they were even women."

"You think they were men?"

"Of course."

"Why?"

"All the master art thieves are. Just as all the master artists are."

Bartholomew winced at the chauvinism.

"What are the museum's chances of getting the statues back?"

Doyle thought for a moment. "Actually, better than you might expect. We're not talking about a bunch of rolled-up canvases that could be hidden anywhere. We're talking about two eight-foot-tall stone statues that probably weigh half a ton each. And another thing: The art underworld's going to have some idea of who might want them. And who might have pulled the job off. I have some dealer friends who. . . ." And with that he decided he'd said enough, and just smiled with a roguish twinkle in his eye.

The reporter turned to the camera. "We've been talking to Dr. Sean Padraig Doyle, formerly of Harvard and author of *The Eye of the Beholder*. . . ."

Turning off the television set, Bartholomew realized something: Dr. D was positioning himself to be hired as the museum's consultant on the recovery. But he feared Doyle was wrong about one thing–terribly wrong. The thieves may not have been skilled professionals. They may not have even been men. They may have been nuns. Real ones.

9 | darkness at noon

Brother Bartholomew's fears grew darker at the noonday service of Sext. The abbey observed the monastic hours or "offices"—brief services of Gregorian chant. Members who worked uptown were unable to attend the daytime ones, but the Religious—Brothers, Sisters, and clergy—attended if at all possible.

At worship, visitors and guests sat towards the back of the nave, on rows of cane chairs facing the altar. Abbey members sat closer and "antiphonally"—facing one another across the center aisle—the men on the south side singing one verse, the women on the north side replying with the next. It was a new way of sitting, adopted when they moved into their new basilica. Actually it was a very old way of sitting, in keeping with the time-honored tradition of religious communities. But it was new to Faith Abbey.

Bartholomew, still strongly opinionated about most things despite all efforts to the contrary, was of the strong opinion that he was going to loathe it. It would be like worshipping in a fishbowl!

But the moment he tried it, he loved it. It was a visual reminder that they were *family*—gathered by God to serve Him there together. And to help one another keep Him at the center of their lives. Looking across the aisle, one could easily see who was nodding off or domed out, who was happy and who wasn't. It didn't matter. They'd been rowing in the same boat for so long, they'd long since ceased judging one another. A lot of familial love flowed back and forth across the aisle.

Sisters and Brothers were expected to practice "custody of the eyes"—avoiding looking at members of the opposite sex, religious or otherwise, during services. But this noon Bartholomew could not help noticing the scarlet sunburns on the three Sisters here on an eighteen-month exchange program from Spain. No one else was so burned—yet they'd all been at the same picnic. Which had clouded over before anyone could get broiled.

And they *were* there, he reminded himself. He remembered catching a glimpse of Maria Immaculata at the volleyball net as he left to join the Chief. Or had he seen her earlier, on his way out to the flats? It didn't matter; she was there. But those sunburns. . . .

He was able to put all of this out of his mind that afternoon by concentrating on the needs of Novice Nicholas. At the abbey it was a tradition that each novice ask the older monk who had been the most help to him, to be his robe-bearer at the vows service and formally help him don his habit for the first time. Koli had asked Bartholomew, who said it would be an honor. Which was what Anselm had said when he'd asked Anselm to do the same thing twenty years before.

Now to help Koli keep his mind off that evening's ceremony, Bartholomew asked him to help prune the apple orchard—eight trees. For a long time, they worked in silence, enjoying the balmy afternoon, the quiet broken only by the *snick, snick* of their clippers.

Then Bartholomew asked, "How are things in the motor pool?"

"You mean, is everything running? It is. Even Matilda."

"What? That old Volvo wagon is still waltzing?"

Koli chuckled. "Remember when we wondered if she could make it to Hyannis? Yesterday she made it over the bridge—in fact, all the way up to Boston. And back!"

"You're kidding! Who took her? I thought everyone was here."

"The Spanish Sisters. They went up for a reunion at the Pops concert with two sisters from their order's motherhouse, over here on the same sort of exchange program with a convent in Framingham. Didn't get back until real late." He chuckled. "Boy, did they get sunburned!"

At Vespers that afternoon, the last service before supper, Bartholomew tried to practice custody of the eyes, but the three red faces across the aisle drew his gaze like a magnet. Nor did Maria Esperanza do any better. Though she instantly looked away, he caught her looking at him.

☙

At supper Bartholomew stopped by Anselm's table. "I need to talk to you."

"Sit down," his old friend responded affably, waving to the only unoccupied chair across the table.

"Privately."

The Senior Brother glanced up at him. "After supper, then, in the library."

It was still daylight when Anselm took his favorite easy chair, facing the window so he could observe the comings and goings at the squirrel-proof bird feeder Bartholomew had made. At least, it should have been squirrel-proof, but the Lower Cape's gray squirrels seemed to have done their graduate work at MIT and were aerialists *extraordinaires* who could have taught the Flying Wallendas a move or two.

As a male cardinal arrived at the bird feeder, the Senior Brother nodded to him and murmured, "Your eminence." Then he turned to Bartholomew, who was pulling up a chair beside him. "They're my favorites," he explained. "I always think their arrival signals the presence of God."

"I'm partial to mockingbirds," the younger monk replied. "They're ego-driven hams. Start imitating their calls, even poorly, and they'll run through their entire repertoire, parlaying with you endlessly." He smiled. "Dueling bird calls."

"So—what's so serious?"

"You know that art theft up in Boston? Where the thieves dressed up as nuns?"

Anselm nodded.

"I think they really were nuns. Our nuns. The Spanish Sisters."

"*What?* Ridiculous! You can't be serious!" Then seeing that he was, he added, "All right, let's have it."

Bartholomew told him the whole story, leaving nothing out.

10 | the three marias

With the Senior Brother listening attentively, Bartholomew relived the events of five months before.

The Sisters in question were over here on an eighteen-month cultural exchange program—three of the abbey's Sisters having gone to their convent in the southern Pyrenees for an equivalent period.

In February, shortly after their arrival, the chief American benefactress of their order, a rich old Beacon Hill dowager, died. Word came from the motherhouse of the Sisters of Mary of Navarre that the three Sisters at Faith Abbey, as well as the two in Framingham, were to attend her funeral at the Cathedral in Boston.

One of them, Maria Constanza, had an international driver's license, but they were new in the country, and finding one's way around Boston was tricky, even for native-born Americans. Plus, there had been a blizzard two days before, and while the main arteries were cleared, the side roads weren't. It was felt that a man from the abbey should take them. Preferably one who spoke Spanish.

Ideally that would be the abbey's resident linguist, Edmond Robertson, a former French and Spanish teacher who was tutoring the newcomers in English. But Ed was also the abbey's resident electronics guru and was away at a technology convention, so the lot fell to Brother Bartholomew.

The funeral was scheduled for 10:00 A.M. On dry roads, in non-rush-hour conditions, the drive to Boston could be done in less than two hours. To be on the safe side, they left at 6:30 A.M.

Normally the three Navarre Sisters would have worn their modern, modified gray habits, which were easy to clean and get around in, much like the beige habits of the abbey Sisters. But that morning, representing their order, they were attired in the traditional habits—long black robes and white wimples— worn only on formal or state occasions. Or high-altar funerals at the Cathedral.

To keep his charges straight in his mind, Bartholomew categorized them. Maria Constanza—short, broad, swarthy, heavy-browed, practical. A doer and a fixer. Maria Immaculata—medium height, thin, fastidious, with quaint rimless glasses and graying hair in a tight bun (now covered by a wimple). And apparently computer literate: It was she who received the e-mail that had set this expedition in motion. Maria Esperanza—tall, soft-spoken, ethereal (some would say spacey), with striking blue eyes—was an artist, and totally right-brained.

At 8:10 the abbey switchboard received a phone call from the diocese that the funeral had been postponed till 2:00, so the Cardinal himself could deliver the eulogy. (Apparently the benefactress's generosity had not been limited to the Southern Pyrenees.)

No problem—Brother Bartholomew had his cell phone with him. Except—he had turned it off for Matins and had forgotten to turn it on again. Thus he did not learn of the postponement until they'd reached the outskirts of Boston. He'd called Dominic, who'd grown up in Southie, for help navigating around the latest change in the ever-changing obstacle course known as the Big Dig.

Suddenly they had four extra hours on their hands. No point going back to the Cape; they'd only have to turn around as soon as they got there. Bartholomew had an idea. The traveling El Greco exhibition was still in town. It had come from the Met in New York and was about to go to the Mellon in Philadelphia. But for three more days it was at the Isabel Langford Eldredge Museum.

If he had to pick a favorite Renaissance artist, it would be El Greco. Bartholomew sensed he was more mystic than master. And that the spirit of God had guided his hand as well as his eye, as he applied layer on layer of light till his canvases were luminous. On three different occasions he'd tried to get up to Boston to see the show, but each time something had come up.

"You like El Greco?" he asked the three Sisters in his schoolboy Spanish. They did, having admired pictures of his pieces in the Prado Museum in Madrid. And Maria Esperanza, the drifty one with the arresting eyes, had family in Toledo, where El Greco had done his last work.

With difficulty he explained to them about the exhibition. They could spend an hour and a half there and still have time to visit Quincy Market and have Polish sausage for lunch, smothered in fried onions and cabbage. While they seemed less than thrilled about his lunch suggestion, all agreed that the opportunity to visit the El Greco exhibition was serendipitous. A gift from God. But how would they pay? No problem, Bartholomew assured them: This would fall well within the parameters of the friary's discretionary fund.

Parking around behind the museum, he led the way to the ticket counter. Where he was greeted with disheartening news: The present time block was full. They could not go in until 11:30. Which made it impossible.

As he related the sad news to the three Sisters from Navarre, only two were paying attention. Maria Esperanza was looking at the guards, one at a time. Now she detached herself and went over to one. After a quiet word with him, he went over to the supervisor. After another quiet *tête-à-tête*, the supervisor came over and had a word with the lady behind the ticket counter. Who smiled and waved to them to come through. Free.

Bartholomew looked at Esperanza in awe. "How did you *do* that?" he whispered, as they went through the turnstile. But she just beamed.

In flawed but firm Spanish, their guide and squad leader now gave them their marching orders. "All right, listen up. Do you all have watches?" They all did. "Good. We meet back here at the front entrance at 11:30. Do not leave the building. And do not be late." Once satisfied they all understood, he dismissed them to go their separate ways.

Bartholomew floated through the exhibition, spending most of his time in front of the three canvases on loan from the Prado—the *Adoration of the Shepherds*, the *Annunciation*, and *Christ Carrying the Cross*. Transfixed by the last, he lost all track of time, and was startled to suddenly realize it was 11:40.

Ten minutes late to his own rendezvous! He went quickly down to the front entrance, where Marias Constanza and Immaculata were waiting. But no sign of Esperanza. And Constanza had been there early.

All right, he said, they would simply have to find her. Constanza would remain there in case she showed up. He and Immaculata, whose English seemed a bit more fluent than Constanza's, would start looking. They would meet back here in fifteen minutes.

Promptly at noon Bartholomew returned, but not Immaculata. Good grief, could *no one* follow orders? Telling Constanza to stay put, he walked swiftly off to check the one place he hadn't been, the Pre-Reformation Wing.

They were there, both of them. Esperanza held what looked like a steno pad, on which she was furiously sketching one of the two statues that stood guard at the wing's entrance. Immaculata was tugging at her sleeve, pointing to her watch, trying to get her to stop and come away. The tall nun ignored her.

Bartholomew, perhaps fifty feet away, was stunned. Instead of boiling up to them, he just stood and gaped at them.

Immaculata caught sight of him and whispered something to Esperanza, who now instantly buried the pad in the voluminous folds of her robe. Cheerfully flustered, the two of them came bustling up to him, apologizing profusely in Spanish and brokenly in English.

Picking up Constanza on the way out, Bartholomew led them swiftly to the car. No time for kielbasa now; they would have to go straight to the Cathedral.

No mention of the reason for the delay was ever made.

&

"Well, that's it," sighed Bartholomew, as he finished. "Now you know as much as I do."

Anselm was nonplussed.

"According to the news," the younger monk summed up, "last night three sunburned nuns in old-fashioned habits broke into the ILE and stole two statues—one of which I'd seen being sketched by one of the Navarre Sisters. Who were wearing old-fashioned habits. Tonight in Vespers there were three sunburned nuns who had been in Boston yesterday at the time of the robbery."

The Senior Brother had nothing to say. Outside at the bird feeder a large black grackle had driven off the cardinal.

Finally he spoke. "As you say, I now know as much as you do. And now that I do, I've no choice but to take it to Mother Michaela."

Bartholomew sighed. "I'm glad someone else knows. But in a way, I'm not. I really like the three Marias."

"Well," said Anselm, getting to his feet slowly, as if he felt every one of his seventy-eight years, "it's out of your hands now."

11 | a matter of principle

"Did we in our own strength confide. . ." as the majestic chords of Martin Luther's hymn thundered down the church's long nave and soared to the high rafters, Bartholomew smiled as he sang. Not just because it was one of his favorites, or because it was several times the amplitude they were accustomed to at morning Mass.

He was recalling the first time they'd sung accompanied by the new organ in their new stone basilica. That instrument, assembled from parts of numerous century-old Skinners, simply overpowered the puny voices of mere mortals. To the point where someone (not Bartholomew) had suggested to Mother Michaela that perhaps the organ might be played . . . softer.

"No!" Her response was instant and unequivocal. "We will sing louder!"

And so they did. And now, as they sang *molto fortissimo*, the mighty organ accompanied them, all stops out, sounding like the voice of God.

"Our striving would be losing. . . ." Which pretty well summed up how he felt about the events of the past three days.

After Mass, Brother Ambrose, on breakfast detail, informed him, "The pleasure of your company is requested in the Abbess's study."

"Now?"

"Now."

Passing through Mother Michaela's outer office, he knocked on her study door, which was ajar.

"Come in, Bart," she called to him cheerily, though she'd not seen who it was. She was on a sofa, in a gray suit that went well with her short gray hair. At her feet were her two toy Manchester Terriers. In a chair to her left was Anselm, and to her right was Hilda, the Senior Sister, who was glaring at Bartholomew with consummate disgust.

Bartholomew shuddered. This was not going to be all skittles and beer. Taking a seat, he took dour note of the fact that Anselm seemed sublimely untroubled, as usual. Idly he wondered who outranked whom. Anselm had been there longer. But he was responsible for only twenty-four Brothers, whereas Hilda had seventy Sisters answering to her.

Mother Michaela spoke. "I gather you have some news that's likely to add substantially to the stress of this already stressful summer."

"Sorry, Mother Michaela. You can't imagine how much I *don't* want to be here."

It was true. He had not felt like this since he was a senior at Dartmouth, years before. According to the college's honor code, anyone who knew of cheating going on was honor-bound to report it. Three of his classmates had taken advantage of a purloined exam. Others knew of it, but apparently were not as bound by honor as he was. He had reported them—and they had never spoken to him again. No, he did not want to be here.

Before he could say anything, Hilda spoke. "I have to say, this is the most ridiculous thing I've ever heard of! Nuns stealing statues! The very idea!"

Anselm turned to her. "That's almost verbatim what I said when I first heard about it." He paused. "I think you'd better hear him out."

But Hilda had a head of steam up and was not about to simmer down. She turned to Mother Michaela. "I've made no secret how I feel about the exchange program! We're short-handed as it is, and then to lose good Sisters! In exchange for unknown quantities who don't know how we do things and sometimes don't even speak our language!"

She relaxed—a little. "But that's not the case with the Sisters from Navarre. They have good attitudes, and they work hard. We all like them. *I* like them." She glared at Bartholomew. "Which is why I don't want to see anything happen that will hurt them!"

"He's not saying they're not good nuns," interposed Anselm, ever the oil on troubled waters. "He's merely relating what he observed. He'd be remiss not to."

Mother Michaela raised her hand. "Let's hear what Bartholomew has to tell us." She turned to him. "Go ahead, and this one time you have permission to tell the long version. Leave nothing out."

So he did.

When he finished, there was a long silence. Then the Senior Sister said, "I say we just forget about this. If there's anything to it, which I still doubt, the police will come up with it eventually."

Mother Michaela shook her head. "We can't forget about it. We might all wish we didn't know what we now know, but we can't *un*-know it. We're before God in this matter, and it's now a matter of principle. A serious one—a man's life is hanging in the balance."

"If only he'd been where he was supposed to be," Bartholomew murmured.

Hilda picked up on it. "What do you mean?"

"According to the latest reports, he was sleeping on duty, sneaking a nap in a storage room next to the wall that was blown out."

"It makes no difference," declared Mother Michaela. "His life is just as precious as anyone else's."

To Hilda she said, "I want him on the Sisters' prayer vigil until he recovers."

If he recovers, thought Bartholomew. And then he rebuked himself for the thought. And chose to believe that God *would* heal him.

The Abbess turned to Anselm. "What do you say, old friend?"

He thought for a moment. "We have a little time. It would be the worst kind of folly to say anything to anyone until we know for certain what happened and that they were involved."

"*If* they were involved," Hilda interjected.

Anselm continued, unperturbed. "We also have in our midst someone with the gift of forensic deduction—if there is such a thing. Until now, this peculiar gift has been at the disposal of the local constabulary." He paused and added, "And Bermuda's."

They laughed.

Noticeably relieved, Mother Michaela turned to Bartholomew. "Pursue this as you would an investigation. But discreetly. No one beyond this room is to know." She paused. "If it turns out as we fear, I will notify the proper authorities."

To Anselm she said, "Bartholomew is to be excused from all responsibilities until the matter is cleared up. But," she turned back to the younger monk, "you are not to let it interfere with your spiritual life here. Your soul is more important than resolving this—situation."

"Yes, Mother."

She got up and, hands clasped behind her, went over to the window overlooking the bay. Gazing at the horizon, as if she could see over it, she murmured, "I only hope she doesn't know."

Hearing her, Bartholomew ventured, "Who?"

"My counterpart over there. Their Mother Superior."

But she did know.

12 | the alavan rioja

Hands clasped behind her, Maria Patientia stood at the low wall of the little terrace attached to her private quarters, enjoying her favorite time of day. There were not many privileges associated with being Mother Superior of the Pamplona convent of the Sisters of Mary of Navarre. This terrace was one of them, and having nothing scheduled for the interlude between supper and Compline was another.

All day she looked forward to this moment. To standing here and watching the last rays of the dying sun burnish the peaks of the surrounding hills—they were too old and rounded to be called mountains—turning them a fiery red-gold. In sharp contrast with the deepening purple behind them, they seemed to glow with a mystical illumination.

Far below, a staccato trumpet call wafted up the hillside, drawing her attention to the outskirts of town, where lights were starting to come on. Soon they would be filled with white-clad farmers, streaming to the center of town for the resumption of the festivities. The town and the region were in the middle of the annual *Fiesta de San Fermín*—the farmers' festival, when everyone who could get there came to Pamplona.

The insistent trumpet call, summoning the partying faithful to resume their eight-day revel, was now joined by other instruments—a drum, a guitar, a violin, more trumpets. Soon this group with its distinctive berets would form a Congo line and dance its way to the central square, to join the other *peñas* gathering there.

Fueled by *vino negro*—wine so raw it was almost black, and so cheap anyone could afford as much as they could hold—the carousing would continue into the small hours of the night. Then those who had beds to go to, would stagger away to them, and those who didn't would find their way to the park, where they would collapse until dawn.

And a remnant, drinking now to stave off crushing hangovers, would wander to the *Plaza de Toros*. There they would watch friends even drunker than they, jump down into the bullring to play *torero* with the relatively harmless "companion cows" that had accompanied the fighting bulls on their renowned run.

The trumpeter below had now been joined by the remainder of the *peña* in joyous celebration of what the night held in store. Maria Patientia smiled. And knew that many of the forty-three sisters for whose souls she was accountable to God were smiling, too. And no doubt tomorrow there would be a fresh flurry of ingenious requests for trips to town on urgent convent business. Which she would grant, because she sensed that God was smiling, too.

She had first come to Pamplona thirty-four years ago, accompanying her father, whose vineyard was on the south-facing hills above San Sebastian on the coast. Each year her father traveled to Pamplona well in advance of the fiesta to make certain the hotels, restaurants, and bistros had enough bottles of good wine and casks of cheap wine.

Twelve-year-old Cristina (as she was known then) was enthralled with the town's preparation—buildings being white-washed, awnings being repaired, chairs and tables receiving fresh coats of paint or varnish. On every prominent façade, men with big paste brushes were putting up the fiesta's bullfight posters, announcing the top matadors who would be coming.

After he had made his commercial calls, he took her to the Cathedral, and she waited in that vast, cool, shadowy interior, while he took the Bishop's order for Communion wine. It was not hard to imagine God's presence in that great stillness. Or that He had created this house of worship and handed it down from on high, though her father had assured her it had taken the town all of the fifteenth century and part of the sixteenth to build it. As she contemplated this, three nuns in long black robes and white wimples drifted past in prayer, and she crossed herself and shuddered. Poor things! What a dreary life they must lead!

As she grew older, Cristina pestered her father to teach her every aspect of the family business, from dressing the vines to harvesting the grapes and marketing the finished vintages. He did so grudgingly, being a Basque of the old school, which held that a woman's place was in the home— quietly in the home. Besides, there was little point; her older brother, Luis, would inherit the vineyard, just as his father and grandfather had before him. But as Luis showed little interest, he tolerated his eager daughter.

For her part, Cristina was desperate for her father's approval, and the longer he withheld it, the harder she strived for it. A quick study, she concentrated on the area of least interest to Luis: marketing. If she were going to shine for her father, it would be here. At sixteen she announced that one day the Baroja label would be as well known in America as any in the Alavan Rioja. A big boast for such a small girl (barely five feet tall), but she had every intention of fulfilling it.

To do so, she informed them at dinner one evening, she would have to go to college, to learn how markets worked and what affected them. One of her cousins had earned a degree in business at the UB, and it sounded exactly right for her.

"No!" exclaimed her father. "He's a man. No woman needs such a thing! No daughter of mine is going to the University of Barcelona!" And since he had only one daughter, that seemed to be the end of it.

Except Cristina had an ally that she knew not of. That evening, after the family had retired, her mother explained to her father that times had changed. Today, to be marriageable, a daughter must have more than a dowry. She must be able to grace her husband's table and entertain his guests—all of whom will have gone to college. For her *not* to go would seriously impair her eligibility.

So Cristina went to college. She took the required courses in business and economics as well as history of art and music, and found time to join a women's choral group. Her father had always said she sang like a nightingale; now she decided to find out what would happen if she got a little training and started treating her voice as an instrument.

What happened was she became a soloist with a depth and range that none of the others could match. She began to learn the old Basque ballads that she knew her father loved. And to accompany herself, she learned the guitar. What a surprise he would have on his next birthday!

Cristina had grown into an attractive young woman. She had lustrous raven hair, which she enjoyed plaiting, and a lithe figure, made more lithe by twice-weekly visits to the UB gym. Her best feature was her deep brown eyes, which often sparkled with delight, but just as often flashed with impatience.

She had no dearth of suitors—handsome for the most part, and a few quite rich. Yet none were as quick as she, and as patience was not one of her virtues, she found she could guard her tongue only so long, despite her mother's earnest admonition.

Their sudden disinterest did not bother her in the least. She was at the UB to learn the variables of supply and demand and the cyclic history of wine growing in the Alavan Rioja—not to acquire a husband.

On her father's birthday at the end of her first summer back home, she brought out the guitar and, in traditional peasant garb, sang a breathtaking medley of old Basque ballads. He was enchanted. So much so that, as the family prepared to attend the annual harvest festival for the winegrowers of the region, which this year was to be held at the Delgado Estate, he suggested she bring her guitar.

It had been an excellent year for the Alavan Rioja, one of the best in recent memory, so the atmosphere that evening was more than festive. It was jubilant. Wine tasting went on for two hours before dinner, and dinner went on for two *more* hours, so that it was approaching midnight when they adjourned. The men gathered down on the patio for cigars and Amontillado, the women in the drawing room for coffee and chocolates.

Having no interest in coffee or chocolate, or the gossip of her mother's friends, Cristina went to the window to look out at the harvest moon. She heard a man singing—outside, below, on a terrace separate from the men's patio. He was seated on a low wall, accompanying himself on the guitar, his white shirt open at the neck, setting off his deep tan. He was tall and sad-looking, even when he was singing a happy ballad. Long face, strong chin, beaked nose, calm eyes—as she watched and listened, she decided he was the best-looking man she had ever seen. Which surprised her, because she was not in the habit of noticing whether men were good-looking or not.

When he started a ballad from the Revolution that had been banned for years, she joined in—harmonizing, always following his lead.

He looked up, surprised. Then waved for her to come out and join him.

She shook her head. She would remain where she was.

He shrugged and bent to the guitar, now singing a traditional lullaby with intricate fingering.

Again she matched him perfectly. And when they had finished, he was more than surprised. He was intrigued. Again he waved to her to come down. Again she smiled and refused. But now she broke silence, calling to him just loud enough for him to hear, "*¡Bravo, Miguel! ¡Otra canción, por favor!*" Instead of playing another, he set his guitar carefully against the wall and went inside. She could hear him coming up the steps to where she was.

13 | miguel y cristina

Miguel stood before her, arms folded across his chest, looking down at her with one eyebrow cocked. "You have me at a disadvantage, Señorita. You know who I am, but I do not know who you are."

"You used to."

"You're from the Alavan?"

She nodded.

"Your family are winegrowers?"

She nodded again.

He frowned and thought back, visiting the different vineyards. "Not Sanchez." He looked at her face for a change in expression, but there was none. "Not Heras." No change.

He went back further. Way back. "Not—Baroja?" Still no change, but her eyes were dancing.

"Wait! The little Baroja girl, with the long pigtails. That was—you?"

"Cristina Isabel Elena Baroja," she announced, making an elegant curtsey.

"Cristina . . ." he murmured. "Didn't we used to call you Tina? Tina, *niña?*"

"You'd better not call me that now!" she declared with mock seriousness.

Properly chastened, he bowed deeply. "Enchanted, *Señorita* Baroja. Miguel Francisco Cortés Delgado, at your service."

She nodded and graciously bid him arise.

"Where did you learn to sing like that?" he asked in wonderment. "You're a nightingale."

She blushed. "My father used to call me that."

"Well, please come down, and let's sing some more. Or would you prefer that I join you up there?"

"No," she said, smiling, "I'll come down—now."

They went down and sat together on the wall of the terrace, singing the old ballads under the harvest moon, taking turns with the melodic lines, experimenting with the harmonies. Bit by bit, the men on the nearby patio gave up their conversation (though not their cigars) and came over. Bit by bit, the ladies gave up their chocolates (though not their whispering) and came out.

They commented on the incomparable sound the two young people made together, and how good they looked together, and how suited they were for each other, and how their families' vineyards were even adjacent to one another.

For Cristina Isabel Elena Baroja, this was the happiest night of her life.

¿🍂

There were not enough hours in the day for Miguel and Cristina to get their talking done. All they did was talk. And talk and talk, as they discovered they felt the same way about practically everything. They would walk and talk, sit and talk, drive and talk, ride horseback and talk. They only time they didn't talk was when they went for top-down drives in Miguel's old blue Alfa Romeo. Then they would have to stop so each could hear what the other was saying. And when they weren't together, they were on the phone.

Their conversations were breathtakingly honest. That was an unspoken rule from the beginning: They would say *exactly* what they thought, no matter how it might affect the other's feelings. So Cristina forgot about guarding her tongue and was pleased to see that she had finally met someone as quick as she, and perhaps even a little wiser.

"Why are you studying law?" she asked one afternoon.

"To help Ferdinand, when he takes over the vineyard."

"Do you like the law?"

"Not particularly."

"What *do* you like?"

"You mean, what would I have done, if I weren't going to help my older brother?"

Cristina nodded.

Miguel thought a moment. "When I was a young lieutenant in the army, my commanding officer urged me to make a career of it. He said I was a natural leader."

"You liked the army? Why?"

"I don't know; I was comfortable in the company of men."

"But not women?"

"You're—different."

They laughed. "You really liked that, leading men?"

"I did."

"Then why did you leave?"

"The family needed me. My father had a heart attack, and the doctor said, if he didn't slow down, the next one would kill him."

"But you're not home; you're going back to Madrid."

He nodded. "Just his knowing I'll be coming back has helped."

They both knew they were falling in love. And that it was happening very quickly. It was clearly fate, and clearly right. They would have three children—a boy, a girl, and then another boy. They would not live with either of their families. They would fix up his grandfather's old place and make it their own.

They would have one dog and two cats. And while they had not decided on the names of their children, the dog, a Great Pyrenees, would be named Alfonso VI after Miguel's favorite king. And the cats would be Manolete and Dominguin, after her father's favorite matadors.

The only thing they were not in agreement on was whether Cristina should continue her studies. Miguel was in his last year of study at the University of Madrid. But Cristina still had two more years at the UB. She said they must wait. He said that was impossible. They were at an impasse—until Cristina decided that she would persuade the UB to let her carry extra courses in the coming year and then take the last courses she needed in the summer. That would enable them to marry at next year's harvest festival.

When Miguel asked Cristina's father for her hand in marriage, Señor Baroja could not have been happier. He'd already begun discussions with Miguel's father on the possible amalgamation of their vineyards, which would make them one of the more prominent in the Alavan. Now the fathers agreed that to celebrate—and symbolize—the imminent union, they would jointly produce a new vintage, actually a very old harvester's red, made from whole grapes without pressing.

It would be called *Miguel y Cristina.*

She ran into difficulty when she presented her proposal to the UB. Despite her outstanding record, her faculty advisor and the academic dean initially refused to consider it. But they had never met anyone, man or woman, with the ferocious intensity and steely resolve of Cristina Isabel Elena Baroja, once her mind was made up. She was more than an irresistible force; she was a *force majeure,* as Miguel called her—a force of nature. And confronted with it, the advisor and the dean—the immovable object known as the UB—moved. She was granted unprecedented permission to complete her degree a year early—three days before her wedding.

Sighing at the fond recollection, Maria Patientia closed her well-thumbed memory album. She would stop there, not turn another page. No reason to ruin a perfectly good evening by dwelling on what had come next.

Below, it was almost dusk. Yet she could still make out a movement in the darkening sky—a female hawk was riding a thermal, circling slowly upward. Higher she came, until she drew level with her. And still she climbed.

Maria Patientia turned her gaze upward. The last vestige of sunlight was gone from the summits above. But she could still see the outline of their brother monastery on the hillside, five hundred meters above. And it seemed that she could barely discern a silhouette at the wall of a little terrace much like her own.

Was he, too, watching the ascending hawk? Did he see her?

14 | afternoon at the prado

Perhaps the only person in the Alavan Rioja who was less than pleased at the prospect of the impending marriage of Cristina and Miguel was someone in his own family. And Miguel learned of it entirely by chance.

He had come home for Easter, though Cristina had not. With her heavy course schedule she could not afford to take even a long weekend away from her studies. On this afternoon Miguel had gone for a ride on his favorite horse—and (as he would write her that evening) discovered that even the most enjoyable pursuits were not nearly as enjoyable without her there to share them.

Walking back from the stable, he was about to re-enter the house when he heard voices from an open window above—the same one at which Cristina had stood that first night. His mother and his grandmother, the family matriarch whom everyone called Doña Pilar, were talking—heatedly. Normally he would have ignored them and gone in, except he heard his name and Cristina's.

"But Mamá!" his mother exclaimed, "She's perfect for Miguel! She's from good family, good lineage! They're even winegrowers, for heaven's sake! And she's a *nice* girl—well mannered, not spoiled. A churchgoer! In fact, it would not surprise me if she was still a virgin!"

"Margarita!"

"Times have changed, Mamá—so much, you would not believe it!" Then, in a pleading tone, "I can't understand what you have against her."

"I have nothing against her," Doña Pilar replied calmly. "I happen to agree with everything you've said about her. And you left out that she's also quick and cheerful and sings like an angel."

"Then what is the matter?" his mother shouted.

"Miguel is not supposed to marry. Her, or anyone else. He belongs to God."

"What are you saying?"

"You know," said Doña Pilar, lowering her voice.

"You're not talking about the diphtheria!"

"Margarita, I prayed for him, that little baby. I took him to church, I put him on the altar, and I gave him to God."

"I was there, Mamá. I drove you, remember?"

"I remember that you were hysterical," recalled Doña Pilar. "Nothing we could do, nothing the doctor could do, brought down the fever. Your baby was going to die! He'd already stopped breathing once!"

"I know that, Mamá!" she cried. "That's why I let you do it! That's why Father Tomás let you do it! There wasn't anything else *to* do!"

"When you give an infant to God, he belongs to God," his grandmother continued. "Not to you, not to Cristina, to God."

"But can't he belong to God and still marry?"

"Of course!" Pause. "But that was not the way I prayed. If God would save that little baby, then when he grew up, he would belong to Him."

"But—"

"And *only* Him. A priest."

There was a long pause, then his mother said in a low but steely voice. "Well, that is *not* going to happen. There *is* going to be a wedding, the most beautiful wedding the Alavan has ever seen. And there *will* be grandchildren—great-grandchildren for you, Mamá."

"I won't live that long."

"Oh, yes, you will! You're too stubborn to go any sooner!"

The two women laughed, and Miguel went into the house.

When he wrote Cristina that evening, he did not mention what he had overheard.

He never mentioned it to anyone. But he never forgot it.

૨ે**

After Easter, Miguel returned to Madrid to prepare for his final examinations. Until now, he had studied hard enough to earn acceptable grades, but no harder. He preferred spending his evenings writing long, patient replies to Cristina's long, impatient letters. Her singing voice may have won him, but her mind intrigued him.

He liked the way she would turn a new concept over in her mind, looking at it this way and that, until she could argue it as well as he could. He liked her insatiable curiosity, and how she would probe until she got an answer. He liked her passion and her politics, particularly when the two combined.

She was a conservative, but also an idealist—an unusual combination in any age. She wished it were 1936, and she were a man, so she could take up her grandfather's Mannlicher and go fight. Not as a Communist or an Anarchist. Not as a Nationalist or a Royalist. As an anti-Fascist Basque Republican. Like their grandfathers.

He calmly, patiently replied that that was forty years ago, and with Franco finally dead, their country could regain its rightful place on the world's stage. And while he could not deny there was still corruption in high places, there always had been. . . . And didn't she think that the wedding guest list was getting a little out of hand?

As law students often did, Miguel and his classmates had formed study groups to help one another prepare. Miguel belonged to one with four other young men, all from family businesses similar to his own. Now, with final examinations approaching, they realized they had to intensify their prep.

Miguel was older than the others in his group, because of his military service, and was willing to push himself harder. So they, fearing their fathers' wrath if they failed to requite themselves with honor, elected him their leader. It fell to him to drill them on what they needed to know, until they did. He didn't mind, as the best way to truly learn something was to coach someone else in it.

At Miguel's suggestion they started breakfasting together—consuming vast quantities of coffee and precedents. And in the evenings he would not allow them supper until they had worked hard from six to ten. They heartily resented it—but grudgingly admitted its necessity.

The only break he allowed them was two hours at lunch. He would eat a quick sandwich, take a quick nap, then go for a leisurely walk, giving his inner tachometer a chance to drop back down to low idle. One afternoon, walking past the *Museo del Prado,* on impulse he went in. He'd been before as a schoolboy, and later as a junior officer stationed in Madrid.

This time, it was not the art that drew him; it was the tranquility. Which the museum's visitors seemed to amplify—taking their time, respecting one another's space and silence, feeding their souls from this masterpiece or that. He joined them.

On this particular afternoon, as he drifted along he probably spent more time in front of the works of Francisco Goya than the others. Normally he didn't care much for Goya—too pandering, too political, or just plain strange. But this afternoon he was caught by the way Goya used light; as he moved from canvas to canvas, he was enthralled. Time flew.

He was standing in front of the *Crucifixion* when he suddenly became aware of how much time had flown. If he left at once, walking as fast as he could, he might just make his next class.

But as he turned to leave, his eyes played a trick on him. Out of the corner of his left eye, he detected movement. Not among the visitors. On the canvas. Which was impossible.

Yet—it seemed that while he was looking at the chest of the figure on the Cross, at the periphery of his vision, the fingers of the left hand were moving. Flexing slowly, in anguish. Trying to clench around the nail that pierced the palm.

And when he focused on that hand, again at the periphery of his vision, it seemed that the right foot, held in place by a nail, was—twisting.

And when he stared at the foot, the top of his eyes seemed to see—or sense—the chest slowly rising, as if the figure were struggling to take a breath.

Shocked, he stepped back. Then took another two steps backward, enabling him to take in the entire painting. No movement.

Of course not! *It was pigment on canvas!*

But now he would have to run. He did not mention his extraordinary experience to any of his friends; he had a reputation to uphold, of being older and wiser. Should he write Cristina? What, and alarm her? Invite her to worry that he was studying too hard? So hard he was hallucinating? Besides, she was studying every bit as hard herself, and he didn't want to disturb her concentration.

He decided it was the product of an overwrought imagination; he really *was* studying so hard he was hallucinating. So he canceled the evening study session, and the morning one. We're all overtired, he told them. Go to bed early, sleep late, and we'll absorb twice as much because of it.

When they realized he wasn't kidding, they cheered him. But when he awoke after nine hours of unbroken sleep, he felt exhausted—which often happens when one finally makes a deposit in the long-overdrawn sleep account. Suitably re-caffeinated, he found that his ability to retain the evolution of land grants was fully restored. In fact, he felt so good, he thought he might try the Prado one more time.

It happened again, exactly as before. As long as he gazed intently at the painting from a distance, nothing moved. But when he went up close and examined a portion, whatever part of the anatomy he was not looking at was moving—in torment.

He had to run to class again.

The next day he had his first exam—an all-day affair. But the day after, he felt compelled to return to the Goya *Crucifixion*. And it happened as before. This time, he left it and went to the El Greco *Crucifixion*. A mystical representation of Christ's death, complete with attendant angels—surely if any depiction were going to move, it would be this one.

He waited. Nothing happened.

Next he visited the Velasquez. Done a generation after the El Greco, it was more true to life, though still idealized, reminding him of carved ivory. It, too, was motionless.

Returning yet again to the Goya, he tried to look at it dispassionately. Working a century and a half after Velasquez and two centuries before now, Goya was a realist. A gritty one, who painted people the way they were. Here, he had portrayed a man—not a vision, not an ivory sculpture—a real man, suffering. In agony, close to death.

And, if you got close enough—moving. It was doing it again.

He went well away from it, over to the side so he could observe the faces of the visitors looking at it—especially any who might linger. A few stayed a long, thoughtful time. But none of their expressions indicated they were witnessing anything out of the ordinary.

As they came away, he wanted to stop them, ask them, "Did you see it? Did it move for you, too?" But they would have thought him mad.

In despair, he thought of asking the old museum guard who'd been on duty there each time. If anyone had ever seen anything, he would surely know of it. He seemed kindly enough. Screwing his courage to the sticking point, he went up to the guard. "The Goya," he nodded toward the *Crucifixion*. "Has anyone ever seen it—" He couldn't finish. The man was already looking at him as if he were mad.

Miguel left the Prado and never returned. And was reasonably successful at putting it out of his mind, as he and his group graduated—two of them, Cum Laude; himself, Magna Cum Laude. Indeed, by the time he reached home, law degree in hand, what had happened at the Prado was out of his mind forever.

Or so he believed.

15 | the call

At home, he immersed himself in the affairs of the vineyards, his family's and hers. Having accompanied Cristina's
father to Pamplona on his annual pre-fiesta trip, Miguel had
endured Señor Baroja showing him off to his customers and
telling them of the impending marriage and the amalgamation
of the Baroja and Delgado vineyards. And his customers,
most of them romantics at heart, as he was, ordered extra
cases of the new vintage bearing the label *Miguel y Cristina.*
    When they came to the Cathedral, he explained that he'd
better see the Bishop alone. The old man did not appreciate
change of any sort.
    On his own for an hour, Miguel was glad to have a respite
from the oppressive heat outside. The Cathedral's five-century-
old stone walls were so thick, not even Pamplona's heat could
penetrate them. He meandered around the shadowy nave,
appreciating the tranquility and the intimacy, which was an
odd way to think of such a large enclosed space.
    In a side alcove, lit by a shaft of natural light from a window
high above, was an elevated, life-sized wooden crucifix. A

thin, gray-robed friar stood in front of it, regarding it impassively, as Miguel entered and stood beside him.

The wood, darkened with age, was still lifelike. Which meant it must have been carved in another century. Modern artists tended to stylize their work, abstract it, impose their own sense of what was meaningful. That was not true of this one, thought Miguel with a shudder. Whoever carved this wanted the onlooker to know *exactly* what Christ was suffering.

All at once, he smiled. This one, at least, was immobile— and staying that way.

The monk glanced at him with a questioning expression.

He must think it odd that I'm smiling at this, Miguel thought. And then he had the strangest compulsion to explain himself, tell this man of God exactly what had happened to him at the Prado, which he'd told no one else. Would he understand?

He looked closely at him. A bemused half-smile seemed to be playing at the corners of his mouth. His gray hair was cropped so close, it was hard to tell how much there was. The dark eyes behind the round, steel-rimmed glasses seemed not unkind. He decided to risk it. The whole episode was so totally bizarre it might be easier to tell a perfect stranger.

When he finished, the monk, took a long time before responding. "I'd come to see the Bishop," he murmured, "but someone's with him. Now I wonder if it wasn't to meet you and hear this."

"You don't think I'm crazy?"

"Do you?"

"I wondered, at first. You know, hallucinating. Sleep deprivation can do that, and I'd been running on about three hours a night for a week. But when I went back the last time, I was well rested." He looked at the other man, pleading. "What's going on?"

The monk chuckled. "You're not crazy. You've had a mystical experience. Such things are not common, but they do happen. Now you must find out why."

At that moment Señor Baroja joined them. "Ah, Dom Peregrino! I was on my way up the hill to see you next. I see you've met my future son-in-law?"

The monk laughed. "In a manner of speaking."

"Well, this is Miguel Delgado, who in ten weeks is marrying my Cristina. Miguel, this is the Abbot of San Fermín."

The two men shook hands.

"You know, Agustín," said the monk, "you don't have to come see me each year. Use the phone. After all these years I'm not about to purchase our wine from anyone else."

"And that's why I will *always* come, Dom. Because I value our friendship as much as you do."

"And because I might give you a very good meal."

Señor Baroja raised his hands, palms up. "I cannot deny it."

The Abbot nodded; it was settled. "Both of you will be my guests for supper this evening." He turned to Miguel. "You may find monastic fare better than you've heard."

"I would be honored."

"Excellent! We'll go up as soon as I finish with the Bishop."

"We'll wait for you at the Bar Txoco."

Miguel had a good time that evening—such a good time that he meant it when, bidding the Abbot farewell, he said he looked forward to coming back. But as he negotiated the steep and narrow road down to the main highway and the hour-long drive back to the coast with Señor Baroja fast asleep beside him, he realized he would not be returning for the food. He needed to talk to the Abbot, and it could not be done by phone.

Actually he returned three times, and with each trip his family—and Cristina's—grew more concerned. Everyone except Doña Pilar. Who was the only one not dumbfounded when, three weeks before the wedding, Miguel announced that he was entering the Monastery of San Fermín.

16 | end of dreams

Cristina was at the UB, studying for her final examination in Epic Literature, one of the last two courses she needed in order to complete her degree, when she looked out the window and saw Miguel's blue Alfa pull up below.

What was he doing here? She was glad to see him, but she had this wretched Epic Lit exam in two days. She ran downstairs and met him outside before he could come in.

"Can we go somewhere and talk?" He asked. He did not look happy.

She led him to a cantina two blocks away. By the time the waitress brought their espressos, she was alarmed. He'd said hardly a word. "Miguel, what is it?"

"I cannot marry you."

"What do you mean? The invitations have gone out; everything's ready. Mother says the presents are overflowing the dining room."

Miguel said nothing.

"Well, *why* can't you?" she demanded, battling to keep her emotions under control. "What is it? What's happened?"

He did his best to tell her.

"You mean, I am losing you because of some kind of sleep-deprivation hallucination? Miguel, that sort of thing happens all the time! I just learned about it. The French poet Rimbaud lived for his hallucinations. When he didn't have enough money for absinthe, he would drink coffee. Endlessly—to stay awake long enough to start hallucinating."

Miguel explained to her that what he had seen was only the beginning. That God had used it to start him thinking about his relationship with God. Now it was all he could think about. And he had become convinced that God had called him to a lifetime of service. As a monk in the monastery of San Fermín in Pamplona.

She nodded and said she understood. But she didn't. Not at all.

"Your life is resolved now; you're taking holy orders. What am *I* supposed to do?"

He shook his head. "I don't know. You might ask God."

She had no intention of doing any such thing. He—if He existed—was either utterly indifferent to her, or monstrously cruel.

She started to cry silently.

He reached out and put a hand on her shaking shoulders, then took it away.

All at once, he got up. "Cristina, I can't bear to see you this way. I want to stay. Help you, somehow. But if I do, I will lose—what I cannot lose." And with that, he got up and left.

Watching him walk away, she went numb. There was no point in studying that evening. Or trying to sleep. Pulling on her running gear, she wandered the streets of Barcelona, mindless of the possible danger and ignoring the overtures of men driving by who were not put off by her baggy sweats.

In her heart she resang every duet, relived every horseback ride, every drive in the old Alfa, every swim, every walk. She reasoned with him, remonstrated with him, pleaded with him. And because she was writing these scripts, they worked out the way she wanted them to. With happy endings, because her logic was irrefutable.

Given: They were in love. More than that, they had pledged their hearts to one another eternally—plighted their troth, as they said in epic literature. They were betrothed. And neither of them could put that asunder. It was forever.

As the sky lightened above the *Plaza de Catalunya*, her case was complete. As the first rays of sun warmed the ancient buildings of the *Barri Gotic* that had stood since Roman times, she was ready. She went back to her room and called Miguel.

He listened with consummate patience and compassion. Yes, of course he loved her. He always would. You cannot turn off a thing like that, like water from a faucet. He just—did not belong to himself anymore, much less to her.

She replayed for him all the shared moments she had spent the night rehearsing for herself. She reminded him of their dreams, their plans, their hopes. The three children—they were going to grow old, watching them grow up, remember? And then watch them have children of their own. She reminded him of Alfonso, of Dominguin and Manolete.

Crying, pleading, rhapsodizing, she spoke for the better part of an hour. He never interrupted. But when she was done, his mind had not changed.

After the call she tried to study, but kept falling asleep. And when night came, she could not sleep. So she resumed her midnight wandering, rehearsing the same scenes, working out the same arguments. But deeper this time, and calmer. More indisputable. At dawn in the *Barri Gotic* she was more ready than the morning before. More resolute. What had he called her? A *force majeure*. Well, he was about to find out just how *majeure*. She was going to move the immovable. *Encore— une force formidable.*

When she called, he was again patient, again compassionate. And again unmoved.

When she called the third morning, the morning of her exam, she could tell he was trying to be patient, trying to be kind. But his compassion was fraying at the edges. When the call ended as before, he suggested, as gently as possible, that she not call about this anymore. His heart was already in the monastery, and his mind was doing its best to catch up.

She took the exam in a blur, not doing nearly as well as she might have, but reasonably confident she'd passed it.

When she called the next morning, the phone rang and rang, until she finally accepted that no one was going to pick it up.

Now what? Her first impulse was to go home. He could hardly ignore her if she were right there in front of him. But what of her final comprehensive exam? It was almost upon her.

She didn't care about it anymore. Still, she had never abandoned a project, never left anything half-done. She would get her degree on schedule. Then she would devote her undivided attention to resolving the situation with Miguel.

In the meantime, the works of Cervantes and Tolstoy and Hugo received her total concentration. Her only time off was after she turned out her light at night, and she spent that convincing herself that it was somehow her fault. Miguel had not betrayed her; she had betrayed him. Been *too* forceful. Too *redoutable*.

From that perspective, she saw how she could change. How she *must* change. As soon as she finished her last exam, she would go home and tell him that. To his face. And ask him to forgive her. Her love for him was undying, but it had also been demanding, not considerate. Well, she had finally seen it. They would live together as *he* wished, not she.

And he, seeing that her meekness was genuine and lasting, would relent. She had driven him to the monastery with her assertive ways. Now he would see how submissive she could be when she set her mind to it. And her will.

But when she arrived home, diploma in hand, he had already left.

Her mother tried to comfort her. Her father was sympathetic, but of little help, being preoccupied with the imminent merger of the families' vineyards, which was going ahead as planned. Love was love, but business was business.

᷊᷋᷉

There *was* one person who might understand—the one she used to go to as a little girl, whenever her mother called on the Delgados. The old woman would have her to tea—formal tea, using her best china and her silver service. Cristina would be super polite, and the old woman would give her tea and sugar cakes—only two, young ladies never had three—and mainly a listening ear, as Cristina told her everything that was happening in her life.

As soon as she entered Doña Pilar's apartment, the tears came. She poured out her heart, exactly as she had years before, when her father had decided she did not need a horse and her mother had felt duty-bound to stand with him.

The old woman, her silver hair piled high and held in place with pearl combs like a diadem, had listened intently and dispensed tea and more than a little sympathy.

Nothing had changed. "Child, you have always been dear to me, as dear as if you were my own."

She smiled and went to the kitchen area to heat water for tea. From the little refrigerator she took out a lemon and thin-sliced it with a sharp paring knife, while Cristina got out the silver sugar bowl with its little white cubes. As Doña Pilar prepared the tea, Cristina set the table with the good china—just as she had as a child. The familiar actions had a soothing effect, as Doña Pilar had undoubtedly known they would.

When they were seated, her hostess poured the tea through a silver strainer and said, "Miguel is also dear to me. My prayers may have restored his life as an infant—and may have directed his life as an adult." She recounted in detail the scene in the country chapel many years ago.

As Cristina listened to the account of divine intervention on behalf of her beloved, she felt as if a door were opening in her heart, and she was looking out on a vista of unimaginable splendor. All she had to do was step over the threshold. . . .

Yet, compelling as it was, she also sensed that if she did step over that threshold, she would lose all control of her life. This God who could reach down and restore a dying infant to full health, could do—*anything*. It was too immense. She shuddered and closed the door.

"I want him back, *abuelita*. I don't want to give him to God, as you did."

The old woman refilled their cups. "But you're *young*, child. You have your whole life ahead of you. Surely there will be another man for you."

Cristina put her cup down sharply on its saucer. "I'm not interested! I had no interest in men before. They were nice enough, but—" she shrugged and smiled, "not very quick. Until Miguel. Who was perfect. *Is* perfect. I've never settled for second best, and I won't now."

"I'm afraid he's taken," said her old friend with a sad smile.

Cristina's jawline firmed. "We'll see."

Three days later she drove to Pamplona herself. The friar on duty at the monastery's entrance informed her that Novice Miguel would not be able to see visitors until he had completed his novitiate. Not even a good friend? A very good friend? Sorry, no exceptions.

Stymied, but only for the moment, Cristina drove carefully back down the winding road toward town. As she did, she noticed two nuns in work habits, cultivating a flower garden in front of what appeared to be a convent. On impulse she stopped and got out. What was this place? The Pamplona chapter of the Sisters of Mary of Navarre. There's a monastery back up there—were they in any way connected to it? Oh, yes, they were the monastery's sister convent.

As Cristina drove away, a radical plan began to form in her mind.

Three days later, she was back at Doña Pilar's apartment for tea. "You have opened my eyes to a new dimension," she declared with enthusiasm, once the tea had been poured.

"One sadly lacking in my life. I go to church on Sunday. You've seen me. But until our talk, I never really thought much about prayer and God—certainly not like you describe Him. But now," she stared out the window at some clouds drifting past, "I'm just beginning to suspect how much I've missed."

The older woman said nothing. Her eyes were on Cristina's face.

"I feel like the first book of my life is now closed," said her guest. "And the second is an adventure that's about to begin. For I, too, am going to take holy orders."

Doña Pilar's eyes widened, and the cup in her hand trembled. "Child, what on earth has—"

"No," replied Cristina with a beatific smile, "nothing on earth, I trust. This is a decision inspired in heaven. Actually, a quite logical one. Since I cannot be the bride of the most perfect man I have ever met, I shall be the bride of the only perfect Man who ever lived. I shall, as Hamlet urged Ophelia, hie me to a nunnery."

Her hostess was nonplussed. "Which order?" she managed to ask.

"The Sisters of Mary of Navarre."

"When?"

"As soon as they'll have me. I've spoken with the Mother Superior, and she's agreed to take me as a postulant for three months, after which I can enter their next novice class, if I—and they—are convinced that it is God's will for me."

Doña Pilar's eyes narrowed. "Where exactly is this convent, Cristina?"

"Pamplona."

Her old friend waited a long time before replying. Then she said slowly, "I hope it is God calling you, my child, and not you calling yourself. Because if it is, you will never be happy there."

"What?" demanded Cristina, incensed. "You think I'm pursuing Miguel? Going to the one place I would be certain of seeing him? You think I'm obsessed? Like Victor Hugo's daughter, vainly following her lieutenant to each posting? I am not her, Doña Pilar! I assure you!"

But afterwards, reflecting on their unsatisfactory meeting, she realized the reason she'd reacted so vehemently was because that was *exactly* who she was—as much in the grip of her fantasy as Adele H ever was. There was one great difference, however. That poor, pathetic creature could not help herself. While she, on the other hand, was cut from a different bolt.

Cristina Isabel Elena Baroja was a force to be reckoned with.

17 | vaya con dios

Miguel was in the second year of his novitiate, three months from his first vows, when the Bishop requested the presence of all of San Fermín's friars at the Cathedral. The Cardinal was coming to celebrate the Eucharist and consecrate their new school, and that meant all hands on deck.

The Sisters of Mary were also present, and while he did not mean to look at them, sometimes as one went forward to receive the Host, one could not always avert one's gaze.

He noticed there was a novice with the Sisters. Who was staring at him. And the harder he tried not to think what was coming to him, the more persistent the thought became. Finally he hazarded another glance. It was Cristina, beyond a doubt. And she was staring at him.

Now what? Should he go to Dom Peregrino when they got home? And tell him what? That he suspected that the woman to whom he'd been betrothed had followed him here and joined their sister convent? The Abbot would think he was grossly flattering himself and would become concerned about his spiritual well-being.

Miguel decided to put her out of his mind, and on subsequent high holy days when all religious gathered at the Cathedral, his custody of the eyes was immaculate. If she was still there, he did not know it.

᠖

Miguel thrived at the monastery. His commanding officer in the army had been correct; he did have a gift for leadership. The Abbot, recognizing it at once, took full advantage of it. He asked Miguel to form and train a choir. Which the new monk did. In the process he also formed a *Schola Gregoriana* for the instruction of the monks in Gregorian Chant.

To help them appreciate what they were singing, he taught them the meaning of the Latin. And when the Abbot informed the Bishop of this, Brother Miguel was recruited to introduce Latin into the curriculum of the Cathedral's new school. The Bishop had studied it as a youth, back when the Mass was in Latin, and he thought it would be an excellent character-building addition. In fact, any student who wanted to learn English or French was expected to take two years of Latin as well. Just like the old days.

Gradually the schola's mastery of chant improved, to the point where the Bishop made a habit of requesting their presence at the Cathedral whenever he wanted to make a favorable impression on visiting dignitaries.

Years later, when the monks of another Spanish monastery made a chant recording that became a surprise worldwide bestseller, a few of the older members of San Fermín's *schola* observed that they were at least as good as those Benedictines over there in Santo Domingo. So why didn't they do their own chant recording?

Miguel—he was Father Miguel now, having gone to seminary and received ordination—laughed. "I'm not sure you would want what goes with that kind of sudden fame. I met the leader of their schola at a conference at Solesmes last summer. They've been inundated with tourists and with reporters wanting interviews. Finally he had to issue a statement to the media, declining all interviews: 'You must understand,' he told them, 'we are monks, not rock stars.'"

One evening Dom Peregrino called Miguel to his quarters. It was May and barely warm enough to sit out on the little terrace. As soon as they had settled beneath the starry night sky, the Abbot came straight to the point. "I am not going to allow my name to go forward for our election in the fall. I'm aware of a movement among the friars to make an exception to our Rule, in order that I might serve a third term, but two is enough. Besides," he said with a smile, "I never have time to garden."

Miguel was stunned. "I cannot conceive of this place with anyone else in charge. Dom Per, you *are* San Fermín!"

"That's just the problem. It is the work, not the man, that matters."

Miguel looked out at the lights of the town far below. "You should know that I'm one of the ones campaigning for an amendment to our Rule."

The Abbot nodded, the half-smile playing at the corners of his mouth. "I suspected as much. The others will follow your lead, Miguel, so I am asking you to stop."

"But—"

The old monk held up his hand. "I have prayed much about this. I believe God would grace me to continue, if I so chose. But I also believe that change now is healthier for the monastery. And I believe God concurs."

Miguel took a deep breath and let it out. "Who, then?"

The Abbot broadly smiled. "You really don't know, do you?"

The younger monk shook his head.

"You, of course. And when I tell the others of my decision, and that I believe you're the one whom God would have follow me, I suspect it will be unanimous."

Miguel sighed. "I was hoping this would never happen."

"Why?"

"Because I am not—" he hesitated, seeking the right word, *"intimate* with Him, as you are. You are married to His presence. I am not. I spend too much time in my own thoughts—and resent it at times when His will clashes with my own." He paused. "You live—beyond surrender. You are abandoned to His will. We are all called to pray without ceasing. I am struggling with that. But Dom Per—you *live* there!"

The Abbot did not reply. The half-smile returned. "You may be closer than you think. However, I will do this: I will hold up my announcement to give you time to do the *Camino*."

Miguel stared at him. "You mean, make the pilgrimage to Santiago de Compostela?"

The Abbot nodded. "Sometimes we must go away to get a clearer perspective on what we have at home."

Miguel returned his gaze to the lights of Pamplona. "How soon do you want me to go?"

"The sooner, the better. The medieval pilgrimage has regained its popularity. It's still cold, and there are already many pilgrims walking the Way; soon, it will be teeming. It's more than seven hundred kilometers, and you should not hurry, so it will take you a month. Will you do it?"

"Of course. You have asked me to."

The old monk shook his head. "Do not take it as a command. Take it as a challenge. With three conditions: you are to go as a civilian, not a priest. If anyone asks, you are a Latin teacher, that is all. Besides, there should be as little conversation as possible. Practice the vocabulary of silence. You are on this journey to learn, not to teach."

Miguel chuckled. "I said the same thing to Bertram this morning when I sent him down to town on an errand."

"Second, pray over each decision, no matter how insignificant, and practice meticulous obedience. If God says stop—stop. If he says fast—fast."

Miguel smiled. Now that he'd wrapped his mind around it, he was looking forward to this—quest. For that was what it was: a quest for intimacy. "And third?" he prompted Dom Peregrino.

"Keep a log of your voyage. At the end of each day, write in it all that God has revealed to you since the previous entry."

He went in to his study and retrieved something from his desk. An old, well-worn, leatherbound notebook, which he handed to Miguel. "Here's mine. Of twenty-six years ago, when our Abbot gave me the same challenge. You might have a look at it before you go."

On the notebook's cover, in the Abbot's elegant script, were three words: *Vaya con Dios.*

&

Four weeks later, a bearded Miguel returned. Tanner and thinner, also quieter and calmer. The friars were overjoyed to have him back, and none more than Dom Peregrino. As Miguel handed him the notebook of his journey, a half-smile played at the corners of his mouth.

18 | maria pat

Cristina fared as well in a world without men as Miguel had in a world without women. Since she had been interested in only one man, away up the hill somewhere and out of reach (for now), she embraced her new life with gusto. The unbroken routine of their daily life—doing the same thing at the same time, day after day—bored her, at first.

But in time she noticed the calming effect it was having on her. She was sleeping through the night now, without waking in the small hours, her mind going at full speed. Best of all, her naturally ebullient spirit seemed to bubble up all the time now—which it had not done in several years.

One morning at Lauds, she realized she actually enjoyed the familiarity of their routine. Familiarity might breed contempt in some; in her it bred only peace.

During her three months as a postulant, Cristina had never left the convent grounds. Once she became a novice, however, she did accompany older sisters down into town whenever they needed her strong back to lift dry goods into their old Fiat truck.

As for challenges, they were immediate and endless. The Mother Superior, recognizing Cristina's ability as a bookkeeper, decided that the time had come to revamp the convent's antiquated and in places non-existent accounting system. She encouraged Novice Cristina to introduce whatever changes she felt necessary.

The old bookkeeper, Maria Sofia, bitterly resented the new methods being implemented—until she discovered that, with Cristina's coaching, she could reconcile their checking account's monthly statement in a few minutes, when it used to take all afternoon—the worst afternoon of the month, as far as Maria Sofia was concerned.

She had been there a year before she finally caught sight of him. The presence of all thirty-two of the Sisters of Mary (and their novice) was required at the Cathedral by the Bishop, for the visit of the Cardinal. They took their places in the choir stalls to the right, across the center aisle from the San Fermín friars.

Maria Ana, who was Novice Mistress for her class of one, had cautioned her not to look at anyone, especially those of the male persuasion. And especially not at any of the friars! She was to keep her eyes downcast, or up at the Cross or over at the Crucifix or the statue of the Blessed Mother. Nowhere else.

But she had not come all this way and spent all this time, not to see the object of her mission. The friars were coming forward in single file to receive the Host. Though her head was bent in prayer, through the tops of her lids she checked them out.

And there he was! The sight of him took her breath away. He was as handsome as ever! No, handsomer!

"Novice Cristina!" Maria Ana hissed. "What are you doing?"

"Sorry, Sister," she whispered, closing her eyes. How could Maria Ana possibly have seen her?

During the closing hymn, she held her hymnal high, and careful not to miss a note, she peered over the top of the hymnal. Aha! She caught him looking back at her! Now he knew she was here!

"Cristina!" It was hardly a whisper. *"Stop that at once!"*

She did. But Maria Ana told on her, and as soon as they got back to the convent, she was called into the Mother Superior's office. When the door was shut, and there were only the two of them, Mother Superior relaxed and smiled. "I understand your mind was not on the things of God during Mass this morning."

Cristina said nothing.

"Was there anyone in particular you were interested in?"

Silence.

The Mother Superior tapped her fingers together. "When we talked before I agreed to allow you to come here, you were a little vague about your circumstances. There was a betrothal, broken. You assured me that you were not on the rebound from a heartbreaking experience. That your newfound love of God was genuine and profound."

She paused and looked at the novice. "This will surprise you: I did not believe you, on either score."

Cristina *was* surprised. Shocked was more like it. She said nothing, but her reaction showed in her face.

The older nun continued. "I prayed much about you and your situation before I admitted you. God sometimes allows us to make a decision—a commitment—that aligns us with His will for us, even when our hearts may be far from what He intends for us."

She paused, but there was no response from the person sitting across the desk from her. "He informed me that your heart was far from what you purported. But that He did want you here. It was His plan for you, as much as you thought it was your own."

Now Cristina did speak—but only to say that she did not know what to say.

The Mother Superior smiled. "You don't have to say anything. All you need to do is know that whether you love God or not, He loves you. And has a plan for you. And hopes that you will want to talk with Him about it."

She looked at the window. "You will have to, one day, Cristina. Because no one can tell you what God's will is for your life. Only you can know that. And you must come to know it."

Cristina nodded. "I will, Mother."

"I hope so." She paused and looked carefully at the novice. "I never asked you the whereabouts of the one you were betrothed to. And I am not going to now. Because if he is here, if he is at San Fermín, then I would have to act upon that knowledge."

She sighed and shook her head. "God wants you here. I have no idea why, but I'm glad you're with us. He has already blessed us greatly through the gifts He has imparted to you. Now go and talk with Him. And if you would like to share with me anything the two of you discuss, I will be happy to hear it."

"Thank you, Mother," said Cristina, arising. "I will do that."

But she never did.

છે.

When a novice took his or her first vows, in many orders it was customary for them to assume a new name, the spiritual name that would be theirs for the rest of their life as a religious. Sometimes they would keep their Christian name. Or ask God for the name He would have them assume.

Traditionally the Sisters of Mary of Navarre took a virtue that reflected their personality. Cristina became Maria Patientia—not because patience was one of her virtues, but because she hoped it would one day become one.

As the years passed, Maria Pat continued to thrive. The Mother Superior, recognizing her gift for music and her exceptional singing ability, asked her to do something about the convent's singing, which was, in a word (her word), abysmal. Even on something as familiar as the doxology, the thirty-two Sisters managed to come up with thirty-two different ways it should be sung. Maria Pat was given *carte blanche*—"Just *do* something!"

Drawing on her experience in the choral group at the UB, she found a first and second soprano and a first and second alto, and started working with them. She taught them how to breathe, where to position their voices, how to listen to one another and to themselves, how to blend, how to read music, and above all, to keep their eyes on her as she conducted them. She worked them hard, but made it fun.

In six months her quartet was ready to perform for the Mother Superior. When she heard them, she clapped for joy. It was a miracle, she informed them, and she meant it.

Now Maria Pat had more than *carte blanche*. This was to be her primary responsibility. Everyone was to cooperate with her and do anything she asked.

She had two more potential first sopranos and three more seconds and commensurate altos. She made her original four voices take responsibility for each section, and set *them* to training the newcomers. And they would rehearse together for an hour a day. Every day.

In six more months the choir comprised nearly half the convent. They gave a concert that brought tears to the Mother Superior's eyes. And when they repeated the concert at the Cathedral, the Bishop, who liked to think of himself as an encourager of the arts, was dumbfounded. He requisitioned Maria Pat to work with the Cathedral choir, which was deplorable (albeit not abysmal), and to start a choir in the school, as young voices were badly needed to augment the Cathedral's increasingly creaky forays.

Maria Pat started with the young ones exactly as she had with the Sisters—working them hard but making it fun—and achieved similar results. When the children's choir gave a Christmas concert, the Cathedral was packed out, standing room only—and people said there were license plates on the cars outside all the way from San Sebastian and Zaragoza, even one from Madrid.

The concert went flawlessly. It had been announced for 8:00, and while people were still finding seats as the town bell began to strike the hour, the moment the last ring died away, she gave the downbeat. Eight o'clock meant eight o'clock.

The applause at the end was tumultuous. It came in waves, pleading for encores. She gave them one: *Silent Night,* in German. People wept.

At the reception afterwards, they told her it was a religious experience. That this would be the most meaningful Christmas in years. There was an agent from the Madrid office of Angel Records, who had heard rumors of this choir. Now he wanted to talk about a recording. The Bishop declared the concert would henceforth be an annual event, and that she had better get started on her program for the Easter concert, which he had just decided to have.

Driving home in the company of her four section leaders, who were still bubbling, she realized she'd never been so happy in her life—well, almost never. But the pain that had brought her here had dulled with the passing of years. Even seeing Miguel in the Cathedral from time to time did not reopen the old wound.

She was still not on speaking terms with God, because she had not given up her heart's desire. But they were getting along. He had answered so many of her prayers, and He was obviously pleased with the choir. The old saying was, He gave you an assignment to see how well you carried it out. If you did well, He didn't give you a chance to rest. He gave you three more.

When she got home, there was a message that the Mother Superior wanted to see her.

"I wanted to save the best news for last, Maria Pat." Her eyes were sparkling. "As a result of your work in the school, we have received not one, but three requests from young girls who want to enter the next novice class." She looked at Maria Pat, eyes brimming. "Do you realize they will be our first novices since you came sixteen years ago?"

Maria Pat just shook her head. Maybe this was the happiest night, after all.

19 | popcorn for lunch

The recording of Basque children's songs was a phenomenal success. *Bright Hope,* performed by the Youth Choir of the Cathedral of Pamplona, did not sell five million copies worldwide in the first year, as the chant recording of the Santo Domingo Benedictines had. But every Basque, at home or abroad, bought it.

When the convent's beloved Mother Superior passed away (their rule had been amended to allow her to serve in perpetuity), Maria Patientia was elected to replace her. Actually it was more of an acclamation than an election.

Maria Sofia, their now-ancient bookkeeper, summed up the convent's feelings for her. Maria Pat (or "Impat," as she dubbed her whenever she was pushed out of her comfort zone) had almost single-handedly brought the chapter into the twentieth century—just in time for it to join the twenty-first.

None of the Sisters had any desire to run against her. All believed it was God's will she become their new Mother Superior—His holy, perfect, white-line-down-the-center will.

Maria Pat was not so sure. And she told Him so after her investiture, when she stood out on the Mother Superior's little terrace for the first time.

She looked to the hills, whence cameth her help. "Well, you got me into this." Then she smiled. "No, *I* got me into this. But you let me do it. Was this what you had in mind, all along? Did you use the whole Miguel thing to get me here?"

She waited, but as usual there was no answer. No still, small voice in the depths of her heart. Others seemed to be able to hear Him, but not her. It used to make her angry, as if He were deliberately withholding Himself from her. But over the years she'd gotten used to His silence. They had an understanding. She would do her best for Him—no, her utmost—and He would bless it. She would ask Him to guide her, and then act as if she really believed He was. It had seemed to work, so far.

"Well," she said, preparing to go back in, "I must say, I never saw today coming! And now that I'm Mother Maria Pat, I'm more than a little curious to see what you're going to do next."

Silence. But as she left the terrace, she sensed He was smiling.

The next morning she received a call from the Bishop's office. They realized it was short notice, but could she join the Bishop for a working lunch?

The answer was yes—as it always was when a request came from that office. But as she drove down the twisting road, she was mystified. Surely this was not merely to congratulate her on her election? No, that wily old tactician always had more than one bee in his bonnet.

But not in a month of Sundays could she have imagined what he had in mind.

&

She had never been invited into his inner office before. There at a table, covered with crisp white linen, was himself. And on his left one other guest: Miguel.

Close your mouth, she warned herself; the Bishop's watching you. And remember, it's *Dom* Miguel; he was elected Abbot last year.

They did her the courtesy of rising, and she nodded warmly to them, as the Bishop bade her take the place of honor to his right. "You know the Abbot, I presume," said the Bishop, as they sat down.

"Yes, we've met at various musical events."

"Hers and mine," added Miguel, chuckling. "There seem to be more and more of them."

The Bishop nodded with enthusiasm. "Which is why we are breaking bread together." He turned to Miguel. "Your cantors, Dom, have gained a reputation for classical purity in Gregorian Chant that has, shall I say, drawn favorable attention from," he paused, "certain quarters."

My God, she thought, he's on someone's short list for Cardinal! And hopes to ride in on a revised perception of this diocese—that Miguel and I have been largely responsible for!

"And Mother Maria Patientia," he said, and then chuckled. "Goodness, that's a mouthful! Would you mind if we called you Maria Pat, which, I gather, your closest friends call you?"

She smiled and nodded, thinking, you can call me Mary Poppins if you want to, as long as you have that big silver cross around your neck. But who told you my nickname?

The Bishop continued. "Your youth choir—*our* youth choir—has put Pamplona on the map!" He shook his head. "I mean, for something other than the Running of the Bulls."

She waited for what was coming next. So did Miguel.

"I want us to have a sacred music festival!"

They were shocked—as he obviously hoped they would be.

"Ours is *not* to be a cultural event, like Granada's or Vitoria's jazz festivals. Or Barcelona's or San Sebastian's film festivals." He paused. "Nor is it to be something for the casual to come to and experience, like Holy Week at Valencia or Seville."

Having defined it by what he did *not* want it to be, he awaited their input.

Neither spoke. But both were cogitating, as the Bishop rang for more coffee.

"I think it should be in the spring," said Miguel finally. "As a run-up towards Easter."

Maria Pat shook her head. "Lent would be the *worst* time to have it," she declared, as usual not wasting time being tactful. "Everyone's focus will be internal, readying their own Passiontide programs. Do it in the fall—late enough to get the summer people gone; early enough not to bump into people's Advent preparations."

Miguel nodded. "She's right. Fall would be best. October—just ahead of the onset of the bitter cold."

She looked at the Bishop. "Whom do we want to attract?"

Before their host could respond, Miguel said, "I think the heart of it ought to be a masters' schola—hands-on workshops led by masters. We'll invite some of the most gifted instructors in Europe—"

"In the world," she interjected.

"In the world. For a week of workshops. Let our choral directors, masters of music, organists, musicians, learn from the best."

"And then in the evenings," she added, expanding the vision, "we can have open concerts of sacred music, to give people a feel for what we are doing."

"What God is doing," corrected Miguel.

"What God is doing."

The Bishop nodded. "They would help defray the costs."

"But they can never detract from the scholas," added Miguel, keeping the vision on course.

"It won't be just music," she went on, undeterred. "Eventually our sacred festival will be for all the arts. Liturgical dance, drama—even oratorio!"

"Yes!" exclaimed Miguel. "A showplace where God can encourage all who love Him, to worship Him with all the creative gifts He has given them."

"The Pamplona Festival of the Sacred Arts!" declared the Bishop, sealing it with his approval. "With evening concerts at the Cathedral—the *host* Cathedral," he concluded, beaming.

The three of them sat in silence, savoring what God had just done.

Then the ideas started popcorning again.

"Venues," said Miguel, announcing the next topic.

"The Cathedral, of course," said the Bishop.

Miguel nodded. "Yes, but only for the evening performances. In the daytime, we'll need workshop sites, places to serve meals, and tranquil settings for meditation."

"Your place," she mused. "Mine is pretty dowdy."

Miguel was surprised. "I'd heard the record sales enabled you to upgrade—everything."

She nodded and smiled at the Bishop. "We did get a generous stipend, and got new beds and a new kitchen. We're still on the waiting list for a truck to replace the Fiat."

For once, the Bishop was ahead of them. "Both of your places," he said settling it. "Most churches have a limited music budget. Few of those who come are paid what they deserve. They'll be used to modest accommodations. And you both have the personnel to take care of them."

They nodded.

"Well," said the Bishop in a deeply pleased tone of finality, "we've made excellent progress. For our first planning session."

They looked at him, surprised.

"What?" he asked, responding to the unspoken query. "Obviously this is close to my heart. We will meet for lunch the first Wednesday of each month—and as we get close to our first festival, it will be weekly. Meanwhile, it would probably be good for you to check out each other's facilities. Whatever you agree that you need—within reason, of course— notify my secretary."

They were speechless. An unusual state for either of them.

He stood up, signaling that they really were finished.

They stood, as well.

"Oh, one more thing: I want you two to collaborate on this. Closely." He turned to Miguel. "I've been listening to the two of you. You work well together. Both strongly opinionated. That's good. But, Dom," he said, turning to Miguel, "don't discount her input just because she's a woman; she thinks like we do."

Thanks, she thought, keeping her smile firmly in place.

As the Bishop bade them farewell until next time, he again urged them to work together on the smallest details. "Normally I would never suggest such a thing, to religious of the opposite gender, even at your advanced age. But you've both demonstrated your maturity, and two heads are always better than one."

As they walked out to their cars, she wondered what he meant by that advanced age comment. Miguel was forty-eight; she was forty-three.

Miguel was talking. "Probably the easiest way to keep in touch would be by e-mail." He hesitated. "You, um, do know how to use a computer."

I'm not even going to answer that, she thought, still smiling. The Church really was a man's world.

If they ever had occasion to cyber-chat, he went on, he had a wry suggestion for their electronic *noms de plume,* which would, of course, be kept to themselves, as neither of them had ever revealed their long-ago liaison. Certainly the Bishop was unaware of it, or he would never have suggested such a collaboration—even at their advanced age.

His suggestion: they would be Heloise and Abelard.

20 | heloise & abelard

Dusk had become night, yet Mother Maria Patientia lingered on her terrace. Not out of choice. Her memory album had reopened and was turning its own pages. Following the Bishop's recommendation, she and three of her most capable organizers drove up the winding road to San Fermín. Constanza—transportation and logistics; Immaculata— lighting, sound systems, and all other things to do with wires and computers; Esperanza—artistic consultant. Her core team— each with a capable younger assistant, to whom they would teach all they knew. Because as soon as the first festival was over, they were leaving for eighteen months in America.

The motherhouse had requested three sisters from the Pamplona convent to join two from their own, going over on a multiple exchange program. On the premise that no one Sister (or three) should ever be indispensable, Maria Pat had picked them precisely because they were so crucial to the success of the PFSA (Pamplona Festival for the Sacred Arts). She urged them to train their replacements well; the second PFSA must go off as well as the first.

As they drove up, they realized that none of them had ever been here before. Which the Abbot perceived when he greeted them. Good! He would give them the grand tour himself. He showed them the modern kitchen, the refectory, the chapel, the dormitory facilities that could house thirty guests.

What would happen to the friars who lived there? This being an active, outdoor-oriented monastery, explained the Abbot, they had an ample supply of four-man tents. And a comparatively flat hayfield carved out of the hillside for the grazing of the three cows that kept them in fresh milk and butter.

He had saved the best for last—their cloister. It, not the chapel, was the spiritual heart of their community—where they came, separately or together, to pray and reflect. Rectangular on an east–west axis, it was completely enclosed, with a columned, sheltered walkway around the perimeter. If they were processing into the chapel for a formal occasion, they would line up and begin here.

The center of the cloister was open to the elements and given to a rose garden with every variety of rose known to Navarre. It was a high-maintenance undertaking requiring constant attention. But the results were breathtaking. And between the seven columns on the north side were six ancient statues of saints. On the south side, however, there were only four—and two bare pedestals.

Dom Miguel explained that for more than nine hundred years, nearly as long as the monastery itself had been in operation, there had been twelve saints here, guarding the monastery, praying for it, hearing the prayers of the monks who walked the cloister. Now there were only ten.

What happened?

In 1917, the Abbot, without the knowledge of the friars, much less their approval, apparently sold two of them—San Fermín and Santa Benedicta. When the monks returned from the three-hour Good Friday service at the Cathedral, they were gone. The Abbot said he'd sold them to gain access to the new aqueduct, instead of having to rely on their dried-up wells.

Then what happened?

A week later the Abbot disappeared. Also the mayor, who had arranged the sale. No one ever saw them again, though the mayor's new motorcar was found wrecked.

"Do you have any idea what became of the statues?" asked Mother Maria Patientia.

"Only this—One of the monks remembered hearing of an agent for an American museum being in town around that time. There was some speculation that the mayor and the Abbot had colluded on the sale, split the proceeds, and were themselves the victims of foul play." He smiled. "But really, no one knows."

They looked at the ten saints—and the two pedestals. Esperanza was standing close to one of the statues. She reached out and lightly touched its face—caressed it, really. "The workmanship is remarkable," she murmured, more to herself than them. "Especially for the eleventh century. There is more subtlety here," she looked into the stone eyes, "than one would expect."

"I can tell you this," added Dom Miguel almost wistfully. "Ever since that Good Friday, the friars of San Fermín have been praying daily for the return of those statues. Each of us who walks here prays for them." He paused, a catch in his voice. "And we believe one day God will answer our prayers."

They reflected on that, gazing in silence at the empty pedestals, as a breeze stirred the pink roses clustered around their bases. There was a milky haze in the sky, so the roses barely cast a shadow.

❧

The first annual PFSA was a success, beyond the Bishop's fondest expectation. The Cardinal came—and went away impressed. Radio Madrid came—and announced that next year they would carry two of the evening concerts live. People came—so many that not only were all costs covered, but next year they would need to have advance ticket sales on the

Internet. Best of all, most of the church musicians and choral directors who came, said they'd be coming back.

As the Bishop had directed, she and Miguel had worked closely. Planning every aspect of the first PFSA required no less. As the event grew closer, they were often cyber-chatting several times a day. And gradually the incredible communication that had once been the hallmark of their relationship—and with it, the romantic magic—began to return.

As she had always hoped it would. She knew she should fight it. Ask God's help laying it quickly to rest, before it took hold. But if she asked Him, He would. So—she didn't.

And so she noticed that Miguel was actually more handsome than that night they'd sung together twenty-five years ago. There was the same sparkle in the deep, dark eyes—but strong character lines were now etched into the long face. And the more she dwelled on them, the more she realized that the obsession that had once gripped her—brought her here in the first place—was not dead, as she'd supposed. It had been merely dormant.

And was now reawakening. Strong as ever. Stronger.

At the Bishop's luncheons she would look at him with such love in her eyes that he started being careful never to let their eyes meet. Fortunately the Bishop seemed oblivious to the chemistry between them, or perhaps he was overlooking it, for the sake of the PFSA.

Alas, Miguel was obviously *not* experiencing a reawakening of the old magic. While he clearly enjoyed working and planning with her, that was as far as he allowed it to go. Which became painfully clear the evening they were cyber-chatting, and she'd tried to push it further.

HELOISE: You know the farewell dinner on the last night, after the evening concert? Why not have the attendees do an informal skit, recapping their week?

ABELARD: Brilliant! I love that!

HELOISE: It's nothing. I toss off brilliance like that all the time!

ABELARD: You're amazing! You know, it's been fun working with you. All I could see was the downside potential.

HELOISE: For disaster.

ABELARD: Yes. I'd forgotten how quick you were. How refreshing to have someone tracking with you, even before you put it into words.

HELOISE: You didn't forget. You never knew. But you should have, from our duets. If you had the melody, I'd layer in the harmony, go to counterpoint on the third verse. If you wanted to harmonize, I'd take the lead.

ABELARD: People who didn't know us thought we were professionals. They couldn't believe we were just kids.

HELOISE: Love can do that.

ABELARD: Careful. . . .

HELOISE: Ever think about those times? When we used to sing together?

ABELARD: No. And if I did, I wouldn't tell you.

HELOISE: Inappropriate.

ABELARD: Yes.

HELOISE: I think about them sometimes.

ABELARD: Look, I enjoy working with you. I enjoy talking to you. I more than enjoy it. It's a treat. So don't spoil it.

HELOISE: Sorry.

ABELARD: If we can keep this on a nonpersonal level, it can go on. Otherwise. . . .

HELOISE: Otherwise?

ABELARD: It's over.

HELOISE: You could kill it? Just like that?

ABELARD: Just like that.

HELOISE: But if we can keep it at an appropriate level. . . .

ABELARD: It can continue.

HELOISE: Which we both want.

ABELARD: Which we both want.

HELOISE: You know, I was thinking—on Skit Night, the students will be making fun of us. Of the masters and especially you and me, since we're the organizers. Everyone will be having a good time. What if, at the end, you and I—were to sing them one or two of the old songs?

ABELARD: No.

HELOISE: No, you want to sing something else? Or no, not a good idea?

ABELARD: What do you think?

HELOISE: Bad idea. Why?

ABELARD: You know why.

HELOISE: Tell me.

[long pause]

HELOISE: You there?

ABELARD: I'm here.

HELOISE: Tell me why you won't sing with me.

ABELARD: All right, I'll tell you. Once. And this will be the
            last time. Because from now on, you and I are
            going to keep our CC and/or talk strictly on
            PFSA matters. Except on Sunday afternoons,
            from 2:00 to 4:00, when we can talk or CC about
            anything we want—as long it stays appropriate.
            Just conversation between two friends. But if
            you ever try to take it away from that, it's over.
            And I mean OVER.

HELOISE: You've had that little speech prepared for some
            time now, haven't you? For just such a contin-
            gency. In case she got—inappropriate. And/or
            difficult.

            [long pause]

HELOISE: I'm sorry. You were going to tell me why you
            won't sing with me.

            [long pause]

HELOISE: Once. You said you'd tell me once. The last time.

ABELARD: All right. I won't sing with you, because the way
            we used to sing—it was like dancing. Ballroom
            dancing—two voices flowing together so smoothly,
            so perfectly, they're as one. Perfect anticipation,
            perfect harmony. Flying. Our voices like two
            doves, wheeling, soaring together. As one.

HELOISE: You HAVE thought about it! That's beautiful,
            Miguel! I love that!

ABELARD: You'll never hear it from me again.

HELOISE: But you said it. I have it. That's enough.

ABELARD: You'd better delete it. The whole thing. And from
            now on, only on Sunday afternoon, 2:00 to 4:00.
            Appropriate. Or never again. Do you understand?

HELOISE: I do.

ABELARD: Agreed?

HELOISE: Agreed.

But she did not agree. And while she deleted their conversation in case he ever asked her, she printed it out first and folded it and stuck it in the back of her personal Bible.

21 | a means to an end

True to her word, the moment the Sacred Arts Festival concluded, Mother Maria Patientia had packed off her core Sisters to the convent of Faith Abbey on Cape Cod, Massachusetts.

Constanza, Immaculata, Esperanza—she missed them. And the convent missed them terribly. It would be weeks before the three Sisters from America would be familiar enough with their way of doing things to start pulling their own weight.

And then, out of the blue, came that extraordinary e-mail from Immaculata to her private computer, with scans of Esperanza's two sketches attached!

She remembered the morning they visited the San Fermín cloister, and the conviction with which Miguel stated the belief that God would one day answer their prayers and those of three generations of friars before them. Well, maybe He would.

There was no question that Esperanza's sketches bore an unmistakable resemblance to the ten remaining figures in the

San Fermín cloister. And no one at the museum seemed to
know where the two statues had come from. Something about
a fire destroying records. All they knew was that they had
arrived in time to flank the entrance at the opening of the Pre-
Reformation wing in 1917—the year that the statues had been
sold.

To Maria Pat there was no question where they had come
from. Or where they belonged. The only question was, how to
get them back.

Holding printouts of the sketches in her hand that
evening, she weighed her next step. She ought to call Miguel,
or at least e-mail him. Send him the sketches and leave the rest
in his hands. But if she did, he would have only one recourse:
to open a correspondence with the museum. Explain to them
the sad deficiency of their present cloister setting. Suggest that
perhaps negotiations might be entered into, for the eventual
return of the statues.

And what would be their likely reply? They would be
extremely grateful for having been apprised of the origin of
the statues, and would be even more grateful if he could send
photographs of the other ten, since they were obviously done
at the same time by the same sculptor. Also, any information
he could provide on the period, locale, and other work of said
sculptor would be most appreciated.

But as to their eventual return, since they had obviously
been acquired through legitimate channels by accepted business procedure, their return was regrettably out of the question.

In other words, since they were purchased and not stolen,
and since they'd been in the museum for nearly ninety years,
Miguel could correspond till his stone grave marker joined the
others on the hill behind the monastery, and it would not
change anything.

The moment she told him, he would put in motion the
sequence of events that she had just foreseen with such clarity.

But what if—she *didn't* tell him? Could there be a different
sequence? A different outcome?

She was not even sure what she had in mind—yet. But she was pretty sure it would not meet with God's approval.

That night, out on the terrace, she'd had it out with Him. It was, as usual, a one-sided conversation. But it was conclusive, and she recalled it verbatim.

"I know you're not going to tell me what I want to hear," she'd said for openers, looking up at the stars. "That is, even if I could hear you in my heart, as others seem to."

Silence. As she expected.

"And I know if I could hear you, you'd remind me that the end can *never* justify the means."

The stars were listening.

"But tonight I prefer Trotsky's take on that: 'The end may justify the means, as long as there is something that justifies the end.'"

She smiled. "You know, I almost *can* hear you now. I think you just said *Gobbledygook!* Well, a lot of Marxism *was* gobbledygook. But look what they accomplished!"

The stars were not pleased.

She sighed. "I'm not going to ask you to bless whatever I decide to do. In fact, I am not going to talk to you about it at all. Because even if I couldn't hear you, I would then have to act upon my conscience—on what I'd suspect you'd say if I *could* hear you."

She stopped and smiled. "You know, a conscience is not much of a conversationalist. All it knows how to say is 'no.'"

Serious again, she said, "The moment I ask you, it becomes a matter of principle. Of doing what I know is right."

She shrugged. "So—I'm not going to ask. Because for once I want things to work out the way *I* want them to. I don't know how yet, but I'm going to get those statues back. Because their return will force Miguel into the relationship with me that *I* want. Not the one you want, or he wants. The one *I* want! Every time he goes into that cloister and sees those statues back where they belong, he will be grateful all over again. Every single day. They will be the gift that keeps on giving— forever."

She shivered. Before turning to go in, she took a last look at the stars. "I'm going ahead, with or without you. I know you love Miguel. And I know you've heard every prayer of every monk for every year they've been praying. I hope, for their sake, you'll cover this. But I'm *not* asking you to."

And with that, she went indoors and e-mailed Immaculata, requesting a private cyber-chat session with her core sisters— her three best friends. For *if* they decided to join her, it would be on that basis—as friends. On a strictly voluntary, extremely hazardous mission.

22 | to a table down at norma's

Chief Dan Burke, in civilian clothes, was already at Norma's when Brother Bartholomew arrived. He'd taken the most prominent table, the one in front of the window, because his monk friend had told him there was something urgent he needed to talk about.

As Bartholomew joined him, his mother, who ran the place for the invalided Norma, came over with a clean mug and a brimming pot of coffee. She had warned them about the weird acoustics in Norma's Café. Conversations at the table one would assume would be the most private—the one over in the corner—could be overheard quite easily at the galley range. Whereas the table in the front window was actually quite private.

Nearly eighty but looking a good ten years younger, Isabel Doane poured his coffee and asked in a voice that could not be overheard, "Something up?"

The Chief smiled. "Ask him. It's his party."

She looked expectantly at her son, who was in the abbey's modified work habit—a blue denim work shirt with a small blue cross embroidered over the heart, and khakis.

He smiled and shook his head. "Sorry, Mother. Not this one."

Her face registered her disappointment, but she kept smiling; they did let her in on some things, and she had even helped them a time or two, filling them in on town gossip. And certain things overheard.

When they were alone, Chief Burke said, "Okay, shoot."

"You know anyone on the force up in Boston? I need to find out how the investigation's going on that museum heist."

"The two statues from the Isabel Langford Eldredge Museum?"

His friend nodded.

"Last I heard, it was dead in the water. No leads."

"You know anyone?" he asked again.

The Chief nodded. "I have an uncle in homicide up there. He could probably find out."

"I want to go up and talk to whoever's in charge of the case."

The Chief raised his eyebrows. "You want to tell me what this is all about?"

"I wish I could."

His friend looked out the window. "Something to do with the Abbey."

"In a way." Bartholomew looked up from his coffee and waited.

"Well," said the Chief, "I can't very well ask my uncle to arrange for this religious Brother, who's a friend of mine, to talk to the inspector. But," he leaned back in his chair and smiled, "I suppose I could go with you. I'd need a reason, though."

"That special advisory from Homeland Security?"

The Chief thought about it. "That might work. And if they failed to see the connection, I would simply tell them I was not in a position to divulge anything. Which would be basically true—since I don't know anything that could be divulged."

Bartholomew shook his head, in mock awe at the convoluted reasoning.

"Jesuitical thinking," explained the Chief.

The next day in Boston they talked to the lieutenant in charge of the investigation. Who failed to see any remote connection between the ILE robbery and Homeland Security. But this was Arleigh Burke's nephew, so it must be all right.

They had nothing. One set of prints on the glass of water that the night security guard had offered the sunstruck nun. With no FBI match. That was all, and the weird fact that they'd used an early form of gelignite. Why weird? "Because everything else was so well thought out and high-tech, you'd think they'd use a modern explosive, like Semtex or C4. Not some unstable World War I explosive used in trench warfare. Definitely weird."

"What about the night security guard's description of the thieves?" Bartholomew asked.

"What description? We have three paragraphs of detail on the habits they were wearing—and three lines on the nuns themselves. The sunstruck one was medium. The other two weren't—one was short, the other tall. Helpful, right?"

The description meant nothing to anyone—except Bartholomew, who did his best to mask his interest.

"But if the other guard, who's still in a coma over at Mass General, dies," the lieutenant concluded, "this one will be going over to your uncle's bailiwick." He looked at Chief Burke. "Homicide."

Neither of them spoke, as the Chief piloted the old white Bravada out of the city. Finally he said, "Well, this has certainly been an interesting afternoon."

"Sorry, Dan." But he offered no more than that.

The Chief glanced at his monk friend. "Except you seemed to register something when he gave that description of the nuns."

"What description?" replied Bartholomew with a chuckle, hoping to disarm his friend. "Short, tall, and in between?"

"Yeah, that one," the Chief replied, not disarmed.

When his friend was not forthcoming, he sighed sadly. "We go back a long ways, you and I. And you've helped me a lot these past four years. And not just in police work. So—we'll just count this day towards that."

Bartholomew nodded. It felt strange, not being able to tell his old friend, with whom he'd recently worked so closely, anything about what he was working on. Or that the trip to Boston had actually been quite productive.

All he had to do now was get alone, where he could do some forensic thinking. He hoped the tide was out. He could do with a walk on the flats.

But first he would check on Pangur Ban.

23 | pangur farewell

As soon as he got home, Brother Bartholomew went to his room. The old friary cat was curled on the foot of his bed, pretty much as he had been for the past few days. Sitting down on the bed next to him, he gently stroked the back of his old friend's neck, till a feeble purr came. The cat opened his eyes and recognized him. Then closed them again—but kept purring.

Choking up, Bartholomew prayed. Should I have him put to sleep? There's not much quality of life here.

Be patient; he has only a little while longer. He just needs you to love him.

Suddenly silent sobs wracked Bartholomew.

The purring ceased. His old friend was asleep again.

Gripped by another wave of grief, the monk got up, pulled his windbreaker back on, and headed out onto the flats.

Leaving his shoes and socks at the stone jetty, he drifted northward towards Eastham, trying to put his old companion out of his mind. Let the sun and haze do their work.

There were a few people out on the vast open stretches—a mother with two little girls in sundresses, a little tow-headed boy with a sand bucket. In the distance, a flick of red against the haze—an older boy with a kite.

At the horizon the milky wash blended seamlessly with the pellucid waters of the bay, making it impossible to tell where sea ended and sky began. The dark and rusted hull of the distant target ship seemed suspended—a ghost ship in a pearl sky.

Beguiled, he felt as if he were part of a seaside painting by a French Impressionist. . . .

Sun-besotted, in love with the light, day after day he would come out here in his broad-brimmed hat and white linen duster, paint box and fresh canvas clamped under one arm, balky easel under the other. He kept coming back, because the flats kept changing. And they were changing now, as he gazed at the tiny summer cottages along the shore, gray-white sea birds snugged down in the dune grass.

Bartholomew sighed and shook his head. Reverie-time was over. Time to get to work.

It was pretty obvious that they'd done it. What was not as obvious was why.

Rule out the professional art theft angle. Hilda was right; they were not that type. Their disguise worked so well, because it was no disguise at all. That was a masterstroke—whoever decided that they should pull it off in their old habits.

Did that mean there *was* a mastermind?

Had to be. The whole thing was too well thought out—the "1812 Overture," the speed of the removal—all of it.

What about the gelignite?

The one unmasterful touch. Low tech. Old tech. Something left over from the Spanish Civil War. . . . Which brought him back to why.

Nothing came. Over the years he'd learned that when an answer was not emerging, instead of cudgeling the conundrum, if he just backed away from it and left it alone for a spell, it would sometimes resolve itself.

Trust the process, he reminded himself. He relaxed and drifted, letting his attention be caught by the reflection of the sun on the surface of a little pool of trapped water. A breeze stirred it, and the sun became thousands of diamonds.

And the answer came: Because the statues had some unique importance to them. That day in the museum Esperanza, who knew his instructions, had disappeared. And nearly made them all late. To sketch those two statues.

Why hadn't she just bought a disposable camera? No money. And the museum probably didn't allow photos. Most didn't.

Where did she get the steno pad and pen? From the bookshop. Or an office. People had a hard time saying no to her. Which meant she could speak English—not fluently, perhaps, but a lot better than she was letting on.

So why was the sketch so important? That was key—and he'd reached another impasse. Trust the process. He wandered on.

She was making the sketches for someone else.

Who?

Someone to whom they would be as important, or maybe even more important.

Incidentally, they were also important to Immaculata. She was trying to persuade Esperanza to leave, but not trying hard enough to simply make her stop. Until he came on the scene. And when they apologized, neither of them mentioned the sketches.

So they were all in it together. All three of them. Who were the sketches for?

Someone—not there. Back home, maybe.

Impasse. Drift. Nothing. Leave it.

Try another angle. What about the statues themselves?

All he knew was what Doyle said on TV. Twelfth or thirteenth century, from France or Italy or Spain.

Or Spain.

What had they said in the car on the way up? They were local girls. Who seldom traveled. Esperanza had family in

Toledo. Chances were, the others had not been more than a dozen miles from Pamplona. Ergo, whatever the statues reminded them of, was in the vicinity of Pamplona.

And so was the person she was doing the sketches for.

So the bottom question was still—why? Were there other statues like them back home? Were these—missing?

His arms suddenly felt clammy, and he glanced at them. Goose bumps. He was onto something—or getting close.

⇜

When he got back to the friary, the Senior Brother met him at the door. "Pangur's gone," he said softly. He put an arm around Bartholomew's shoulders, as the latter wept. When the grief subsided, he said gently, "Don't think you're over the worst of it; it'll be back. When it comes, don't hurry it or ignore it. Just let it run its course."

Bartholomew nodded, wiping his eyes.

That evening after supper, in the last rays of the sun, they had a burial service in the little pet cemetery behind the friary. The Brothers were there, and the calligraphy guild, and a number of the abbey children who had come to know him. They sang "All creatures, great and small."

Then a Brother played "Ashoken Farewell" on the violin, and each older child put a shovelful of dirt on the little pine box, with the youngest ones putting a flower on it.

Finally Bartholomew planted a dogwood sapling at the foot of it. One of the Brothers had to finish it for him. Grief came in waves.

By Mass the following morning, Bartholomew felt some-what better, though he'd not slept much without Pangur Ban at the foot of his bed. It had been a hard night.

After the service, as he was returning his processional robe and green scapular to his peg in the vesting corridor, Ed Robertson came up to him.

"Brother Bart, I need a favor. I've got to go to San Diego tomorrow for a weeklong television directors' workshop. Normally I tutor the Navarre Sisters in English tomorrow afternoon. You subbed for me once before; would you mind taking that hour for me and next week, too?"

"Happy to," said the monk, smiling. He'd been wanting to talk to them, but could not figure how to do it without raising their suspicion. "What do I have to do?"

Ed exhaled, noticeably relieved. "Just get them practicing their English."

"How good are they?"

The former teacher thought about that. "You know, I'm not

sure. They're learning really fast, but—sometimes I get the funny feeling they're more fluent than they're acting." He shrugged. "Holy mystery. Well, thanks; I owe you one."

"No problem. Where do I meet with them?"

"Conference room in the creative arts building."

The next afternoon it was raining hard, so everyone was glad to be indoors. When he joined the three exchange Sisters they giggled and greeted him in unison: "Good afternoon, Brother Bartholomew."

"*Buenas tardes, mis hermanas,*" he replied with a polite bow. And then added with enthusiasm, "*¡Vivan las tres Marías!*"

They all laughed.

Nodding towards the streaming window, he asked, "The rain in Spain—*does* it stay mainly on the plain?"

They looked at him like he'd just grown another head.

Nodding again, he simplified. "It's raining."

They all smiled and nodded emphatically. "Much rain!" said Maria Constanza.

"Long rain," added Maria Esperanza, glad to be able to make a contribution

"Flowers need much long rain," summarized Maria Immaculata, showing off.

"Very good!" responded Bartholomew, clapping. "Now, each of you tell me: What do you like best about your life here in the abbey?" He looked at Constanza first.

"Your trucks work good."

From their drive up to Boston for the funeral, Bartholomew recalled that she was the Sister who fixed things at home. "Your trucks at home don't work well?"

"We have two. One big, one little. The big one, Generalissimo, gives me big headache!"

"Generalissimo Franco?"

"No!" declared Constanza. "Generalissimo Fiat!" and they all laughed.

"You drive a Fiat truck at home!" Bartholomew deduced.

"When he decides to go. Sometimes he needs, how you say—*persuasion.*" Making a fist, she smacked the imagined truck upside its fuel pump. They laughed harder, including Bartholomew. So far, so good.

"Maria Immaculata—what do you like most?"

"Ice cream!" she declared.

"Why?"

"Cone better," she replied simply.

"Until you spill," giggled Maria Esperanza. She and Constanza laughed. Esperanza mimed an imaginary cone dripping on the front of her habit. As she greatly exaggerated Immaculata's horrified response, all of them laughed. Obviously Immaculata's religious name reflected a well-known and much-teased trait.

He turned to Esperanza. "And you? What do you like?"

"Having time to draw!" She took an imaginary charcoal pencil to an imaginary pad.

"You don't have time at home?"

"Not like here."

"Tell me about home."

The three Marias looked at one another. Esperanza spoke up. "Our convent has forty-three Sisters."

"Go on," coaxed Bartholomew, turning to Immaculata.

"It is nine centuries old."

"Really!" he exclaimed, genuinely impressed. He turned to Constanza. "Who is in charge?"

"Mother Superior," the swarthy one answered promptly.

"Tell me about her."

"Nothing to tell."

"Her name?"

"Maria Patientia."

"Why?"

When Constanza was not forthcoming, he turned to the other two. "Anyone?"

"She is much bright," explained Immaculata, tapping her temple, "and much fast."

Bartholomew nodded and smiled. "And so," he paused to think of the most graceful way of putting it, "with someone not so bright or so fast, she is not always—*patientia?*"

They smiled and nodded.

"What do all of you look forward to about going home?"

"Fiesta!" cried Esperanza. And then more haltingly in English, "Each year we have the festival. Of our main saint, Fermín. Bullfights, parties, everyone comes."

Bartholomew chuckled. "I've heard of your fiesta."

"And next year," Esperanza added, "we celebrate the monastery's thousandth birthday!"

"Really," replied Bartholomew, shaking his head. "A thousand years!"

The other two threw a look at Esperanza, who abruptly lost her enthusiasm.

Thereafter, much of their fluency in English seemed to drain away, as they gave Bartholomew the simplest of answers to his queries.

When the session was over, they thanked him and pointed out it was no longer much rain outside.

As he left, he felt he was getting closer. To what, he wasn't sure, but—closer.

25 | two circles

That evening after supper, as Bartholomew glanced through *The Boston Globe*, his eye fell on an item at the back of the local news section. The Isabel Langford Eldredge Museum had retained the consulting services of antique art specialist Sean Padraig Doyle, author of *The Eye of the Beholder*. Formerly of Harvard and now in private practice, Dr. Doyle would oversee the recovery of their stolen statues.

Bartholomew smiled. His old friend and mentor had gotten the position he'd obviously been angling for in that interview after the robbery. Which made him the only person other than the police who might have any knowledge, no matter how specious, of the statues' whereabouts. And since the police had nothing, like it or not, he was going to have to have a word with Dr. D.

He did not look forward to it. Not wanting to know why Doyle had left Dartmouth, he had made no effort to contact him—then or now. But Mother Michaela had charged him to investigate the theft thoroughly, to ascertain any involvement of the Navarre Sisters. He was going to have to see Doyle.

Four days later the opportunity arose. Brother Ambrose was flying to Nebraska to visit his father, who'd had a massive heart attack. Ambrose asked Bartholomew to take him to the airport, since both of them knew he'd need some help getting ready for what was certain to be a traumatic trip.

Bartholomew called Doyle to see if they could meet afterwards. Finding him was not that difficult, though the chilly reception of the History of Art Department's secretary indicated that Dr. Doyle's *persona* was no longer *grata* at Harvard.

Sounding genuinely pleased to hear from him, Doyle suggested they meet at 4:30 at the Black Rose.

It was precisely 4:30 as Bartholomew entered the dim interior of the old Irish pub. Doyle was already at the bar, a pint of Guinness in front of him—actually half a pint, which upon seeing Bartholomew he downed and ordered another for each of them. "Well, Andrew, me boy, tell me all ye've been up to since the green machine finished with us."

"For openers, it's Brother Bartholomew now, not Andrew."

"Are you serious?" He squinted at the monk. "By God, you *are!* Well, tell me all about it, and don't skip a jot or a tittle."

Bartholomew filled him in on the gist of it, leaving out the forensic adventures of the past four years.

"You always were a serious one," Doyle said appreciatively when he'd finished. "You could laugh, but you seldom smiled." He ordered another round, but Bartholomew put his hand over the top of his nearly empty glass and shook his head.

"I've got a long drive ahead of me. Tell me about you."

Doyle did not go into the details of his abrupt departure from the Hanover campus, beyond alluding to an evening of too much Irish whiskey and too much Irish charm. Living on his publisher's advance, he took a year off to produce *The Eye of the Beholder,* into which he poured all his passion for his field. The *New Yorker* had taken a liking to it, as had the NYTBR, and it had become an instant backlist success.

"I read it, Dr. D, and arranged to get a copy for our library. It was brilliant. The Irish may not be the best administrators, but when it comes to the written word they are a race of geniuses. In fact, English Lit might as well be called Irish Lit, once you get to the twentieth century. You did your heritage proud."

Doyle beamed. "Andrew, or whatever you call yourself these days, I always considered you a man of discriminating taste."

The luck of the Irish continued to hold for Doyle. As it happened, Harvard had an opening in its History of Art Department the following year, and the author of the acclaimed *The Eye of the Beholder* was a luminous addition to their short list of candidates. It didn't hurt that Doyle had been at Trinity College Dublin on a Fulbright at the same time as the head of the department.

The next ten years passed uneventfully, and then—"'Twas the night before Christmas' a year ago. Our department was havin' a wee celebration, and the head's wife, with perhaps a bit too much nog in her noggin, decided to find out if all those outrageous rumors were true."

He stared soulfully into the black liquid in his glass, as it released its tiny bubbles.

"So?" Bartholomew prompted, fearing that his friend might soon lose track of everything.

"So I was careful to do me carrying-on off-campus. And the pooh-bahs at Harvard decided to ignore the wild oats of their wild Colonial boyo."

"Until the Christmas party."

"Trouble was," said Doyle, his brogue growing ever thicker, "I'd had a few meself. I should have resisted. In the daylight I surely *would* have resisted. But—" his voice trailed off, and he just shook his head.

"Well," said Bartholomew, "tell me about your new adventure. In that television interview you intimated that you knew certain people who knew certain people who might know . . . all very *sub rosa*." He chuckled. "Do you *really* have entree into the art underworld? Or was that just to impress the ILE?"

Doyle looked carefully around before replying, then lowered his voice till Bartholomew could barely hear him. "It's not who you know; it's who they *think* you know. And it works both ways. The art thieves think I know certain people. So does the museum. And the people in the middle—the real ones—will eventually get in touch with me."

Bartholomew smiled. "Sounds a bit chimerical, to say the least. Like something out of Graham Greene. What exactly *do* you know?"

"Beyond what I said in that interview?"

Bartholomew nodded.

"I know the statues are *not* being held for ransom. We'd have heard something by now. *I'd* have heard something, since it's now known that I am the go-between. It's also known privately—*very* privately—that half a million dollars might be in the offing for their safe return."

"No takers?"

"Not so far. And each day makes it less likely that it's a ransom deal." He chuckled. "At the very least, there'd have been some indication that half a million is laughably low."

"So if ransom's not the motive—what is?"

"It's an eccentric. Probably someone who's seen those statues for years and always thought they'd look perfect at the entrance of his formal garden on some obscure estate. He finally did something about it. That would be my guess."

"How long before you have to come up with something concrete?"

"To justify the exorbitant retainer I've insisted on? Let's just say I'd better have something solid by the end of the year, or," he shuddered, "there's a small liberal arts college in Dubuque that's looking to start a History of Art Department— a very small college." He shuddered again, and ordered another Guinness.

"You must have some plan."

"I'm letting it be known that I'd pay handsomely for information of any sort. And the museum would pay *very* handsomely if it turned out to lead to something. Beyond that?" He shrugged. "I hear Dubuque is really quite charming in the early spring."

"And even that has produced—nothing?"

Doyle looked at him and tilted his head, then shook it as if to clear the muzzies—and, too late, Bartholomew realized that he had asked one question too many.

"Now why would a monastic be so interested in an art heist?" Doyle ruminated. "So interested that he would locate and call up a friend he's not clapped eyes on for twenty-six years? Just to renew old acquaintances?"

"I told you," said Bartholomew lightly, "I saw the piece in the paper and got the impulse to call you."

"So, ye did, Laddie, so ye did." He looked at him, his eyes narrowing. "Or—the piece in the newspaper is doing exactly what it was intended to, bringing someone who knows something into my circle of proximity." As he spoke, he traced two circles on a little pool of moisture on the bar—one circle for Bartholomew, another for himself. And then he drew the first one over to the second.

Bartholomew laughed but did not smile. If this were chess, he had just lost his rook. How to lighten, how to divert—

At that moment the new singing group, Little Skellig, launched into their first set piece of the evening, a sad old ballad that Dyer-Bennett had recorded, and Doyle and Doane had often sung along with him, *Down by the Salley Garden*. They joined in now, verse upon mournful verse, of young lovers whose moment was forever lost.

When it was over, both men were moist of eye and thick of throat. Bartholomew took advantage of the emotional moment. He said huskily, "Dr. D, this has been an afternoon I'll not soon forget!" Seemingly overcome, he shook his head and waved the bartender over, paying for what they'd had and what his friend might have. And left.

In the car he wondered if Doyle had gone for it. He'd been careful not to say where his friary was, or even in what general direction. With luck, he would never see him again.

But he did not hold out much hope. Sean Padraig Doyle had the luck of the Irish, and his overly inquisitive monk friend was now the biggest lead he had. The only lead.

Three days later it was time for Bartholomew's second English session with the Navarre Sisters. Since it was a warm, sunny August day, he suggested they spend it out on the flats.

"Truth?" asked Esperanza.

"Truth."

They almost knocked him over on their way out the door.

Out on the broad reach of sand, barefoot and without time constraint, they seemed like children playing.

"Tell me about Pamplona," Bartholomew ventured.

"First, you tell," responded Immaculata.

"Tell what?"

"What you know about our country and our town."

He thought for a moment. "Well, I've read Malraux and Orwell and Hemingway on your war and also Hemingway on your bullfighting."

Esperanza clapped her hands. "Papa put us on the map!"

Immaculata glared at her. "Pamplona was important a thousand years before Hemingway," she declared with disgust.

Bartholomew looked at her, eyebrows raised.

"Pamplona was most important town on the *Camino*, other than the destination—Santiago de Compostela."

"The *Camino?*"

"The Way of Saint James."

The monk stopped, his feet ankle-deep in a pool between sandbars. "The pilgrimage," he murmured.

Immaculata nodded. "Once, as many pilgrims went to Santiago as to Rome."

"So Pamplona really is more than a thousand years old."

They all nodded.

"I must go there some day."

"We will take you to all the sites you must see," said Constanza with enthusiasm. "*I* will drive."

Bartholomew stopped parallel to the farthest-out sapling marking the channel to the harbor. They had come a mile, and it was time to turn around.

He remembered something else about Pamplona. "You know what your town is best known for, other than the bull-fights and the fiesta?"

They looked at him and drew a blank. "It is the home of Miguel."

They were shocked. "You know the Abbot?"

His eyebrows knit. "I don't think he's an Abbot." He gave them another hint: "Among American aficionados, his nickname was Big Mig." He paused. They still didn't get it. "Miguel Indurain! The greatest cyclist who ever lived! Five-time winner of the Tour de France!"

"Oh."

"I know his uncle," said Constanza.

The tide was coming in now, quickly enough that they had to head for shore. Already two charter fishing boats were circling out in the deep water, waiting for the tide to come in enough to admit them to the marsh creek harbor grandly known as Eastport.

Esperanza looked out at the boats behind them. "Portuguese?"

"Nope, local Cape Codders. The Portuguese are commercial fishermen."

"What does that mean?" asked Immaculata.

"They sell their catch to the market. These," he waved to the charter boats, "are for sport."

He pointed north, but the Provincetown Tower was occluded by the haze. "You know, I'd like to take you up there sometime and show you P-Town. Very picturesque."

"We know!" said Esperanza with enthusiasm. "Sister Hilda took us for the Blessing."

"The Blessing of the Fleet?" Each year, on the last Sunday of June, in celebration of the Feast of Corpus Christi, the commercial fishing fleet received a blessing from the Bishop. The boats, decked out in pennants and bunting, paraded in single file past the end of the wharf, from which the Bishop prayed for each and sprinkled it with Holy Water.

Esperanza nodded. "We were on one that belonged to friends of Sister Hilda, the *Jubileu*. A trawler owned by the Silviera family—seafarers on both sides. From Oporto. Our two Sisters from Framingham joined us. We sang the seven-fold Amen."

"Everyone was much pleased!" Immaculata added. "The Bishop waved. I think our boat won."

"It wasn't a competition," corrected Constanza. "But they do want us back next year."

Bartholomew was nonplussed. "You three amaze me! Just when I think I know you, I realize I know nothing."

They all laughed.

As they got closer to the abbey, Bartholomew shifted the conversation to current events, global, then national, then local. They were just going over the walkway to the Caulfields' yard when he asked if they'd heard about the robbery of two statues up in Boston.

Suddenly, like a balloon rapidly deflating, all the fun went out of their outing. They nodded and shrugged and murmured assent, as if to say, yes, they'd heard, but hadn't paid much attention to it. He thought of mentioning that they'd seen them on their field trip–funeral day. Esperanza had even sketched one. But it was too soon to bring the heat.

He did say one thing, after they'd washed off their feet and were donning their shoes. "I understand the guard who was injured in the blast is still in a coma."

No one responded.

Then Esperanza said softly, "I pray for him every day."

27 | esperanza, call home

No one could remember who donated Old Ben to the convent. The antique grandfather clock had always been there in the foyer of the main entrance. It kept remarkably accurate time, gaining or losing less than a minute a week, depending on the humidity. It chimed every quarter-hour, with a deeper tone for tolling the hour. Encased in cherry wood, the chimes had a rich, mellow sound. Newly-arrived Postulants sometimes complained that Ben kept them awake, though after a night or two, none seemed to notice.

On this night the last stroke of three had just died away when three silhouettes filed silently past Ben and queued at the front door. The lead figure opened the door a crack and surveyed the Common in all directions. Satisfied that there was no one abroad, she opened the door wider, and the three slipped out, shutting it noiselessly behind them.

They went to the creative arts building, where the tall one extracted the key from beneath the second pot of geraniums in the right-hand window box, and let them in. Without turning on a light, they went into the administration office, drew down the window shade, and booted up the computer. In a moment the medium, thin one was into Hotmail, where she had an e-mail address. She quickly typed up an e-mail in Spanish, requesting an emergency transfer of funds to their account at the Cape Cod Five Cents Savings Bank, to cover an inadvertent overdraft.

But instead of sending it, she minimized the e-mail window, leaving it ready to be summoned instantly should someone suddenly materialize and wonder what on earth they were doing in the arts building at 3:15 in the morning. At home, they would explain, the Sister responsible for the bursar's office was on the Internet only one hour a day, from 9:00 to 10:00, and there was a six-hour time differential. And since they needed an immediate response. . . .

With luck they would never have to use that story. And now Immaculata got down to the real reason for their being there. In a moment she was cyber-chatting live with MP@SoMoN.sp.

MI: We're all here.

MP: You said you needed to talk.

MI: We do. Something's come up that could be a problem.

MP: First, is there any change in the guard's condition?

MI: Unfortunately, no. We are all praying for him. And so are all the abbey Sisters. He is at the top of their abbey prayer vigil. We're not sure why, but suspect it may have something to do with the problem we need to tell you about.

MP: We're praying here too, though no one but me knows why.

MI: Esperanza says he's in God's hands, and that He will not let him die.

MP: I hope she is speaking in her mystical voice. Now fill
        me in on where we are with the parcels.

MI: The parcels are secure.

MP: Where?

MI: The abbey has a great deal of enclosed storage space
        in what were once commercial greenhouses.
        Fortunately they did an inventory in June and won't
        do another for at least a year. There are religious arti-
        facts of every size and description stored there, so if
        anyone happens to look under the tarpaulin we put
        over them, they won't think anything of them.

MP: Well done! What about the boat?

MI: We've code-named her the Jubilatté. We were on her
        for the Blessing of the Fleet and have been invited
        back next year. She's a Portuguese trawler with a
        winch and boom on board, so we should have no
        trouble loading them when the time comes.

MP: Is the captain with us?

MI: Cesario? Mostly. His wife, Rita, is a daily communi-
        cant and is distantly related to Esperanza. She's
        fallen in love with our project and assures us her hus-
        band will be 100% by the time we need him.

MP: Your cover story?

MI: We're working on it. We may blanket them with
        flowers, our gift to the J-Boat, a sort of floating float
        for the Blessing. The captain has gotten a taste for
        having the premier ship in that event.

MP: Tell me about the freighter.

MI: Rita has a cousin who's captain of a tramp steamer
        out of Lisbon. He goes all over the world, and he's
        willing to carry the parcels across for us.

MP: Can we count on him?

MI: We can't be *sure* of anything, MP. But we're told he
       does have some say over his ports of call. His name
       is Mario Bordalo. She's talked to him, and he's
       intrigued. He'll do it for the Blessed Mother. In July.

MP: I wanted to get them over here in the spring.

MI: We know. But there's a problem. *He* has a problem.
       His rudder is broken. He's in drydock in Valparaiso,
       where his cousin talked to him. It shouldn't take
       much longer, but in Venezuela nothing is ever cer-
       tain. And that's backed up his itinerary everywhere.

MP: When can we get them?

MI: At this point all he will confirm is that he will clear
       New York two days before the Blessing. That means
       he can rendezvous with the J-boat on Georges Bank
       after the Blessing. He should make Lisbon ten days
       later.

MP: That's ten months from now! But I suppose there's
       nothing we can do. What's the new problem?

MI: There's a monk here who took us to the funeral and
       just before it to the museum. He saw Esperanza
       sketching one of the parcels. And he knows we have
       the old formal habits that the guard described,
       because we were wearing them for the funeral.

MP: So?

MI: We think he suspects something.

MP: Why?

MI: He's starting to ask questions—all very innocent,
       except he has a reputation around here for being
       some kind of amateur sleuth. He's helped the local
       constabulary solve crimes. And now he's found out
       how old the monastery is.

MP: How did he find that out?

MI: Esperanza told him.

MP: Put her on.

ME: Yes, Mother?

MP: Maria Esperanza, I want you to practice the vocabu-
       lary of silence. Do you understand?

ME: Yes, Mother. I'm sorry.

MP: Forgiven. We must all be so careful.

ME: We will be. Until next Tuesday?

MP: Next Tuesday. Now get some sleep.

⁊⋒

Maria Patientia left her computer and walked out onto the
terrace adjacent to her quarters. It was a little late for an attack
of conscience, let alone "My God, what have I done?" She
knew exactly what she had done, and what she was doing. She
was proceeding without His blessing, which she had deliberately avoided asking for.

Other than the night watchman, her only qualm was that
she had put three other souls in peril—three who loved and
trusted her. If the whole thing turned sour, went totally wrong,
there would be disgrace and ruin, of course. And long prison
terms for all of them. That was the problem. She deserved
whatever came; they didn't.

And what of the guard hovering between life and death in
a coma?

How many things had she not considered when she
embarked on this course? And none could be reconsidered
now.

Did she have regrets? Yes. If she could rewind time to
three months ago, would she do differently?

She thought about that. No.

The die is cast, she thought, looking up at the milky haze. We're going ahead, with or without you.

28 | death angel

Two days later, Bartholomew was pruning in the rose garden when his cell phone went off.

"Brother Bart?" It was Susan Saxon, their guest coordinator. She was bubbling. "We've just had the most wonderful visit with someone writing an article for the Sunday *Globe* magazine on religious art in Massachusetts. His thesis is that it's gone about as far forward as it can go, and what's happening now is we're beginning to rediscover some of the great treasures of the past. I've shown him the church, and he's blown away by our mosaics and frescoes!"

A chill went through Bartholomew. "What's his name?"

"Dr. Sean Doyle. The most charming man!" She waited, then continued, a little disappointed that he did not share her enthusiasm. "Anyway, he wants to interview some of our religious, and I thought of you. Can you come to the guesthouse? I'm giving him tea on the sun porch."

"Sure, give me a couple of minutes to clean up."

How did he find me? Bartholomew wondered, as he washed his hands and put on a more presentable shirt. He had not bothered to keep Dartmouth informed of his whereabouts, so their alumni association had no record of him. Oh, well, he's here, and that's that.

Joining them on the sun porch, he was relieved to see that the whites of Doyle's eyes really were white, not streaked with red. Nor was the nose red, and there were no red rims around his pupils. Dr. D was, in fact, bright-eyed and bushy-tailed.

All at once he realized he was glad to see him. Apparently the feeling was reciprocated, for Doyle jumped up and stuck out his hand.

"Boyo! 'Tis good to see you now!"

Susan looked at them, astonished. "You know each other?"

Both men nodded.

"He was my History of Art professor in college," Bartholomew explained. "A pretty good one, too."

"Well," said Susan with a smile, relieved that Brother Bartholomew was showing a little more enthusiasm, "I'll leave you two to it." She got up to leave, saying to Bartholomew, "When you're done, would you take your professor over to the creative arts building? He ought to see what the guilds are doing now."

Bartholomew waited until she was out of earshot. "You didn't come here to see mosaics and frescoes," he said softly. "You came to see me."

"No, laddie, you're wrong there. I am doing the article. And I *am* impressed with what you all are doing here. It's like you've brought over artisans from Italy to do what they used to do better than anyone, anywhere."

"Actually, we have. Brought over a master mosaicist from Ravenna and a master fresco artist from Florence, and sent apprentices over there to study under them. We have a stone carver from France, a bronze sculptor for the doors, and overseeing everything, an Irish genius who makes it all come together."

Doyle laughed. "Sure'n I'm not surprised to hear that! We *did* save Western Civilization, after all, as that darlin' man Tom Cahill made clear."

Bartholomew chuckled. "Come on now, how did you find me?"

"Well, the green machine was no help. And since you somehow neglected to tell me the name of this place or its whereabouts, all I had to go on was your status as a monastic. And since you'd come by car, I figured your monastery had to be within a hundred miles."

He shook his head. "Ah, Google is a marvelous invention! Eventually I narrowed it down to the likely ones, then started making calls." He paused and put on an exaggerated brogue. "Now would there be, by any chance, a monk named Bartholomew in that lovely place?"

"I'm impressed, Dr. D. You missed your calling. Or maybe you've found it."

Doyle sighed and smiled. "I need your help, boyo. We both know the investigation is going nowhere. And the five bits in the newspapers? And the four interviews on the telly? Not one bite. Not even a nibble. Except you."

Bartholomew said nothing.

Doyle looked at him. "You're not going to help me, are you."

"Believe me, I would if I could, but—" He shrugged and smiled. It wasn't a lie, exactly.

He stood up and said, "Come on, I'll show you the creative arts building. You should see what's in the works. Then I'm going to have to get back to work."

As they walked over to where the guilds did their creating, Doyle said, "I'm going to feature your abbey in my article. Something very special is going on here."

Room by room Bartholomew showed him what the stained glass people were doing, and the calligraphers—his responsibility—and the mosaicists and the stone carvers and the artists.

"I feel like I've stepped back into the Renaissance," Doyle murmured appreciatively.

Finally they came to the large room used by the artists and sculptors. Several were at work, including, at the far end of the room, Maria Esperanza. She was doing a large charcoal drawing on a big pad, and Doyle was drawn to it, as if by a magnet.

The picture was of a sculpted angel, almost life-size, his wings semi-folded. His because, while angels were supposed to be without gender, this one was definitely male. Illumined by a shaft of light from somewhere above, he bore a solemn, arresting expression, and his right hand was outstretched, as if he were summoning the beholder.

Beckoning—Bartholomew thought—like a death angel. One so three-dimensional it seemed almost alive. He shuddered. Focus! What does the background tell you? Not much. Vague, dim, cavernous—it seemed to be the interior of a cathedral.

Working on neutral brown paper, Maria Esperanza had completed layering in the charcoal shading, and with a white piece of chalk was now applying highlights. Fascinated, the two men watched her work.

Finally Doyle broke the silence. "Excuse me, but where have you seen this?"

She smiled and looked at him blankly, then turned to Bartholomew for the translation.

"She's Spanish," he quickly explained, "over here on an exchange program." He told her in his schoolboy Spanish what Doyle had just asked, though he was pretty sure she'd understood the English.

Smiling, she nodded and tapped her temple.

"You *imagined* this?" asked Doyle, incredulous. He looked at the drawing, then at her. And rubbed his chin. "Whereabouts in Spain are you from?"

Bartholomew translated, and she replied "Navarre."

"Whereabouts in Navarre?"

She understood that. "Pamplona." She looked at Bartholomew, with a questioning glance.

He told her in Spanish that this man was gathering material for an article on religious art. And then added that he was also investigating the robbery at the Isabel Langford Eldredge Museum.

A flicker of alarm passed over her face before the smile returned. It was only for an instant, but both men saw it.

As Bartholomew walked Doyle back to his car, the latter asked, "You told her I was working for the museum—why?"

The monk shrugged. "No reason."

But as he waved to his departing friend, he asked himself the same question: Why *had* he told her?

29 | brother jonathan

It was the day of the vows service. In the evening, first-vowed members would make their final vows, and novices would be admitted into the Brotherhood and Sisterhood. For the inductees and the abbey family witnessing it, it would be as solemn—and joyful—as the sacrament of holy matrimony. Which in a sense it was.

Perceiving Novice Nicholas's mounting tension, after lunch Bartholomew suggested they take a bike ride.

"Don't we have work to do?" Koli asked.

"We do. But I'm declaring a holiday. We'll go out to Coast Guard Beach."

Riding out on the bike path, Bartholomew kept the speed down so they could talk. As he suspected, Koli had much on his mind.

"You think I'll make a good Brother?"

"You'll be fine."

"No, seriously."

"I *am* serious."

They rode on for a bit. "I'm not so much worried about now. I'm thinking about down the road—twenty or thirty years from now."

Bartholomew glanced at him with a dour smile. "Beware the dogs of noonday?" A young monk burning with zeal, on fire for God, had little problem with doubt or regret. But later, in late middle age, as he looked down the long, lonely corridor of his remaining years. . . .

"Yeah," admitted Koli, "something like that. Will I—ever want to leave?"

"Oh, probably," responded Bartholomew, keeping it light. "We all do, at one time or another."

"But will I actually do it?"

The monk hesitated. "Honestly? I don't know. You won't have to. Not if God has called you, and you know it. He'll give you the strength to stay."

"Did He give it to you?"

His older friend nodded.

"Can I ask what it was?"

Resentment flashed across Bartholomew's face, but he took a deep breath and smiled. "Normally I'd say it's none of your business. But Koli, this is not a normal time for you. It's a momentous time. So—I'll tell you."

They crossed the Mid-Cape and glided past the octagonal National Seashore house where, as a park ranger, he once gave lectures before entering the friary. Entering the cool, shaded path that wound through the trees to the beach, he resumed.

"Was I ever tempted to leave? Four years ago I came this close." He held up thumb and forefinger with a sliver of day-light between them. "When I joined the novitiate, I was deeply in love. Almost got married. Leaving her was the hardest thing I ever had to do." He paused. "Until I had to do it again."

Koli almost responded, then waited.

"God well knows the void we religious have in our hearts—in our lives—when we choose not to take a life partner. It's all right to have such a hole, as long as we acknowledge it and ask Him to keep it filled with His love."

He glanced at Koli riding beside him. Did he understand? He seemed to.

"My problem was, I'd not acknowledged the emptiness. So, seventeen years later when I met her again, I was not prepared for the shock. My feelings for her were as strong as they'd been the last time I saw her. As were hers for me. She'd never married. And now she wanted what she'd been denied. She wanted me. Out of the Brotherhood. And God help me—I wanted to go."

Koli, mouth open, stared at him.

Bartholomew redirected their attention to the path in front of them. And smiled. "But I also wanted to stay. And I knew God wanted me to. In the end, that's what it turned on."

"Did you ever regret it?"

"No. Once it was settled, it was settled."

Koli seemed relieved. "And that was the only time you considered leaving. Or was it?"

It was an honest question, thought Bartholomew; it deserved an honest answer. He could remember his own misgivings at the threshold Koli faced.

"There was one other time," he went on, his voice barely audible. "Last year. About the time I hurt you—remember, in the orchard?"

Koli didn't say anything, but he remembered.

"*All* at once, all of our life . . . stopped making a whole lot of sense. In fact, it made no sense at all."

Koli said nothing. But Bartholomew, glancing at him, sensed that he'd been assailed with exactly the same thought. Recently. Today.

"I'd lost touch with God," the older man went on. "And without Him—without knowing that you're in the center of His will—*none* of this makes any sense."

Koli nodded emphatically; he *had* been thinking along the same lines.

"I mean," continued Bartholomew, "why would anyone in their right mind want to live this way? Why would they relinquish the right to own, to choose, and to marry? Give up control of one's time or space?" He paused. "Give up the right to make the final decision?"

Koli nodded again.

"They wouldn't. Unless they *knew* beyond the shadow of a doubt that He had called them to. Called them to love Him with all their heart and mind and soul and being—here. In this community of like-minded believers. Then," he shrugged and smiled, "it makes perfect sense!"

Koli grinned. This was helping.

"That's why I went down to Bermuda. To get reconnected—or else."

"Or else what?"

Bartholomew thought for a moment. "Or else leave."

"Leave? Why?"

"Because not to leave would be dishonest."

They had arrived at Coast Guard Beach. From the promontory in front of the old lifesaving station which once had surfboats that could run out to rescue shipwrecked sailors, Bartholomew pointed to the beach far below. "When I was a boy, all of that was paved. There was a road down there from here, and a parking lot, and even a long line of cabanas to change in."

"What happened?"

"You never heard of the Blizzard of Seventy-Eight?" Apparently not. "Well, the storm surge here was *fourteen feet* above mean high tide. It took away—everything."

As they were about to remount for the journey home, Bartholomew caught his gaze. "Koli, do you *know* God wants you to become a Brother?"

"Absolutely!" cried the novice. "We've been over it many times, He and I. He brought me here because this is the place I will be the most happy, serving Him. And you know what? I really am! I'm just nervous, that's all."

Bartholomew laughed. "You'll be fine!" Which, he realized, was what he'd said at the start of this conversation.

૨&

That evening was indeed a solemn occasion. The entire abbey membership processed in their robes, with white scapulars. First came the Cross, flanked by two candle bearers. Then the most senior members, followed by the choir, the Brothers and Sisters, and the newer members, with the clergy and the Abbess coming last.

The lights in the basilica were dimmed, so that the candles along the first rank of seats on either side of the center aisle would provide most of the illumination. The nave was redolent with incense, and the organ was playing the opening bars of Mozart's "Coronation Mass."

As always, the Eucharist would be the center, the heart of their worship. Bartholomew thought about that, as he and Koli found their designated seats. He had not liked it when, years before, they had begun having daily Mass. To him, Holy Communion was special—so special that he feared it would become ordinary if they did it every day. Familiarity breeds contempt.

So he wrestled with it, until the first weekday morning he went forward to receive. As he knelt at the altar, waiting for the priest to bring the Body and the Blood, suddenly he had a picture come to mind. Of ancient Rome. The pillars and temples and steps were all of white marble. Except it wasn't white; it was grimy and tarnished and stained.

Then as he watched, a crimson flood, as if a dam had burst, came roaring into the city, washing up the steps, the columns, the temples, covering everything. When it receded and drained away, it left the marble as it had been originally—white and pure and gleaming.

There were tears in his eyes as the priest offered him the chalice.

His attention was brought back to the present as the choir began the lyrical, soaring Kyrie. Was it his imagination? Or was the soprano section augmented—invisibly augmented? He gazed into the dim rafters above, half expecting to see triangular points of light—the tips of angel wings. He didn't see any—but that didn't mean they weren't there.

When it came time for Koli to go forward, make his vow, and receive his robe and his ring, Bartholomew accompanied him. Too late, it occurred to him that they probably should have practiced what they were about to do, ahead of time.

And sure enough, as he held up the robe, the newly minted monk somehow got his head in the armhole. Which meant disrobing and re-robing. To the stifled amusement of the abbey family.

When they finally got it right, and the new Brother's head emerged from the folds of his robe, he whispered, "Did we win?"

It was meant only for Bartholomew's ears, but such were the acoustics of the bandshell-like apse that all the nearest members heard it. And burst out laughing. Which caused those behind them to ask what was so funny. Then they laughed. Then the next laughed, and the next, till holy hilarity pealed down the nave.

And heaven and earth rejoiced at the addition of Brother Jonathan into the fold.

30 | the unthinkable

Plymouth was cold and gray even for November. A fog coming in from the bay could do that—suddenly drop the temperature by fifteen degrees or more.

Bartholomew sat at a window table of the designated second-floor restaurant overlooking the harbor. Doyle had picked it, and Doyle was late.

Actually, it was a compromise. Doyle wanted the meeting; Bartholomew saw no point to it. Then Doyle had gotten hard-nosed. "We'll meet halfway then. Or would you rather I come down there and arrange an interview with your three Spanish Sisters?"

"I'll come to Plymouth." And after he'd agreed, he realized that this, too, was a test. What he should have said was, "Fine, come ahead. No skin off my nose."

So now here he was, drinking coffee, waiting for SPD to arrive. He glanced at his watch; where *was* the man?

His eye fell on a group of four men at another window table. They, too, were drinking coffee and were huddled with heads close together, talking earnestly, leaving their meals untouched. One was older and bearded, mid-forties, two were in their twenties, and one, also bearded, was in between. All had dark hair, dark eyes, dark skin. Middle Eastern.

He was doing it, he rebuked himself. Profiling.

But after what the Chief had said last summer about the confidential alert from Homeland Security, they were *supposed* to be suspicious of anything that might be suspicious. It was their civic duty.

Did he want to live in a Big Brother state? The Rule of Fear, instead of the Rule of Law? Where did it end? When the Berlin Wall came down, it came out that the East German secret police—the *Stasi*—had dossiers on one out of three of their fellow countrymen! Did he want that?

No. What he wanted was not to have to worry about some demonically possessed agent of hell, bent on blowing up the Pilgrim Nuclear Power Station.

Ridiculous, seeing terrorists under every bush—yet what of the actor James Woods, who, according to news reports, had witnessed a terrorist dry run a month before 9-11? He had reported it to airline authorities and had been ignored. The horror to come was simply unthinkable.

Well, so was the destruction of Pilgrim. And he could do something. The way to the men's room went right by their table. Doyle was still nowhere to be seen. He got up and went.

They were definitely speaking some Middle Eastern language, and they did not see him coming until the last moment. Their leader leaned way forward, apparently making a point to the younger man across the table—but in the process covering what was spread on the table. Not before Bartholomew caught a glimpse of it, however. It was a map of the local coastline.

When he returned from the men's room, the map was gone, and they were speaking English. As he passed, his eyes happened to meet the youngest one's. It was barely for an instant, but Bartholomew saw something that troubled him.

Doyle was waiting at the bar for him.

"Sorry, boyo, for the delay. The troopers were out in force

on Route Three. I got pinched, trying not to be late." He looked at Bartholomew. "What is it, laddie? You look as if you've seen a ghost!"

"Something like that," he admitted. "The Ghost of Christmas Future—I hope not!"

Doyle might have pursued it, but he had his own problems. They each ordered a salad, and Doyle came out with it. "Andrew—Bartholomew—why can't we work together?"

"I don't know what you mean."

"What I mean is, you're my only hope of avoiding Dubuque. The museum's running out of patience. I've a friend on the board there, a lovely widow, but she's told me she can't keep the wolves at bay much longer."

"Dr. D, I'm sorry, but—"

"For auld lang syne, lad," he implored his friend. "For auld lang syne!"

Feeling deeply tugged, the monk just shook his head.

"That sister from Pamplona, the one who drew the angel," Doyle ruminated. "I keep thinking about her. She's connected with it somehow. . . . Wouldn't it be something if the thieves really *were* nuns?"

"The missing statues," Bartholomew quickly interjected, "were they angels?" He knew perfectly well they weren't, but he had to throw Doyle off the scent.

The art expert frowned. "No, I've seen an etching of the entrance. They were just a pair of old saints, male and female."

"No wings, no connection," said the monk cheerily.

Doyle smiled, too. "Are you Irish, by any chance?"

"With a family name like Doane, it's more than likely back there somewhere."

"Not too far back, I suspect," said Doyle, still smiling, "judging from the way you spin the blarney."

"What do you mean?"

"I mean last week I went over to talk to the lieutenant in charge of the investigation. And he mentioned that you and the Eastport police chief had been up to see him right after the robbery."

Bartholomew felt as if a mule had just kicked him in the stomach. He must have looked it, for Doyle added, "That's not idle curiosity, boyo. So I'm going to ask you one more time: Do you know where the statues are?"

"As God is my witness," Bartholomew replied emphatically, "I don't."

Doyle sighed. "I believe you. Where your soul spends eternity is too important to you, for you to lie to me. But you do know where they might be?"

"No."

"At least you know where they originally came from."

"No."

"Well, you know something!" he exclaimed, starting to get angry. "And you're not going to tell me what."

The monk said nothing—and hoped that he showed nothing.

Doyle paid for their lunch, and as they were leaving, he said, "I've one more card to play, before they pull the plug on me. I'm going over there."

"To do what?"

"To try to find two empty pedestals whose statues went missing about ninety years ago. I think I'll start in Spain. Northern Spain. Navarre, to be exact. Maybe Pamplona." He looked at Bartholomew sharply, who returned his look with what he hoped was a benign expression. "Think I'll find any-thing?"

Bartholomew shrugged, and they said goodbye, not as warmly as either of them would have liked.

On the way out, Bartholomew lagged behind to ask the waitress who'd brought their salads, about the four men who'd been at the table by the window earlier.

"Oh, that's Abou-Ali and his two sons. They're a land-scaping crew. Family business. Been here for years. And today they were joined by their cousin, just over from Riyadh. They brought him here for lunch, as a treat."

She looked at Bartholomew and tilted her head, adding pointedly, "I think it's a shame what's happening to perfectly innocent Middle Eastern people, because of 9-11. What's being done to them—not by us, by you outsiders—is nothing less than shameful!"

Duly chastened, Bartholomew thanked her for lunch. And made a mental note to tell Dan about the incident.

31 | memorial day remembrance

"You looked at him!" declared the cousin from Riyadh, turning to look into the eyes of the younger brother in the back seat. They were sitting in the cousin's rental car, parked facing the seawall above the beach.

Khalid stared back at him, mouth open, eyes widening.

"Well?" prompted his father, also turning to face him.

"I—I don't think so," Khalid managed.

The cousin turned to the father in the front passenger seat. "You assured me both of their hearts were firm. But I wonder about the younger one."

"They both went to camp-school in Riyadh before we came over. They hate the infidel. Nothing has changed."

The cousin's expression did not soften. "That was ten years ago. A long time. Imperceptible softening can happen in that length of time."

"It hasn't!" the father insisted.

The cousin looked in the rearview mirror at the older brother, who until now had not spoken. When he had the younger man's eyes, he asked softly, "Has it?"

Ahmed hesitated—and the cousin picked it up immediately. "Tell me now. Everything," he commanded in a quiet but forceful tone. "*Now!*"

Ahmed, his voice quavering, murmured, "Khalid has met a young woman. A Saudi. Her family is from Riyadh, like ours. She helps at a day-care center in Plymouth."

Khalid glared at his brother and said nothing.

"Is this true?" his father asked him.

The younger son gave the slightest of nods.

"When did this happen? You have been with me—always."

Khalid didn't answer, but his brother did. "When he went to get us coffee in the morning and in the afternoon. He met her at the coffee shop. She could see him coming from the day-care center, which was across the street, and would come down and meet him there."

Their father looked as if he had been shot. He turned to the cousin. "I knew nothing of this."

The cousin thought for a moment, then smiled. "Well, the damage is not irreparable. Never let him out of your sight. In time, his heart will firm up again. And we do have time. The operation is not until next summer."

He turned again to the younger brother. "Read your Qur'an. What it says about our obligation to slaughter the infidel, once jihad has been declared." He smiled again. "And do not forget the seventy-one virgins awaiting you in Paradise. Surely you can forswear one to gain seventy-one! And your name will be added to those on the Wall of Martyrs, to be revered for perpetuity."

Khalid smiled wanly.

The cousin turned to his father. "I will be honest with you, Abou-Ali, since you have been honest with me. Your family is too important to our operation to turn to another at this late hour. You are the ones chosen by Allah. I know he can count on you." He glanced in the rearview mirror at the occupants of the back seat. "*All* of you."

To their father he concluded, "I will be seeing our leader, when I go home next month. I will tell him you are ready for

Memorial Day. The young one will be fine. But—if his heart
does not firm up. . . ." He did not need to finish the sentence.
They knew what he meant. All of them.

è❧

That evening after supper, Bartholomew asked Anselm if
he could have a word with him.

"How goes the quest?" the Senior Brother asked, when
they were alone in the library.

Bartholomew shook his head. "Not good. I'm starting to
protect the Navarre Sisters—and I don't even know what from."

The older monk seemed preoccupied with a debate at the
bird feeder between four sparrows. "If they would just take
turns," he murmured. "But they're just like us."

"Anselm, I feel myself being drawn into this, like it's a
vortex." He described the meetings with Doyle, and his
instinctive reactions.

Now he had his old friend's undivided attention. "You cannot allow yourself to get personally involved. It's bound to
affect your judgment."

"It already has," admitted Bartholomew in despair. "I'm
acting like an accomplice. I'm even feeling pangs of guilt—and
I haven't done anything!"

The Senior Brother regarded him sternly. "A serious crime
has been committed. A man's life hangs in the balance. Even
if he recovers, there will be long penitentiary sentences."

"If he dies, they'll be a lot longer. It'll be Manslaughter I, at
best. Possibly Murder II, since there was premeditation
involved."

Anselm turned back to the bird feeder. "What exactly
were you asked to do?"

"By Mother Michaela? You were there. Investigate with the
utmost discretion. If there *is* cause for concern, I'm to relate it
to her, and she will take the appropriate action."

The older monk nodded. "And are you doing that?"

"Yes."

"And have you found any tangible evidence of wrong-doing?"

"No."

"Then keep going." He paused and smiled. "And don't take on a load of unwarranted guilt. You're doing exactly what you were asked to do."

Bartholomew smiled and got up. "Thanks. That helps—I think."

His old friend had returned to the nightly drama outside. "Better than television," he murmured, more to himself than Bartholomew. "Just keep one thing in mind," he added, as the younger monk was about to leave. "The end *never* justifies the means."

"Funny you should say that," his younger friend replied. "I was thinking the same thing."

At Compline, the last Hour of the day—the one that traditionally tucked the church into bed—he counted on the chant settling his soul and composing him for sleep.

It didn't. And the absence of Pangur Ban didn't help.

Still unsettled, he grabbed his windbreaker and went out for a walk. Nowhere in particular, just out. Wandering near the creative arts building, he noticed a light in there, going out. Whoever had been working there had just gone to bed.

He entered and turned the light back on. On impulse he drifted over to where Esperanza had been working and looked through the preliminary sketches in the cubicle closest at hand. There were several of the summoning angel, the one he thought of as the death angel.

And there was also a sketch of a new one. As he looked at it, he had the oddest feeling of someone looking at him. Feeling his scalp tighten, he turned slowly around.

There on the big easel was a new drawing he'd not noticed on his way in. Another chalk-and-charcoal rendering of another angel. Female in appearance, but just as arresting and almost alive as the Death Angel had been. This one was holding an open scroll. And with her other hand, she was pointing—at him.

32 | dietary extremes

Tuesday, 3:13 AM. The only light in the creative arts building could not be seen from outside. It was emanating from the monitor of the office's computer. The Midnight Ramblers were in place: Maria Immaculata at the keyboard, Maria Esperanza standing behind her, Maria Constanza by the window, watching for movement.

MP: This morning give me the good news first.

MI: The cover story is in place. As a gift to the Silvieras, owners of the Jubilatté, for their kindness in having us aboard at the last year's Blessing of the Fleet, and in appreciation of their invitation for this year's, we've received permission to create a pair of flower floats for the stern of their boat. We will again sing the seven-fold Amen, and this year if they give a prize for best boat, the Jubilatté will win, hands down.

MP: Everything depends on the rendezvous with the freighter. It's too tight.

MI: I'm afraid it's gotten even tighter. The *Estrela do Mar* is out of drydock now, and out of Valparaiso, but she's two weeks behind. She's steaming to make up lost time, running two knots faster than she's comfortable. But the captain now estimates not leaving New York till June 26, the day before the Blessing. He'll barely make the Georges Bank rendezvous in time for the transfer. Any further delays will ruin everything. Because the J-boat has no place to store the parcels and obviously cannot keep them aboard and fish, too.

MP: If this is the good news, I shudder to ask about the ungood news.

MI: We're now fairly certain that Brother Bartholomew, the monk we told you about, is on to us. He may not have the details, but he knows we're connected to the statues and the robbery.

MP: What makes you so sure?

MI: His questions. And he may not be the only one.

MP: Good grief! Now what?

MI: There was an art expert here from Boston, named Doyle, who's doing a magazine article on contemporary religious art in Massachusetts. He took an interest in Esperanza's drawing for one of the floats.

MP: Was Esperanza there?

MI: Yes.

MP: Put her on.

ME: Yes, Mother?

MP: Did you practice the vocabulary of silence?

ME: As best I could. But here's something: Bartholomew brought him to the creative arts building and acted as my translator. In Spanish he warned me—I think—that the art expert also worked for the museum,

investigating the theft of the statues. I wondered if he
was trying to help us.

MP: Assume not. And be extremely careful. Is there any
       change in the status of the guard?

ME: He's still in the coma. More than five months now.

MP: Keep praying for him. We are praying here, too.

ME: I will, Mother. His name is Dominick, and I feel like
       I've gotten to know him in my prayers. I sense he is
       with God—and wants to stay there, because it is so
       beautiful. That's the way I felt, when I was so sick as a
       child. You all say I'm still more there than here. But
       Dominick's work here is not finished, or God would
       have taken him at once. That's why I know he will
       return. In God's time.

                          ❧

It was the first Sunday in Advent. With the basilica tem-
porarily closed for the installation of the next phase of
mosaics, the abbey's members were cast upon the waters for
Sunday worship. Being an ecumenical lot, they went to various
churches in town. While many went to St. Joan of Arc in
Orleans, Bartholomew and three other Brothers went to the
Episcopal Church of the Holy Spirit in Orleans.

Made of dark barn beams in the form of a Cross, the rus-
tic old structure was nonetheless surrounded by new ancillary
buildings and an expanded parking lot, the result of a quiet,
ongoing revival. Bartholomew had wanted to go to the 7:30
A.M. service, as it followed Rite I, the form and language closest to his beloved *1928 Book of Common Prayer*. But the other
three had wanted to take advantage of the rare opportunity to
sleep past 6:00, so they went to the 9:00 service (Rite II).

Afterwards, he dropped the other three at the friary, then
went to return the car to the abbey's parking lot. In doing so,
he passed the one charter fishing boat yet to be taken out and

set on blocks for winter. It was the *Sara Ann*, Ron Wallace's boat. And despite a chill early December wind, Ron was aboard her, working on the radar.

Not having had a chance to talk to Ron since their adventure in Bermuda the year before, Bartholomew steered the old Volvo over there, then saw he was not alone. A man who'd come in a black pick-up was talking with him.

As Bartholomew turned back toward the parking lot, he realized there was something vaguely familiar about that man talking to Ron. He'd seen him before. . . .

Walking back from the lot, he noted the black pickup was gone, and Ron was getting into his own truck with *Sara Ann* elegantly lettered on the door. Bartholomew called to him, and he waved.

"How was your season?" he asked.

Ron grimaced. "So-so. Seems to take the Cape six months longer to climb out of a recession than the rest of the country."

"Discretionary income," observed Bartholomew. "Next year should be better."

"It had better be."

"Was that a potential client you were just talking to?"

Ron nodded and smiled. "Yup. An eight-hour on Memorial Day Sunday."

"Isn't that pushing the season a little?"

"A little! Could be colder than a—never mind."

"Where's he from?"

"Plymouth." He frowned. "Odd duck. Some kind of Muslim. A devout one."

"How do you mean?"

"Well, whatever sect he belongs to, its dietary laws are very strict. He asked me if he could bring his charcoal cooker along, so they could prepare their own meat."

Bartholomew nodded. "Was his name Abou-Ali, by any chance?"

"Yeah," responded Ron, surprised. "You know him?"

"Not personally. I saw him in Plymouth last month. He's a landscaper."

"Yeah, that's what he said. He's bringing two sons and a cousin. Party of four."

The monk looked at the boat, trying not to recall his horrific adventure aboard such a boat in Bermuda the year before. "You normally allow someone to bring a grill on board?"

Ron shook his head. "I don't like live fire aboard any boat. But—" he shrugged, "he made me an offer I couldn't refuse. An extra four hundred dollars—in advance." He patted his wallet. "For that kind of jack he can bring his mother-in-law on board and cook *her!*" He winced. "Don't tell Bunny I said that."

Bartholomew smiled. "When are you taking her out?"

"Bunny?"

"The *Sara Ann.*"

"Tomorrow, as a matter of fact. And thanks for the reminder. Once she's out of the water, the season's over, and I owe Bunny dinner out. Guess we'll try John Murphy's new room."

As Ron drove away, Bartholomew was troubled. He had forgotten to tell Dan Burke about the incident up in Plymouth. Now he would have to do so and add this conversation to the pot.

33 | midnight ramble III

It was not 3:13 on a Tuesday morning. It was midnight on the eve of the Feast of the Epiphany—an emergency session called by Mother Maria Patientia. Shivering in the January cold, the Navarre Sisters were in their customary places in the darkened creative arts building.

MP: An art historian from America is in town, asking questions. Name of Sean Padraig Doyle. Is he the one who came down from Boston to do the article?

MI: That's him. Did he come to the convent?

MP: No reason for him to; nothing of antiquarian value here. But I suspect we'll be seeing him anyway. He's been to the monastery.

MI: Did he—

MP: See the pedestals? He did. He's gotten the Abbot's hopes up about their possible return. Of course, I couldn't tell him what we know. I couldn't even ask questions. He must never suspect.

MI: Dear God. If he's seen the empty pedestals, he knows! The only thing he doesn't know is how we're going to get them back there!

MP: All right, everyone's allowed a moment of panic. I had mine yesterday. Now pull yourselves together and keep your wits about you. Is there any way we can move up the timetable?

MI: No. It'll be the grace of God if we can keep to the one we've got!

MP: We'd better start working on an exit strategy.

MI: ??

MP: A fallback plan in the event Doyle does figure out what we're trying to do.

MI: I'm having trouble following you. So is Esperanza. And Constanza.

MP: We need to work out a worst-case scenario—and assume that it's likely.

        [No response]

MP: Anyone there?

MI: We're thinking.

MP: Think faster.

MI: Can't.

MP: All right, break for twenty minutes.

જ⁀

Mother Maria Patientia went out on her terrace. She did not breathe in the fresh morning air. She could scarcely breathe at all. It was not the breathless panic she had felt yesterday. It was an overwhelming sense that they were doomed. To certain, hideous failure.

And now, like a nightmare one could not wake up from, or a movie one was forced to watch, eyes taped open, she saw the whole thing unfolding before her.

The scandal breaking in the newspapers and on national television. The disgrace she has brought on her house, the motherhouse, the entire order. The shock and horror of the Bishop. Of her family. Of Miguel. She dwelt on his sad despair and then his fury.

The trial, the courtroom, wave upon wave of sensational scandal, worldwide. The entire globe witnessing her shame. Hers alone, for she would do her best to absolve the others. Make the courtroom believe that it was her initiative, her scheme. They were only following orders.

And then prison. Where Miguel would never visit, never write, never speak her name again.

No wonder she couldn't breathe!

Oh, God! What have I done?

Silence, of course. She'd made a point of not including Him at the beginning or in the middle; why would she think He'd deal himself back in now?

As she stood at the wall of her terrace, the hawk was circling slowly upward. When it reached her level, she saw it. And thought that if she had a gun, she would shoot it.

૨૦

MP: Well?

MI: When is Fiesta this year?

MP: July 4 to 12.

MI: And the procession?

MP: The eleventh.

MI: Bigger than usual, because of the monastery's thousandth anniversary?

MP: I think I see where you're going. My God, it's brilliant! I love it! Oh, my God, I love you guys!

MI: All the world will be watching.

MP: Well, probably not. But we can do our best to make sure the procession gets as much attention as possible.

MI: So that if the missing statues, disguised as flower floats in the procession, are revealed to be the ones. . . .

MP: World sympathy will be with us!

MI: And if we can somehow get them back on their pedestals. . . .

MP: The world will see they belong there!

ъ♨

To celebrate the Feast of the Epiphany (and the reopening of their basilica), the abbey's liturgical dance group put on a major production called "The Star." Performing interpretive vignettes of aspects of the Wise Men's journey, they danced the entire length of the nave, with the audience seated on either side of the center aisle, facing it.

As with everything else the abbey did in the realm of the creative arts, there was a concerted emphasis on "Excellence to the Glory of God." The dancers were honest, innovative, and inspired, and the audience came away with a fresh appreciation of the faith and commitment of the Magi who had gone toward the Star—at the compelling of God's Spirit in their hearts.

Bartholomew, who had been invited to Dan and Peg Burke's for Thanksgiving, took this opportunity to repay his friends' gracious hospitality. Peg was suitably impressed, and so, to his surprise, was Dan.

"Ballet's not my thing," he confessed at the reception afterwards. "I only came because—"

"Because I said he had to," interjected Peg, laughing. "I knew he'd like it."

"I *did* like it," the Chief said defensively. "It made me think about some things I'd never thought about. And the dancers were great. The women weren't anorexic. And the men," his wife threw him a warning glance, "are the kind you could have a beer with."

Peg turned to their host. "We both loved it, Brother Bart. Thank you so much."

Before they left, their monk friend remembered what he had forgotten to tell the Chief. He drew him aside and told him about the Middle Eastern men with the map in Plymouth, and then the leader hiring Ron to take them out on Memorial Day Sunday. With their cooker.

The Chief frowned. "I'll have a word with Ron tomorrow. And my counterpart up in Plymouth. And maybe Homeland Security."

34 | sleeper wakes

Winter on Cape Cod was never pleasant. People who thought the Cape might be a nice place to live would be advised to winter over there, before investing in a condo. They needed to experience the bone-piercing chill of the north wind over the bay, or see the bay frozen solid and resembling an Arctic ice pack.

That winter on the Cape had been the coldest, wettest, bleakest in anyone's memory. The only saving grace was that the depleted reservoirs, lakes, and aquifer were fully replenished, and for once there would be no hand-wringing drought advisories in the coming summer. But try telling that cheery news to the people who had water in their basements for the first time in twenty or thirty years.

On Ash Wednesday the Navarre Sisters went to Boston, to Massachusetts General Hospital on an errand of mercy. Sister Constanza's international driver's license had expired, and Ed Robertson was involved in a major television shoot, so it fell to Brother Bartholomew to escort them to the hospital. Almost a year from when they had gone up for the funeral.

He made the best use of the time, encouraging them to

use their English, at which they were all gaining a measure of proficiency. But today the three Marias did not seem particularly talkative.

"Tell me about the Sister you are going to visit."

"What's to tell?" asked Constanza. "Maria Fidelia was cleaning the gutters at the Framingham convent yesterday. She was reaching for rotted leaves blocking a downspout, when the ladder slipped. She fell. And now she's in hospital with a badly broken leg."

"There's more to it," offered Esperanza, who appeared to be more in chat mode than the other two. "They told her that the gutters were too dangerous and to leave them to the professionals who were coming next week. She wanted to save the convent the cost, though they said it was already in the maintenance budget. She went ahead anyway, and was reaching for a clot too far, when the ladder started to go. She cried out, "Jesus!" and that's why she landed *next* to a huge boulder, instead of *on* it."

Bartholomew stared at her. It was the most he'd ever heard out of her.

Immaculata also looked at her. "Have you forgotten the vocabulary?"

"I think her vocabulary has grown amazingly," declared Bartholomew, impressed.

But Esperanza knew what she was referring to and lapsed back into silence.

"She has a spiral fracture and is completely immobile, with a halo cast around her leg," Constanza offered.

"That's depressing," observed Bartholomew.

"That's why we're going up to see her."

When they got there, Bartholomew said he'd park the car and wait for them at one of the lower level cafeteria's outdoor tables.

ॐ

Fidelia was delighted to see them. And they were delighted at her delight. As they nattered on, Esperanza slipped out and went to the head nurse's station. She had a word with the head nurse, who got on the phone, then told her what she wanted to know.

Esperanza went back to Fidelia's room, where none of them had noticed her absence. She whispered something to Immaculata, who whispered back, "You have twenty minutes. No more."

Esperanza nodded and slipped away again. She went down to the main floor and followed the head nurse's directions to a different wing and another bank of elevators. She went up to the eighth floor, to Room 813.

The name on the door was Santini, Dominick. Looking in, she saw a man in bed—eyes closed, perfectly still, with all manner of tubes running in and out of him. Next to his bed was the monitor of his vital signs, all of which were slow and steady—as they had been for nearly eight months.

In a chair beside the bed was a gray-haired woman, knitting and occasionally murmuring something to the figure in the bed.

Esperanza went to the head nurse at the nurse's station and had some words with her. As they were talking, the old woman folded her knitting away in a canvas bag, bent over and gently kissed the forehead of the motionless figure, and departed.

The head nurse nodded to Esperanza, who now went in and sat in the chair the older woman had occupied. She took a deep breath and, smiling, leaned so close to the figure in the bed that her lips were almost touching his ear. She closed her eyes. Her lips moved slightly, as did her body in the intensity of her prayer.

There was no movement, no change in the monitor's indicators.

Esperanza arose, eyes still half closed, a beatific smile on her face. She exited the room, thanked the head nurse, and headed for the elevators.

The head nurse did not respond. Her attention was riveted on one of the monitors in the bank in front of her. Without taking her eyes from it, she called for the duty nurse.

"Carol? Come here! Oh, my God!" As the duty nurse approached, she jumped up. "It's 813! He's waking up! *Oh, my God!*"

35 | wall of martyrs

For five months Abou-Ali kept a careful eye on his younger son. When the last leaves had fallen, they raked their clients' lawns and prepared their flowerbeds for winter. At the first sign of snow, they attached a yellow plow to the truck and kept their drives open during the worst winter in years. And when the frost finally came out of the ground, they cleaned up fallen limbs and edged and mulched flowerbeds.

With his father looking on approvingly, Khalid worked as hard as his older brother and gradually turned back into his old self. On the infidels' highest holy day, when they celebrated their prophet's resurrection from the dead, he took his two sons back out to Rocky Point. They again rehearsed the plan, and Ahmed and Khalid seemed equally firm, equally ready.

They knew the name of the boat they would use now, the *Sara Ann*, and her captain, Ron Wallace, and her harbor, Eastport. They had reserved her for Memorial Day. They knew her range was two hundred miles, and her maximum speed was eighteen knots. She was equipped with a good radar with a range of twenty-two miles, and they would be equipped with a handheld Global Positioning System that would fix their position within ten meters.

They had received their life vests, which were actually death vests. They were packed with explosives surrounded with radioactive material, making each of them a living dirty bomb. Moreover, each vest would be hard-wired to the "cooker," which was rigged to detonate if any of the vests were triggered. So that even if they were stopped prematurely before they could get close enough to their target, they would go to paradise, leaving behind a dead zone with a radius of twenty miles. And if the wind were in the right direction, thousands would die from radiation poisoning.

And that was the worst-case scenario, in the event they were interdicted before they could get within three hundred meters of the canal. But they had every confidence they would get right up to its mouth, in which case the reactor would be split open and the devastation would be catastrophic.

The father drove home, satisfied that they were ready. All of them.

He was so certain, in fact, that the following morning—the first really warm day of spring—as a sign of trust he dispatched Khalid without his brother, to bring them coffee.

The younger son returned without delay. And that afternoon he was sent again and again returned promptly.

But the next morning, as they prepared the beds of the largest of their clients' estates, Khalid was working in the front, while his brother and father were working in the back. When his father told Ahmed to send Khalid for the coffee, the younger brother was nowhere to be found. And a bike that had been hanging in the garage was also missing.

Without a word the father got in the truck and headed for the coffee shop. On an isolated, densely wooded stretch of Beaver Dam Road, he saw his son up ahead, bent over the bike, pedaling hard.

Rage swept over him. He gunned the truck toward his son. Who would betray Allah and disgrace his father. Who would bring shame to their family and cause them to be remembered in ignominy, instead of reverence.

Khalid never knew what hit him. At the moment of impact, the truck was doing sixty and accelerating. Bike and rider were sent flying. The young man landed head first on the pavement. He was not wearing a helmet.

But he did not die at once. Neck broken, bleeding from the mouth and left ear, he recognized his father, as the latter bent over him. There were tears in his eyes. He tried to speak. "I'm sorry, Father. I—"

His father did not wait to hear any more. He got back in the truck, backed it up, then shifted into first and ran over his son, making sure the wheels crushed his chest.

When he returned to the estate, he made one comment to his elder son. "Your brother's name will be with ours on the Wall."

Twenty minutes later, the chief of police arrived. "Abou," he said to the father, "I'm afraid I have terrible news. I came to tell you myself."

He told him and Ahmed of the discovery of Khalid, the apparent victim of a hit-and-run accident while riding a bicycle on Beaver Dam Road. Abou-Ali was shocked and inconsolable in his grief. For an hour he wept, and then offered to pay the owner of the estate for the bike Khalid had apparently borrowed.

The owner wouldn't hear of it. Instead, he paid for all the funeral expenses. And the townspeople of Leyden and Plymouth who knew the family, felt the same way. Condolences and sympathy poured in, and were gratefully received by the father and his only surviving son.

36 | dead in the water

It had been a long, cold Lent, but it led to a glorious Easter. The weather cooperated with mostly sunny skies, albeit weak and watery. Only the daffodils seemed unaware of how long it had taken to warm up enough to go outside without a coat on. Like golden trumpets, they lined the path to the church, and one brave bloom had forced its way up through a crack in the asphalt where the driveway ended.

The basilica was resplendent. The liturgical art guild had come up with something at once startling and exhilarating. White bolts of cloth had been tied to the center of the roof beams far above and extended diagonally left, and then right, down to alternate columns on either side.

The effect was that the basilica looked like it was decorated for a medieval wedding of great nobility—Arthur and Guinevere, perhaps. And for Easter, the traditional choir was augmented by the brass choir, with trumpets heralding and tympani rumbling.

At the end of the service, after they had joyously processed out through the great bronze doors, everyone milled about in front of the church, reluctant to leave. A writer on Celtic spirituality, visiting their publishing house, came up to Bartholomew. "You know, I knew there had to be a place like this. Where they worshiped the way you do, with old-fashioned majesty and awe in the presence of God. The Russian Orthodox have that. You do, too."

Bartholomew didn't know what to say.

The visitor smiled. "You're still a hidden work, but others who've been looking and hoping are eventually going to find you."

Bartholomew just smiled—and fervently hoped not. As far as he was concerned, it would be wonderful if God never drew back the curtain on what He was doing here.

Though the visitor's observation cheered him somewhat, he was depressed.

He found Anselm on the old bench in the apple orchard, enjoying being able to sit outside now, with his beloved birds. "You know," he said softly, "if you talk to them, they'll talk back. And it doesn't matter how poorly you imitate their calls. They're just glad to have the attention."

He demonstrated by answering the call of a male cardinal in the top branches of the farthest tree. The bird called again. Anselm answered again—in not too poor an imitation at all, thought Bartholomew.

They went on this way for more than a minute.

Anselm chuckled. "Now, see that mockingbird over there?" He pointed to a gray bird with white flashes on his wings, which had just alighted on the tree next to the cardinal's. "He wants the attention."

All at once Bartholomew laughed. "Anselm, I taught you that! And now you spout bird lore as if you were some meek holy man, in perfect harmony with his natural surroundings."

The old monk looked up at him, and then smiled broadly. "So you did, so you did."

Bartholomew grinned. "That doesn't mean you shouldn't go on doing the Saint Francis thing. It won't hurt our younger friars and novices one bit to believe they have a holy one in their midst."

The Senior Brother patted the bench beside him. "Tell me why you aren't enjoying this Easter Sunday the way you have enjoyed so many others."

"You mean out on my bike? I would be, except I've got to talk to you."

"The investigation," the old monk surmised. "It's not going as you hoped."

"It's not going, period. And that may be what I *am* hoping for. I don't know. That's why I'm here."

Anselm waited.

"The fact is, the whole thing is dead in the water. Nothing's happened since I saw Doyle before Christmas. As far as I know, he's over in Europe somewhere. But he hasn't found anything, or we'd have heard something. He's struggling to keep his retainer, and any positive publicity would help. It's like he's fallen off the face of the earth."

Anselm looked at him carefully and slowly shook his head. "That's not it. Something has hurt you, Bartholomew. What is it?"

The younger monk started to dispute that, then remembered that this was precisely why he'd sought Anselm out. If his old friend picked up that he was hurt somehow, he'd better—

And then he knew what it was. "You heard about the security guard, the one in a coma as a result of the explosion at the ILE?"

Anselm nodded. "He came out of it, didn't he? No brain damage, after being gone all that time?"

"Yup. Good as new."

"Praise God! We were all praying for him."

"Anselm, it happened the day I drove the Navarre Sisters to Mass General. While they were in the hospital!"

The old monk nodded. "You think they had something to do with it."

"You've got to admit, it's a little too much of a coincidence. I think one of them—Esperanza would be my guess—or all of them went to see him and prayed him back."

"You weren't with them?"

"No, they were up there seeing one of their order from Framingham who'd broken her leg. I waited in the cafeteria."

"And they didn't tell you about the guard reviving."

"They didn't say a word. I didn't find out until I read it in the paper the next morning and put two and two together."

The old monk smiled to see the pair of cardinals nest-building. "And you got your feelings hurt."

Bartholomew nodded.

"But why would they tell you? Why would they tell anyone? The *last* thing they want is to be connected in any way to that robbery."

"I know, but—"

"You know what your problem is? You're now so identified with them, you're subconsciously thinking of yourself as part of their team. That's why it hurts when they don't tell you things."

Bartholomew thought about that a long time. Then he said, "God help me, you're right!"

"Well, He'd better help you, because you are on dangerous ground, my friend."

Bartholomew sighed. "You're telling me!" He looked at his old friend. "What should I do?"

"Back away from it. From the whole thing. Be grateful that nothing has happened or appears to be happening. That may be God's mercy, giving you a chance to regain your objectivity, which you have clearly lost."

Bartholomew stood up. "So I should just relax for a while. Trust God."

"Works for me. In fact, it's worked for centuries. Won't hurt to try it."

"Thanks, Anselm. I think I'm going for a bike ride."

As he walked away, he glanced back at his white-haired friend, who was now enrapt in his conversation with the cardinals. The younger friars weren't the only ones grateful for a holy one in their midst.

❧

Bartholomew was just lifting the old Trek from its hooks in the workshop, where it hung upside down like a marsupial, when Brother Jonathan found him.

"Bart? Phone," said the new monk.

"Can it wait? It's Easter Sunday, for crying out loud."

"It's Chief Burke."

With a sigh he went back into the friary.

"Happy Easter," said the Chief. "I'm really sorry to bother you, but we need to talk."

"Two minutes later," Bartholomew replied with a chuckle, "and you would have missed me. I was about to go for a bike ride. A long bike ride."

"Don't you take your cell phone with you?"

"I go on rides to get *away* from that thing!"

"Listen, ride over to Nauset Beach. I'll meet you in the parking lot. It'll only take a few minutes. Then you can go ride your bike, and I can go fish."

Twenty minutes later, Bartholomew pulled up alongside the white Bravada. Dan got out and checked to make sure there was no one else in the parking lot. "Okay, you want the good news, the bad news, or the ugly news?"

"You decide."

"We've had a confidential update from Homeland Security. They've got a fix on the Al Qaeda operative responsible for the distribution of nuclear devices."

"That's good news."

"They're monitoring his communications, but so far he's only referred to twenty-nine of the forty-seven devices suspected to be in this country. And they can't just scoop him up, because they don't want him to know they're on to him."

"That's not good news."

"And apparently there are two other devices considerably larger—and more powerful. One of them is in New England."

Bartholomew shuddered. "That's ugly."

"You're telling me!"

"What are you going to do about it?"

The Chief looked as if he'd just sucked on a lemon. "That's the problem—there's nothing I *can* do that I'm not doing already. I quietly remind our people to keep a weather eye out for *anything* out of the ordinary. And also remind them not to say anything to anyone that might start a panic."

He sighed. "But you can only go to that well so often. Or you start to encounter the cry-wolf syndrome—the bane of Homeland Security. How often can you warn people before their alert buttons start to grow calluses?"

Bartholomew tried to think of something to say that might help. He couldn't.

The Chief smiled. "Thanks for coming out here, Bart. Just venting like this, helps."

"I'll pass the update on to the Rees Howells Brigade. Discreetly, of course; no specifics. By the way, what did you find out about those Middle Eastern landscapers?"

"Oh, they're fine. They live in Leyden, next town up from Plymouth. Been there ten years. Everyone likes them."

Bartholomew said nothing, but his expression indicated how much that did not impress him.

"They cut the *mayor's* grass, for crying out loud! *And* the police chief's."

"What about the trip with Ron?"

"Cancelled. One of the sons was killed in a hit-and-run."

"The younger one?"

"I don't know." The Chief reached in the back of the Bravada and pulled out his fishing gear. "Bart, thanks for coming."

"Keep me posted."

"Count on it. Happy Easter."

"Happy Easter, Dan."

And the two friends went their separate ways.

37 | the non-negotiator

April came in as a lion, but went out as a lamb. And May showers brought June flowers. And the Japanese cherry trees did manage to make it Maytime in Eastport, but they were ten days late, and six weeks behind Washington, D.C. The old saying that Cape Cod had two seasons, winter and the Fourth of July, had never been quite as true as this year. In all, it had been a winter to remember. Or rather, forget—as quickly as possible.

Yet the final Friday in June was doing its best to help eradicate that memory. It was gorgeous! The sort of day that reminded vacationers why they kept coming back to the Cape—and would keep coming, even if the weather was not promising.

Brother Bartholomew, mowing the spacious lawn in front of the abbey aboard the old John Deere, basked in the balmy air. He was carefully cutting against the grain, back and forth, creating a Harris Tweed pattern that would not have been out of place in Fenway Park.

And then he was called to the phone, and his morning was ruined.

It was Doyle, back from the dead. Or at least back from Europe. "I'm coming down there, boyo. This afternoon. I've discovered where the statues originally came from, and that gives me a pretty good idea of what's going on. I want to talk to those Spanish Sisters, and this time you're not putting me off."

"Talk to me first," replied Bartholomew. "Why don't I meet you in Plymouth, like—"

"No! I told you, laddie; I'm coming down there, and I'm going to see them!"

"After you see me, all right?"

Doyle hesitated. "All right. For auld lang syne."

"Good. We'll have dinner at Gordie's."

He was there at the appointed hour. And was able to get a table, though the older, early-supper crowd had taken nearly all of them. From the ceiling hung dozens of quaint signs announcing local businesses and establishments, all carved and lettered by the owner/proprietor. And last year John had come to him and asked, in recognition of his endeavors as the town's amateur sleuth, if he'd be willing to have his name added to the collection. A brass plaque on the back of a deacon's bench now recorded that.

Doyle finally arrived and apologized for a twenty-minute backup at the Sagamore Bridge—one of the things vacationers did *not* like about coming to the Cape. They ordered baby back ribs and onion rings, which Doyle insisted they wash down with Black-and-Tans—a pint of half Guinness and half Harp.

"What *happened* to you over there?" asked Bartholomew, when they'd been served. "I wondered if you'd fallen off the edge of the known world."

"Strangest thing," Doyle mused. "I was in Madrid, asking questions, trying to get a line on the statues, when all of a sudden I got knocked over by a virus. A real mugging! Fever, hallucinations, blacking out, the whole nine yards. Had to be hospitalized. And I was in there for nearly a month. Then another month weak as a kitten, no energy, barely able to walk."

He took a deep draught of his glass. "Needless to say, the museum was not thrilled with a sudden barge-load of medical expenses. My widow friend on the board used up all her cachet and finally had to send me money herself."

Bartholomew looked at him, concerned. "Are you okay?"

"Fit as a fiddle!" Doyle said grinning, and then added, mystified. "I have no idea what it was."

"Are you still on retainer with the ILE?"

Doyle gave a wry chuckle. "Yes—and no. Technically I'm still in their employ. But there'll be no further remuneration unless and until I come up with something bankable, as it were."

As Doyle ordered another pint, Bartholomew decided it was time to get down to brass tacks. "But you did find out where the statues came from."

"I did, laddie. And you know, it was the piece of the puzzle that lined up all the others."

"All right, where?"

"From a monastery in Pamplona. Where there are ten other statues of the same size and antiquity. And two very empty pedestals."

"Were the statues—stolen?" the monk asked, hoping to find something to at least partially justify what had happened.

"Afraid not. It was all quite legal and proper. In 1917 the Abbot arranged the sale to an agent for the museum, and they must have been shipped straight over."

Suddenly Bartholomew was not hungry. And he loved baby back ribs and onion rings. "Why do you want to talk to the Spanish Sisters?"

"Because they did it. Those 'nuns' the guard described? They *were* nuns!"

"*If* they were nuns, what makes you think it's our nuns who did it?" *Our* nuns? Anselm was right. Objectivity had gone out the window.

"Because their convent is just down the hill from the monastery. It's their sister house!"

Bartholomew couldn't breathe. He felt like his world was

caving in. This was the thing he had been hoping for so long would not happen. And now it had. Play for time.

"Could it possibly be coincidence?"

"It might have been," Doyle conceded. "Remote, but possible. Until yesterday."

He didn't want to ask. "What happened yesterday?"

"I went over to Mass General and had a talk with the head nurse who was on duty when the security guard came out of his coma. She recalled a visit by a nun just before it happened— a tall nun with striking blue eyes. Her description exactly fit the Spanish Sister I met with you, when I was down here before. You know the one I mean; the one who drew the angel. Maria what's-her-name."

"Esperanza."

"Yeah, that's the one." Doyle chuckled. "The head nurse was relieved to hear I knew her. Her duty nurse is apparently a little overwrought in the religious department. She's been going around telling everyone it was a miracle, and that the 'nun' was actually an angel in disguise. You ever heard such a thing?"

Bartholomew just smiled weakly. Actually he had—but he was not about to go into it now. Instead, he offered, "Well, knowing that Maria Esperanza is a normal, down-to-earth human being should put the nurse's mind at ease. Both nurses."

Doyle looked at him, head tilted. "I'm not sure I agree with you, boyo."

"What do you mean?"

"I'm not sure she's normal, not atall, atall. In Ireland we know that some people are—'fey.' They see things we don't, and—know things. I think she's one. And down-to-earth? I'm not sure of that, either. That angel she drew? He's been haunting me."

Bartholomew stared at him.

"I mean it!" exclaimed Doyle. "He came to me in a fever dream or hallucination, while I was in hospital in Madrid!"

Bartholomew took a deep breath. Time to get to the heart of the matter. "If you know all this, why don't you go to the police?"

"Because, laddie, I've been hired to effect the return of the museum's stolen property. If those Sisters don't tell them—us—where the statues are, it won't do a bit of good to put them away for ten to twelve years."

Bartholomew ate a rib. "So, what are we doing here? What do you want me to do?"

Doyle wiped barbecue sauce off his chin and fingers. "I want you to act as the go-between. I want to negotiate. With you—and only with you—for the return of those statues."

Bartholomew chewed a back rib, which he would have enjoyed under other circumstances. "First of all, I'm not authorized to do any such thing. And I'm not saying I'm willing to do this, or even admit your wild hypothesis has any legitimacy. But—if it did—what would you, or the ILE, be willing to put on the table?"

Doyle tilted his glass and emptied it. Then looked at his former student. And friend. "I think that for the safe return of the statues, the Isabel Langford Eldredge Museum *might* be willing to forego pressing criminal charges. But someone would have to pay for the damage done to the building, and the catastrophic health expenses incurred by the guard during his months on life support."

Bartholomew thought for a while. "You mentioned once that there might be half a million available for the statues' safe return." He paused. "How much did it cost to repair the back wall of that wing? Probably under a hundred thousand dollars. And life support? Figure ten thousand a week, for what," he calculated the time, "forty weeks? That's still under the amount your side was willing to put up."

Doyle looked at him with new appreciation. "You're good, boyo," he said softly. "Shall I take that back to my people?"

"No! Don't take anything back to anyone! I'm not negotiating here! I was just trying to find out what you had in mind."

Doyle put up his hands and smiled, "Of course, of course! And now that you know, you can—um—pray about it."

"You won't interview the Navarre Sisters?"

"Let's say I won't—tonight. But I'm staying in town, and I'll see you tomorrow. When hopefully you'll have authorization to make a deal. Because I certainly will." And with that, he stuck out his hand.

After a moment's hesitation, Bartholomew shook it.

38 | do ask, do tell

Brother Bartholomew went immediately to the Senior Brother, who alerted the Abbess, who called a special meeting. In ten minutes Anselm, Hilda, and Bartholomew were in her office. He summarized the situation, then related what had just transpired with Doyle, including the terms he had not negotiated.

Hilda attempted to refute the irrefutable evidence, then acidly remarked to Bartholomew, "Well, I hope you're happy."

"What do you mean?"

"You've turned the Navarre Sisters into common criminals! It's what you set out to do, wasn't it? Prove your little theory?"

Mother Michaela turned to her. "He only did what I asked him to. What *we* asked him to. He was acting on behalf of the entire abbey."

She turned to Bartholomew. "Thank you. I know you did not want to find out what you did. In fact, I suspect you had a hard time remaining objective."

Anselm chuckled. "I didn't say a word to her, Bart."

Bartholomew smiled and nodded. "My objectivity went out the window a long time ago. I love the three Marias; how can you help it?"

Hilda's scowl softened—somewhat.

Mother Michaela got them back on track. "We are now ninety-nine percent certain that our Spanish Sisters stole the two statues and presumably know of their whereabouts. We can further assume that their intent is to get them back on their pedestals in the cloister of their brother house."

She paused and looked at each of them. "And now that we know that—before God, what are we to do?"

"Nothing," said Hilda.

"Which would make us accessories after the fact," said Bartholomew with a sigh.

"Not if you hadn't done your blasted snooping. What part of 'Don't ask'—as in 'Don't ask, don't tell'—do you not understand?"

"Hilda," rejoined Mother Michaela, an edge in her tone, "*he did it at my direction.*"

Hilda said nothing. She did nod. Reluctantly.

"You were going to inform your counterpart over there," Anselm reminded the Abbess, "if we indeed learned there was anything to inform her of."

Mother Michaela nodded. "Thank you, Anselm. I shall inform her forthwith."

"Um, Mother Michaela?" Bartholomew raised his eyebrows. "You might want to wait. "It's 3:30 A.M. over there."

She nodded. "We'll give her time to wake up. But then we'll have to go to the authorities. I'll leave that to you, Bart. Your relationship with Chief Burke makes you the logical one. You can tell him you're speaking for me, and he has my blessing to do," she sighed, "whatever needs to be done."

Anselm raised a hand. "I wonder if we might not go to Dr. Doyle first. I mean, if the museum is willing to drop charges— and thanks to our non-negotiator here, perhaps even damages—ought we not approach their representative first? Bart said he was spending the night in town."

"Point well taken, dear friend. I think we can let matters rest until we have *our* morning coffee. Those stone statues are not about to go anywhere suddenly."

But they were.

≥●

First-time visitors to Faith Abbey invariably commented on the extraordinary sense of peace they experienced as soon as they set foot on the grounds. The tranquility was palpable.

Those who lived there, however, knew at what price that peace was purchased. It required everyone doing what they were supposed to do, when they were supposed to do it, no matter how inconvenient. In this regard, the abbey's 350 members resembled the crew of an aircraft carrier in a battle zone. As long as everyone carried out their assignment, the mission would be accomplished smoothly. The flight deck of a carrier might seem peaceful (except in the middle of a launch), but a vast, coordinated effort below decks went into that soothing hum.

Many hands made light work—and often the right hand did not know what the left hand was doing. Abbey members performed their duties without knowledge of others' tasks—unless there was a need to know. So it was that Bartholomew did not know the Navarre Sisters were preparing angel floats for the Blessing of the Fleet, until Hilda informed him the following morning.

And no one had told Hilda that the angels were being picked up early that same morning. Or that the Navarre Sisters accompanied them. With all their personal gear. In fact, none of that came to light until their chairs were empty at Lauds.

Belatedly realizing what was afoot, Bartholomew called the Senior Brother on his cell phone. "Anselm, there's no time to talk to Doyle now. I think we've got to bring the police in on this right away!"

The Senior Brother agreed, and Bartholomew ran to the old red pickup, jumped in, and gunned out of the Friary parking lot, scattering gravel in all directions.

39 | level red

At the police station, the duty officer had standing orders to show Brother Bartholomew to the Chief's office, if the latter's door was open. The door was ajar, and he nodded him in that direction.

The monk was about to knock on the door, when he heard the Chief's end of a quiet but tense exchange. "Get everyone in here, as fast as possible!" Pause. "I don't care where they are. I need them *here! Now!*" And he hung up.

Bartholomew went in. "Dan, what *is* it?"

"Level Red," he muttered, "for real. Half an hour ago they intercepted satellite phone traffic. Whatever they've been planning, it's going down *today! Bandershnoogy!*" he cried, uttering the second strongest of his substitute curses. He called out to the duty officer. "Arnold? Where *is* everybody?"

"They're coming, Chief! On the double!"

Bartholomew tilted his head. "Dan, you might want to check with Ron Wallace, to see if those landscapers rebooked."

"I can't!" declared the Chief, totally frustrated and out of patience. "He's on an eight-hour! They all are! The harbor's empty! That's the *first* thing I checked!"

"I just—"

"I told you! Those guys cleared!"

The monk smiled and held up both hands. "Hey, I'm one of *us*, remember?"

The Chief exhaled and smiled. "Of course! Sorry."

Bartholomew grimaced. "I don't want to beat a dead horse here, but—"

"But what? C'mon, if your *hobussing* intuition is at work again, I want to know about it!"

"Well, you might want to call Bunny Wallace to see if she knows who Ron's got out with him."

Scowling, the Chief flipped through his Rolodex and made the call.

"Bunny? Dan Burke. You don't happen to know who Ron's got with him now, do you?"

He turned to Bartholomew, "She's checking the trip schedule on his desk." Pause. "Oh, no! Thanks, Bunny," he hung up gently and then shouted, *"Birds Eye Frozen Peas!"*

Bartholomew stared at him. The Chief nodded. "You were right. It's them. Party of three, with the cooker."

He went out into the main office and briefed the duty officer, concluding, "We're going to the harbor, Arnold. Send the first car to get here after us. Have the rest stand by here. Brief Homeland Security. They'll tell you who else to tell. I want the dispatcher ready to patch me through to them, soon as I call in."

He looked at his watch. "How long a head start do they have?"

The duty officer glanced at the tide chart taped to the desk next to the duty roster. "If they left with the others, it would have been about thirty, forty minutes ago."

"C'mon," he shouted to Bart, "we're going to the harbor!"

But when they got there, every serviceable boat was out earning money or chasing fish, or both. And on top of

everything, a fog bank had crept in on little cat feet and set-
tled down on them for the day. It was impenetrable. What
Navy pilots called EBAW (the opposite of CAVU)—Even the
Birds Are Walking.

The Chief was beside himself. "I'm about to start using
language I promised the Blessed Mother I'd never use again! If
we had a boat, we might at least *try* to catch them. Anything
beats just standing here!"

Bartholomew gaped at him. "And do *what*, Dan? Scare
them to death with *that?*" He pointed to the Chief's holstered
Smith & Wesson .38 Special. "These people are terrorists. Real
ones! And you can bet they're armed with more than box
cutters."

Red-faced, the Chief bit back the words on the tip of his
tongue. "All right, Brother Serenity, what would *you* suggest?"

"Homeland Security's undoubtedly got something with a
little heft in the ballistics department, and it's probably
already en route here, via the FBI."

He glanced up the creek, where his eye fell on a craft they
had overlooked—the Friary's own day sailor. He chuckled. "Of
course, if you *really* want to go after them, we could probably
use the *Bluebird* over there."

The Chief winced as he surveyed the slightly listing, paint-
peeling outboard with the half-cabin big enough for one man
standing.

Seeing his dismay, Bartholomew laughed. "When you're
up beggar's creek without a paddle, you don't look down your
nose at the only game in town!"

Dan stared at him, then smiled at the mash of mangled
maxims.

"I'll grant she's not much to look at," his monk friend went
on. "Someone just gave her to us last month—I suspect because
they were tired of perpetually fixing her up. Now she's ours to
perpetually fix up, except none of us has had any time to
spend on her. But she does run—if we can find Ambrose. He
grew up on a farm and has a way with small engines."

"Get him, and tell him to hurry!"

The Chief started walking towards the dilapidated day sailor, while Bartholomew phoned the abbey switchboard and asked them to locate Ambrose and have him come to the harbor on the double.

The Chief waved him over. "The State Police have patched me through to Homeland Security, who've patched me through to Agent di Lorenzo, the FBI case officer. He's up in the AWACS aircraft, about twenty thousand feet over the bay. He wants a description of those guys, as best you can remember."

Bartholomew took the phone and did his best. Then he asked, "What about calling the skipper on his cell phone? Or the ship-to-shore?"

"Too risky," replied the case officer. "From the intercepts, we're pretty sure these guys have wired themselves up as live, dirty bombs—explosives encased in highly radioactive uranium. If they're caught before they get into Plymouth harbor, they'll blow their device anyway, and themselves with it. Even if they're in the middle of the bay, the fallout will devastate whatever is downwind. Right now the wind's from the south—which means Boston."

Ambrose arrived, and in three minutes the *Bluebird* was underway with Ambrose at the wheel, the Chief forward, scanning the fog-bound horizon, and Brother Bartholomew remembering how much he hated small boats and had vowed never to set foot on one again.

Put-put-put—the *Bluebird* nosed her way out of the harbor, and Ambrose gave her full throttle—which meant all of eight knots. Which could not even euphemistically be considered hot pursuit.

In all the frenetic activity, Bartholomew had forgotten the departure of the other boat, the one he had gone to the station to tell Chief Burke about.

40 | angels unaware

Fog enshrouded the *Bluebird* to the point where Brother Ambrose had to follow his Compass, with occasional course corrections through the Chief's cell phone, which was set on speakerphone so they could all hear what was said.

The fog was working in their favor. Not only was it slowing all boats out on the bay, it was masking the presence of an AWACS aircraft overhead, which was part of the Counterterrorism task force. High enough not to paint on any of the fishing boats' surface radar, including the *Sara Ann's*, its own look-down radar could see everything from Plymouth harbor to Barnstable, Eastport, Wellfleet, and Provincetown— and every vessel in between.

By a process of elimination, they had isolated the *Sara Ann,* the only blip not meandering around, looking for fish. It was making straight for Plymouth, as was the *Bluebird,* twenty miles behind her. The case officer requested they keep that distance (as if they had any choice), lest they spook the terrorists.

"Do they have a GPS?" the Chief asked the case officer over the cell phone on speaker mode.

"We have to assume they have. They'll know where they are, and their radar will tell them where everyone else is. Helmsman, steer two-seven-three."

"Roger, two-seven-three," Ambrose replied, making the slight adjustment to starboard, until the compass settled on that heading.

"How far are they from Plymouth?" asked Chief Burke.

"At their present speed? About fifty-one minutes." He paused. "But we'll have to stop them in the next thirty-two minutes if we're going to save Pilgrim Station."

"What are you guys going to do?" asked the Chief.

The case officer hesitated. "We're working on it. The problem is, we've got to take them by surprise. Kill them all before they know what hit them. That rules out the Coast Guard or any powerboats, for that matter. They'd just blow themselves up and turn the bay into a radioactive dead zone."

They motored along for a spell, thinking about that.

"Of course," di Lorenzo resumed, "we may have to do that anyway. Blow them out of the water. We can't let them detonate that thing anywhere near Pilgrim."

"You're going to kill all of them?" asked the Chief. "Including the skipper?"

"Afraid so. Can't take any chances."

"But he's a friend."

"Can't be helped. There's no time to evacuate the shoreline, so we're talking hundreds of lives here, anyway—and if there's fallout, thousands. And if Pilgrim blows—"

"I get the picture," murmured the Chief. "It's just that I've known Ron Wallace most of my life."

"I'm sorry," said di Lorenzo. "There just isn't any other way."

"If this were a James Bond movie," observed Bartholomew wryly, "about now, a flight of good guys would be descending silently on hang gliders."

"Say that again?" asked the case officer.

"I wasn't being serious," the monk apologized.

"Not hang gliders," mused the case officer, thinking out loud. "But skydiver parachutes. . . . Big vents, big airfoil, highly maneuverable. . . . Vectored in by the AWACS air controllers. . . . The Seals have them, and we've got access to a Seal detachment. . . ." Pause. "I'll get back to you."

The Chief looked over at Bartholomew. "I don't believe you! What's a monk doing, going to James Bond movies?"

"Late-night television," replied Bartholomew with a shrug. "I couldn't sleep."

The case officer came back on the phone. "Got 'em! They're leaving Hanscomb Field now. And will be over the target in twelve minutes. But—they could only find two of them."

"That's not a lot of good guys," Bartholomew murmured, not for the case officer's ears. "Must be a low-budget film."

Di Lorenzo heard him. "One Seal is worth ten ordinary soldiers," he tartly replied. "They'll use concussion grenades. Stun everybody."

"Not kill them?" asked the Chief.

"If they can get close enough, they won't have to. Besides, they're worth much more to us alive."

Bartholomew was about to ask why, when a cry from ahead of them in the fog draw all eyes forward. Someone was in the water.

Ambrose steered for the swimmer, while Bartholomew looked around for something to throw. He found a line tied to a buoy. Good, the buoy would float. He hurried forward and got ready.

As they came close, they recognized him. It was Ron Wallace! Bartholomew tossed him the buoy, which Ron caught, and they soon had him alongside and then on board.

He was as surprised to see them, as they were him. "What are you guys doing out here?"

"Oh, just going for a cruise in the fog," quipped Bartholomew. "How about yourself?"

"Bit of a swim. After all these years of wondering what it would be like to just plop in—I did."

The Chief told him what they were really about, and Ron explained, "I had a funny feeling about those guys when they hooked into a couple of big bluefish and didn't even get excited. While they were absorbed in reeling in their fish, I snuck a look under the tarp covering their cooker. That was no cooker, let me tell you!"

"Would you believe a nuclear device?"

"I figured it was something like that. So I disabled the radar and—slipped over the side. I stayed under for as long as I could hold my breath, counting on the fog to conceal me when I surfaced. It did. Except—now I was in the middle of the bay, with everyone fishing somewhere else, and it being too far to swim to shore."

He laughed. "I kept thinking, this is a really stupid way for a charter fisherman to die!" Too late he remembered how Bartholomew's father had died. He just winced and shook his head at the monk.

Who smiled and asked, "How'd you dismantle the radar without drawing attention to yourself?"

Ron smiled and fished in his pocket, and held up a fuse. "I didn't want to wreck it. Those things are expensive!"

The case officer came on the line. "They'll be away in two minutes. Coming in high, about twelve thousand feet, so they won't hear the plane above the sound of their own engine. The Seals will free-fall most of the way, then at two thousand they'll deploy their chutes."

"How far behind are we now?" asked Bartholomew.

"About twelve miles. They must have spent a fair amount of time looking for the captain, before deciding he couldn't hurt them."

There was some radio traffic in the background, then di Lorenzo came back on. "They're away!" he declared. "And each of them has an air controller up here on a separate 'scope, who will vector them in and put them right on top of the boat." He laughed. "A little slower than what they're trained for—lining up interceptors with bombers at Mach One plus!"

"Angels, unaware," Bartholomew murmured with a faint smile. Then to the case officer he asked, "How long before—" he couldn't bring himself to finish it.

"Before you or they are blown to kingdom come?" came the voice over the speaker phone. "Four minutes from right—*now*. Start sweating, boys."

A chill went through Bartholomew. Until that instant, it had not occurred to him that his life might be over in—he checked his watch—three minutes and thirty-two seconds.

His life didn't exactly flash before his eyes; it sort of fast-forwarded. Except time did its accordion thing, as it occasionally does in moments of extreme peril. A car spinning, or turning end on end, with the driver acutely aware of each millisecond.

Fishing with his father, 'Nam, Dartmouth, Laurel, the Friary, the Brothers, Pangur Ban—who would be waiting for him. That was nice. He was grateful that his last meeting with his mother had been rancor-free, unlike earlier years. He would not want her torturing herself that they had parted on less than amicable terms.

He felt calm, but one look at his knuckles whitening on the boat's rail put the lie to that.

Think about something else. The terrorists. He turned to the cell phone. "You said they were worth much more to you alive. How?"

"If we can get close enough to stun them with concussion grenades, we'll be able to question them. Find out who their coordinator is."

"You're not going to—"

"What, torture them? We don't do that. This is America!"

"But they don't know that we don't, right?"

"Exactly! Let them assume we're as ruthless as they are. And we can do an awfully convincing job of faking that. Two-minute warning, gentlemen. Silence from here on in."

Bartholomew braced himself for the blinding flash of light that not even the fog could dissipate, and then the shockwave, which would undoubtedly flip the *Bluebird*. He said his last prayers—for his Brothers, his mother, his abbey family, his friends like Dan and Peg—and composed himself for death.

It didn't come.

Nothing came.

Two minutes became three and then four. . . .

"We got 'em!" exulted the case officer. "All three of them! Captain Wallace, steer two-six-five to retrieve your vessel. Unharmed. But don't try to cook anything on that cooker. Bravo Zulu, gentlemen! Well done. You deserve the thanks of a grateful nation. Of course, you'll never get it, because the less said about this little operation, the better. We clear on that?"

"Clear," responded the Chief, and the others nodded.

"When the threat level is reduced a click or two, you can congratulate yourselves that you had a part in that. Silently, of course."

"Of course," the Chief answered for them.

After they caught up with the *Sara Ann,* the senior Seal, a lieutenant, requested the Chief and Bartholomew ride back with him on the *Sara Ann,* for a debrief. Bartholomew apologized to Ambrose, who would have to go back alone, and joined the Chief and the lieutenant in the stern, while the other Seal guarded the zip-strapped suspects, who were just coming around.

The Chief called the station and gave the word for everyone to stand down. Those off-duty could return to their families.

When they finished pooling everything they knew, Bartholomew realized he had to tell the Chief what he had forgotten about—until now.

He did. The whole story, which took them all the way back to Eastport.

When he finished, the Chief smiled. "If you'd told me yesterday, it might have seemed like a big thing. Today?" he chuckled, "ain't no big thing. What do you want to do?"

Bartholomew was at a loss for words. "What do you mean?"

"Well, do you want me to pursue it aggressively from my end? Or do you want to deal with this Doyle fellow first?"

Bartholomew was even more at a loss.

"Look, Bart, after today I owe you one—a big one." He chuckled and looked back at the western horizon, which was now clear of fog. "So does Plymouth." He looked northwest. "So does Boston."

Bartholomew smiled. "Let me get back to you on that."

41 | the third option

There were two pairs of muddy shoes outside the door to the Abbess's study, a man's and a woman's, both sturdy and sensible. The Senior Brother and Sister were already there, deduced Bartholomew, adding his pair to the collection.

He entered on a heated exchange.

"He *had* to have known!" Hilda declared. "Everyone in the abbey knows they were working on those floats!"

Anselm shook his head. "I didn't," he said calmly. "If Bart had known, he'd have said something."

"Let's ask him," said Mother Michaela, seeing him enter. "Bart, did you know the Navarre Sisters were working on two floats for the Blessing of the Fleet?"

"Not until Hilda told me yesterday."

"You see?" said Anselm to Hilda.

"But I should have," added Bartholomew, unwilling for his Brother to mitigate his circumstances. "I saw Esperanza's two angel drawings. Actually, both of them. I should have probed into what they were of—or at least, for."

He turned to the abbess. "To be honest, Mother Michaela? I don't think I wanted to know."

She nodded. "None of us wanted to know. I certainly did not want to believe that my counterpart over there, Mother Maria Patientia, knew anything about this." She looked out the window. "But now that I have spoken with her—" her voice trailed off, and she slowly shook her head. "Complete lack of surprise, on her part. And resignation to the inevitable. She's called her Sisters home, the ones here and at the convent in Framingham."

Hilda was subdued. "They told us they were going to accompany the floats up to Provincetown for any final touches that might be needed. They were going to spend the night with my friends, the Silvieras, the owners, who would drive them back here after the Blessing tomorrow." She sighed. "But with all their gear cleared out, I doubt very much we're going to be seeing them again."

Mother Michaela appeared lost in thought. "I still find it hard to believe," she wondered aloud, "that anyone with souls entrusted into her care, could jeopardize them that way."

No one had an answer.

"Well," she said, collecting herself, "now we must decide on our next step." She turned to Bartholomew. "You've informed the proper authorities."

"Yes, Mother. I told Chief Burke this afternoon. I meant to, first thing this morning, but something a little bigger came up."

"About which, you are not at liberty to say," surmised Anselm with a smile.

"That's right," confirmed Bartholomew, also smiling.

"But which may have something to do with the possible confidential Level Red that our EMT's were alerted to."

"Which may," Bartholomew concurred.

"And which, judging from your relaxed demeanor, we may assume has been averted—or at least downgraded."

"That would be a safe assumption."

Mother Michaela brought them back. "What was his response?"

"Well," he paused to consider how to put it, without revealing more than he already had. "Let's just say that the Chief is willing to let us decide how *we* would like things to proceed. He can pursue it aggressively, or allow us time to negotiate an arrangement with the museum. Or simply let matters take their course."

Mother Michaela looked around the group. "What do you think?"

They looked at one another. No one had a recommendation. And in making none, they were, in effect, choosing the third option. To let matters take their course.

Mother Michaela summed it up. "Property has been stolen. The perpetrators did so while under our roof and our care. The property must be returned to its rightful owner."

She paused to observe the sun setting over the bay. Other than Chesapeake Bay, the inner crook of the elbow of Cape Cod was the only place on the Eastern Seaboard where it was possible to see an over-the-water sunset. Cars were already thick at the far end of the harbor parking lot. In the summertime people drove a long way to watch from there, applauding as the last sliver of sun sank beneath the horizon.

This evening the sunset was spectacular. A mackerel sky caused the deepening crimson hues to fan out from the entire horizon—as if God Himself were celebrating the thwarting of a horror that would have eclipsed 9-11.

Mother Michaela let the beauty sink in, then picked up her thought in a bemused tone. "The question is, who—in God's eyes—*is* the rightful owner?"

She turned to Bartholomew. "I'm afraid your assignment is not yet finished. We need to explore all avenues. Find this man Doyle and see where the museum stands. I should think it would be in everyone's interest to handle this thing as quietly as possible."

Anselm frowned. "You're not suggesting—a cover-up?"

"Of course not! God would never bless such a thing! In fact, I suspect it would invite an avalanche of bad publicity. That which was whispered in darkness will be shouted from the housetops!" She sighed. "But if the museum can be satisfied, and the statues returned, and charges against the Navarre Sisters dropped, would that not be the best possible outcome?"

They nodded.

"I'll go see Doyle immediately," stated Bartholomew. "This time, empowered to negotiate."

He went to the Cove Motel, where Doyle was staying, only to find that he'd checked out. When? Four hours earlier. Why? He said he'd come to see a niece, but when he learned she'd left, there was no reason for him to stay.

There was one more place for Bartholomew to go: Provincetown. From Sister Hilda, he learned the name and address of the captain, and the name of his boat. First, he went to his home.

The captain's wife, Rita, seemed to know English—at first. But with each question he asked, her understanding deteriorated, till she did not understand a word he was saying—even though she'd lived in America nearly all her life.

There was only one thing left to do. He went home, spent the night, and came back early, just after dawn and well before preparations for the Blessing got underway. He went down to the wharf, where some of the captains and their families were decorating their boats with pennants and bunting they'd collected all year long or saved from last year for this occasion.

One boat was not in her slip: the *Jubileu*. Cesario Silviera had the best boat last year and was certain to repeat this year, with his amazing angel floats. But he was nowhere to be seen. Apparently the *Jubileu* had gone fishing.

He went to the harbormaster's office, which was closed—doubly closed, for Sunday and for the Blessing. With great difficulty he located the harbormaster, who was in a dockside restaurant, having a breakfast of Portuguese sausage and sweetbread—exactly the breakfast Bartholomew himself would have ordered. With even greater difficulty, he persuaded the harbormaster to leave his breakfast and open his closed office, to call the missing captain on the ship-to-shore.

"You sure this is an emergency?" the irate harbormaster queried, when they got there. "Cesario filed for the Grand Banks yesterday."

"Any mention of passengers or cargo?"

"Nope. Just him and the crew."

"Why did he skip the Blessing of the Fleet?"

"How should I know? Listen, what kind of an emergency is this?"

"It's about to become a police emergency, if you don't get him on the radio." Bartholomew was bluffing—but he was also sure Dan would call his counterpart in P-Town if he asked him to.

The harbormaster dialed in the frequency and attempted to raise the trawler. "She's not responding."

On a hunch, Bartholomew said, "Call Rita and see if she's heard from her husband."

He did. She had. He'd called her by cell phone before sailing out of cellular range. He told her he was having some trouble with his radio but would have it fixed in a day or so.

The conversation was conducted in perfect English.

42 | end of the affair

Summer sunsets in Pamplona were consistent—hazy, shimmering, mellow—the time of day and the conditions that movie directors dubbed "the golden hour," when everything seemed almost magical.

That Sunday evening had lost all its magic for Mother Maria Patientia as she stood out on her terrace. The afternoon's cyber-chat with Dom Miguel had started horribly and ended worse. She had carefully deleted all traces of the exchange from her computer, but it was not so easily deleted from her memory. In fact, it kept popping up.

ABELARD: What have you done?

HELOISE: What do you mean?

ABELARD: The man Doyle who was here last week, who
            asked all the questions about the statues missing
            from our cloister. He seemed to know the
            answers before I could tell him. Then he asked

about your convent. Were there any Sisters from there in America? In Massachusetts? I told him he should ask you those questions. He said he tried. He was told that only you could answer such questions, and you were unavailable.

HELOISE: I was on a three-day cleansing fast—from people, as well as from food.

ABELARD: Then I repeat: What have you done?

              [no response]

ABELARD: ??

HELOISE: It's a surprise.

ABELARD: A surprise?

HELOISE: For your millennium celebration.

ABELARD: Some surprises are not appreciated, when they are not inspired or graced by God. Is this one?

ABELARD: ??

HELOISE: I don't know.

ABELARD: After all these years, have you still not surrendered to Him?

ABELARD: ??

ABELARD: What are we to do?

HELOISE: I don't know.

And she didn't. In all her life, she had not had such a disaster—let alone *caused* one. And it was worse than he suspected. Much worse.

Knowing that their objective could no longer be achieved quietly, that, indeed, there was now no way of avoiding an international incident—a *scandale* that would see their name spread across the front page of every newspaper in the world—

she had decided to exercise damage control in the only court available to her—the court of world opinion.

She had put a call in to her nephew, the chief television correspondent for Radio Madrid.

"Raul? If you will have a camera crew in Pamplona for the grand procession on the next to last day of the fiesta, you'll have an exclusive that will have CNN, Reuters, and the BBC begging you for your footage."

"What kind of story?"

"I can't tell you that. But bring your *best* crew. And come a day early, to get background shots. And is your English up? Because you're going to want to do two takes—in Spanish and then in English."

Raul was unimpressed. "You're going to have to give me a hint, Aunt Cristina. What you're asking costs a lot of money. Even if it wasn't on such short notice. We schedule months in advance, and you're talking barely two weeks from now."

She hesitated. "It has to do with the thousandth anniversary of the monastery."

Impatience tinged his reply. "We already covered that! At the beginning of the year, remember?"

"That was less than a minute. What I'm talking about will be your lead story on the evening news. On everyone's evening news!"

Raul Baroja had gotten where he was, thanks in large part to a healthy professional skepticism. "If you were not a Mother Superior, I'd wonder if you'd been into the Amontillado."

"I *am* a Mother Superior, and I'm telling you the truth!"

He sighed. "All right. It'll take massive rescheduling, but I'll be there."

"I have your word?"

"You do."

"You won't be sorry."

"I hope not."

But now she wondered if she was the one who would be sorry. No, not *would* be. Already was.

Because even if world opinion *were* to line up in sympathy with them, even if all of Navarre—all of Spain—were to rejoice, there would still be only the taste of ashes in her mouth. Her beloved Miguel would never soften. He would never speak to her again.

And all this purgatory she had endured all these years—a soul in limbo, surviving on a fantasy—would be bereft of even that chimera. Her barely endurable existence would become durance vile.

The sky had grown dark. The lights had come on in the outskirts of town below. She looked down at them. It was a fifty-meter drop from where she stood to the rocks below. The lights seemed to beckon.

They would say she slipped. Her three closest friends would know the truth. And Miguel would know. But would he even care?

She sat down on the low terrace wall, raised her feet up on it, and hugged her knees. Now all she would have to do is lean and—her misery would be ended.

Taking a deep breath, she started to lean.

43 | the bargain

Maria Pat stopped leaning. The name Dante had come to mind. She'd read his *Inferno*, knew in her heart that the vision of Hell he'd been given was probably accurate. That the next-to-bottom circle was reserved for suicides. Had Dante ever known this torment? This agony of soul?

She shifted closer to the edge. The distant lights again beckoned. Just lean a little. . . .

Something made her look up. At other lights. Pinpricks of light. Fainter. Tinier. But not colder. Not indifferent. Listening.

Was it—too late?

In her heart, a reply seemed to form. *It is never too late.*

There had been times in the past when it seemed God was answering her in this fashion. But "Maria Impat" had dismissed them. One mystic in the convent was enough! She loved Esperanza, but she'd had to work long and hard to inculcate in her a modicum of wisdom, to keep her from blurting out every interior thing God spoke to her heart. That was all the Bishop needed: *two* "inner locutionists" in his diocese!

But now—with no one to love her, not even God. . . . She again looked down at the welcoming lights below.

It's never too late.

It *is* too late, she cried inside, even as the thought came: You're doing it. The thing you said you'd never do.

She ignored that thought. And pointed out, what's done is done! And cannot be undone.

Its outcome can be affected.

How?

Are all things possible in me?

Yes. But why would you—?

Because I love you.

After all I've done?

I watched you do it.

Why didn't you stop me?

You didn't want me to.

She had to think about that. Walk and think. She swung her legs off the wall and stood up. And began slowly pacing the terrace, lost in thought. Looking up, not down.

Then she stopped. And thought: How come we never did this before, just talked like this?

You didn't want to.

Why?

Because if you could hear me, you would have to decide.

Decide what?

Whether you would do what I wanted, or what you wanted.

Talking on through the night, they gradually got down to bedrock: She had never forgiven Him for taking her beloved from her, at the very threshold of marital bliss. After that, despite numerous overtures—of which He reminded her—she had steadfastly refused to surrender her heart to Him.

She would ask His help, and He would give it, many times. She would ask Him to heal others, and He would. In response to her prayers, He would provide sustenance when they needed it, resolve tangled situations, reconcile broken relationships. There was very little He would not do for her.

And she had thanked Him. And praised Him with her music and her choirs.

But she would not give Him her heart. Not after what He had done to her.

Until now. Until she was overshadowed by this looming, catastrophic disaster, wrought by her own hand. Until she was so desperate that her only other option was to spend eternity with the others who had refused to remain on earth till the end of their days.

"All right," she whispered aloud. "If you will somehow rescue this—cataclysm that I have brought down upon us all, I will give you my heart."

And—

"Isn't that enough?

Silence.

"Very well, and I will abandon myself to your will."

And—

"You're pushing it."

Silence.

"All right! But in that case, I'm upping *my* side of the bargain: If you restore everything to the way it was—only much better on every side, for all concerned—then," and now she hesitated. If she said the next words, everything would be in play, and there would be no taking anything back.

She looked at the stars. Waiting.

She took a deep breath—and forever altered the course of her life.

"Then I will give up Miguel. Give him to you. And never again dream of him, or think of him, in an inappropriate fashion, even for a moment."

She was shaking. Silently crying. Grieving—for what had never happened.

44 | night flight

Gazing out the window at the night sky, Brother Bartholomew prayed for the gift of sleep. He never slept on night flights. He tried a sleeping pill once, but it only numbed him out. It did nothing to still the activity of his mind, which was like an unruly child in church.

He went back over the events that had brought him to this pass, a window seat on the exit aisle, with no seat in front of him, and no one in the seat next to him. Poor man's First Class. . . .

For all intents and purposes, the Navarre Sisters had disappeared. He had called the Framingham convent. Their two were gone as well. Having received an urgent request to return home at once, they'd departed early Saturday morning, about the same time the Faith Abbey Marias had sailed away into the fog. And they, too, had neglected to leave their host convent any travel information—flight numbers, departure and arrival times, emergency contact numbers. Nothing.

They'd simply vanished.

Back in Eastport from his fruitless foray to Provincetown, Bartholomew had wanted to go out on the flats, to get his head straight. But the tide was in, so he went on a bike ride. A long one—out the bike path to the Mid-Cape and on to Wellfleet Harbor. He didn't push it; it was a thinking ride—forensic thinking.

What to make of it all? He scarcely knew where to begin. Follow the money. Or in this case, the statues.

The trawler must have come down to Eastport around dawn and picked up the statues and the three Sisters. All of them aboard the trawler, ready to sing in the stern for the Blessing of the Fleet like last year, only this time with two angel floats.

Except something spooked them. What? Maybe someone saw him and Doyle meeting at Gordie's. Or it could have been the switchboard Sister, mentioning Doyle's call for him.

There was one other possibility: Hilda had tipped them. No, that was unthinkable. Would he have done it, in her place? No. But he might have been tempted.

Back to the statues. The trawler's owners, Cesario and Rita, were obviously in on it, not for any money. For God. For Him, he might be willing to aid and abet grand larceny, and at the very least risk losing his license. The trawler was capable of taking them all the way across, but it was a big ocean and a small boat. A small, dirty, commercial fishing boat, with its own crew, and no private quarters for five nuns.

They had to have more help. Transshipping help. Maria Esperanza had mentioned something about the owners' families back in Portugal. They were seafarers. Out of Lisbon? No, Oporto. Suppose—a cousin or a brother ran a freighter. There were an awful lot of ships out there flying Portuguese flags of convenience off their fantails. What if they transferred the statues to one of them out at sea? That's what he would do, if he were they.

What about the Sisters? They would not have stayed in America, as in all likelihood it would not be long before the police would be looking for them. Did they fly over? Or stay with the statues? There was only one way to find out.

When he got back from his ride he called Dan, who was home watching the Red Sox. Could he come to the station in the morning to check airline manifests? And could an officer help him, in case it was necessary to verify that it was police business?

Again, after Saturday's adventure, the Chief agreed, but Bartholomew realized that he'd used up all his chits. The next morning, with occasional help from Officer Whipple, he called every overseas airline and asked them to check their manifests for each day from last Saturday till next. He was looking for five Spanish nuns traveling together from Logan or JFK, to Pamplona, via Madrid, Frankfurt, London, or Paris. He did have their names, but that was all he had. And yes, it was police business.

It took all day, and in the end he'd come up with nothing (other than the Delta–Iberia promotion, of which he was now taking advantage). He told Otis Whipple he had a new appreciation of police work, and the latter assured him this was far closer to what they spent much of their time doing, rather than the impression he might have gotten on television.

They hadn't flown. Which meant they were on the freighter, steaming east with their precious cargo.

He'd gone to Mother Michaela and told her of his suspicions.

She thought for a long time. "I don't think you're done—or we're done."

He nodded. "I don't either, Mother Michaela."

"I think you're supposed to go over there, see the thing through." She paused and smiled at him. "But I don't know why. God must have something more for you to do."

"That's what I've been feeling, too, for most of the afternoon."

"Is your passport up to date?"

"I think so; I haven't used it in a long time."

"How quickly can you leave?"

"Soon as I can get a flight."

"Good. I want you over there before they arrive. See their Mother Superior. And the Abbot. And let me know what you think."

"I will, Mother."

෨෪

The cabin lights were out. The second movie was over. Most of the passengers were curled up and covered with blankets, heads tucked into pillows, asleep. One or two, like him, were transatlantic insomniacs, reading by the solitary spotlights above their seats.

He gazed out the window and down. The night was so clear, there was no cloud cover beneath them. He could see all the way down to the surface of the ocean, thirty thousand feet below. In the faint light of a new crescent moon, it glistened like wet, black slate.

The sliver of moon was narrow enough that the stars were icy points of light. And ahead of them, barely visible if he rested his forehead against the Plexiglas of the window, were two towering cumulus buildups—twin white spires, snow-covered Alpine peaks. It was a magical night.

And in his imagination he was out there soaring in it. Held by the same spell that had caught the great poet-aviators of the dawn of flight—Malraux, Saint-Exupéry, Beryl Markham. He smiled to recall her. Hemingway, reading *West with the Night*, said she was the best of them all. Not pilots. Writers.

He imagined himself slipping into the cockpit of the *Spirit of Eastport* and checking its rudimentary instruments. Compass: 091 Magnetic (for Madrid). Fuel tank: three-quarters full (and they were half-way there). Altimeter: 10,000 feet. Airspeed indicator: 112mph. Turn-and-bank indicator: steady as she goes. He listened carefully to the nine air-cooled cylinders in the 220-horsepower engine, for any roughness that would indicate a sticking valve or a fouled plug.

She was fine. Banking her briefly to pass between the two spires, he brought her back to zero-niner-one and settled back to enjoy the flight, comforted by the steady drone of the faithful Curtiss-Wright Whirlwind. On and on he flew . . . sleep was coming . . . and now he was back home in bed, Pangur Ban curled up at his feet. . . .

At that moment someone sat ungently down in the seat next to him. And peered over at him, to see if he was really asleep.

It was Doyle.

45 | interrupted journey

Brother Bartholomew kept his eyes shut, hoping against hope that Doyle would leave him alone. No such luck.

"I couldn't sleep, either," announced the Irishman cheerfully, undeterred by the monk's apparent slumber. "On these night flights, I'm a third-movie man." He nodded toward the galley. "They carry a third one, in case anyone is still awake and wants to watch."

Then why don't you go back to your seat and watch it, thought Bartholomew, maintaining his feigned sleep.

"I would have watched it, except I saw the back of your head move a moment ago, and thought perhaps you and I ought to have a little chat."

Doyle rang for the flight attendant, and when she came, asked her for another Jamison's. She informed him that he had exhausted their supply. Did they still have any Bailey's Irish Cream? They did. He would have one of those. On the rocks.

Bartholomew gave up and opened his eyes. "Did you follow me?"

"Not exactly. When I called the friary to find out where you were—we had a meeting in the morning, you'll recall—the lady on the switchboard—"

"Whoa," interrupted Bartholomew. "We did *not* have a meeting. "You *wanted* a meeting. I did not commit to it."

Doyle shrugged. "Whatever. She said you were called away."

"I was." He was not about to tell Doyle about the terrorists.

"I asked her how long you would be away. You hadn't said. A day, a week? She didn't know. But if I left my name and number, she'd see you got it."

The flight attendant appeared with his drink, and asked Bartholomew if he would care for anything. He ordered Bloody Mary mix—with nothing to mix in it.

"So," Doyle went on, "I told her who I was, and that I was the one doing the article on the abbey's art program. She knew about it and was quite enthusiastic. I said that on my last visit I'd interviewed a Sister from Spain, Maria Esperanza. I had some follow-up questions for her—would she be available? No, she was away. How long for? She didn't know."

Doyle chuckled. "Then I'm afraid I had a wee bit of fun with her. Sure'n Maria Esperanza didn't go off with Brother Bartholomew? No! What about the other two Spanish Sisters— were they away, too? Yes. You're sure they're not all together? What did I just say! Well, how can you be certain? Because the Sisters left by boat!"

Doyle winked at Bartholomew. "The ah-hah moment! One by land, three by sea! I didn't know where they were going, but I figured you did. So I called back this morning, losing my Dear brogue, and posing as the Dartmouth Alumni Association, trying to track down a former student, Andrew Doane, for a semi-unsolicited testimonial."

He chuckled and rang for another Bailey's. "Fortunately a different lady was on the switchboard. I was transferred to the Friary, where they informed me you'd gone abroad for an extended trip, and that you'd left that afternoon. After that, it was simple: Go to Logan, stake out Terminal E, wait for you to show up, and in the meantime, see if there were any special deals going to Spain. There was this one. Which you were booked on."

The flight attendant returned with his drink and another Bloody Mary mix for Bartholomew.

Taking a sip, Doyle leaned towards him and got down to cases. "Look, boyo, we're both operating on a diminished budget." When his monk friend raised his eyebrows, he sighed and said, "They've pulled the plug on my life support. Given me my final retainer. That's it; no more expenses, nothing. If I come up with the statues, well and good. They'll reconsider. But as of now? *Kaput.* Thanks to my widow, I'm ticketed round-trip to Pamplona, and I've got about eight hundred dollars in Traveler's Checks. Then I'm tapped out."

To his surprise, Bartholomew found himself feeling almost sorry for Doyle. As an implacable, relentless Javert character, he was pretty nonthreatening.

"You must be going my way," concluded Doyle, "and for the same reason."

Bartholomew said nothing. If he were to be honest, he didn't know exactly why he was going—and wouldn't have told him if he did.

What do you say," Doyle pleaded. "Shall we pool our resources?"

"Let me think about it."

Doyle exhaled and grinned, immensely relieved at not being summarily rejected. He rang for the flight attendant, who soon appeared, smiling, as always, but with something in her eyes that indicated she was probably going to refuse him another drink.

Doyle beamed at her and said, his brogue suddenly thickening, "Ye know, lass, ye'd love Ireland."

"I've been there. I do love it."

"Ah, now, if ye came with me, we'd motor up to County Mayo, and there we'd climb our national treasure, Crough Patrick. And we'd watch the first rays of sun turn Clew Bay all silvery and awaken the wee isle of Clare, stronghold of the great pirate queen and patriot, Grace O'Malley, whose bones reside in the Cistercian abbey there. Then, as the roosters of Killadoon greet the morning, I would write a poem that caught the highlights of your golden tresses, with the first rays of sun just behind them."

Bartholomew's eyes widened. His friend was weaving a spell over her. No wonder he got in so much trouble! Who could resist that charming line?

The flight attendant couldn't. Laughing, she fetched him another Bailey's.

Bartholomew shook his head. "You're a menace, Dr. D. You should be a banned substance!"

"Sure'n what would ye be meaning by that, laddie?" he asked, keeping up the brogue.

"No one—man, woman, or dog—can resist you."

"Well, now," he said, making no attempt to hide his pleasure at Bartholomew's appreciation, "enough about me. You must tell me—now, without delay—how you became a holy man in the making."

Bartholomew smiled. "Some morning, when the dew is tiny diamonds and the sparrows are yawning, and it's coffee ye be drinkin' with naught else in it, I'll regale ye with the likes of that."

"No, tell me now," Doyle murmured—and abruptly fell asleep.

Carefully, Bartholomew removed his glass, raised his tray table, and slipped out into the aisle. Finding two empty seats together, he climbed back into the cockpit of the *Spirit of Eastport*. Altitude? 10,000. Bearing? Zero-niner-two. Fuel mixture? Lean and clean. Engine? Smooth and uneventful. Icing? None. And with Pangur Ban dozing beneath his seat, he flew on into the night.

46 | deus ex machina

"Please return your seatbacks and tray tables to their full-upright position. The Captain says we'll be landing in Madrid in fifteen minutes."

Yawning with the sparrows, Bartholomew raised the shade next to him. Daylight came flooding in, and with it the realization of how much he had needed even that wisp of sleep. It had sharpened his mind. No way could he travel with Doyle; their motivations were diametrically opposed. In fact, he would have to part company with him at the earliest possible opportunity.

Easier said than done. Doyle, he was coming to see, was remarkably resourceful. Not as implacable as Javert, perhaps, but certainly as persistent.

Something else came to him in the clarity of first light. If the captain and his freighter were Portuguese, he needed to be going to going to Portugal, not Spain. Figure the freighter would take ten or eleven days to reach—what, Lisbon? That meant it would make port on or about the seventh of July, a week from now and four days before the end of the annual fiesta, which he'd checked out on the Internet before he left.

And now he was remembering something else. The Navarre Sisters said this year was special—something about it being the thousandth anniversary of the monastery. The monastery! Where the statues were from! The statues, which were disguised as flower-covered angel floats that would fit unnoticed into a parade or—a *procession*. Like the religious procession on the next to last day of the fiesta.

The last piece of his puzzle had just fallen into place.

He looked up four rows, to where Doyle was surfacing. Too bad he could not share with him the greatest ah-hah moment of all. Instead, he had all the more reason to distance himself from Doyle, as far and as quickly as possible, if the Navarre Sisters were going to have a chance—

Whoa, he was doing it again, he told himself. Crossing the line. Losing his objectivity. Like a naturalist on the Masai Mara, observing a pack of a dozen hyenas about to surprise a lone lioness at a kill and take her down. She didn't have a chance. A true naturalist would remain resolutely objective, letting nature take its course. But Bartholomew was reaching back for his .270 Winchester with its Zeiss scope, about to even the odds a little.

They filed off the plane and through Customs, Doyle sticking to him like glue. When they had collected their baggage, Doyle said, "Let's get breakfast; I'm famished!" He led them along to the terminal's café. They entered and took a table, Doyle quickly perusing the menu—and scowling. "You read Spanish?"

"A little," responded Bartholomew.

"Well, here," he groaned, handing him the menu. "And see if there's anything alcoholic, to wash down the *huevos*. Even a *cerveza* will do." He flashed a wan smile. "Beggars can't be choosers, and beggars we are."

The monk glanced at the menu, and looked up at him with a sad smile. "Sorry."

Doyle took the name of God and His Mother and the Holy Family in vain. "Come on," he said standing up. "We've got three hours before the plane to Pamplona. And this is the capital of this bloomin' country! There's got to be *some* place that's serving, this early in the morning! We need some of the hair of the dog!"

Bartholomew just looked up at him, smiling. "The dog didn't bite me."

Doyle was obviously torn. If he left, his monk friend might not be here when he returned. But if he didn't, the leprechauns that were teasing him would soon turn mean. He assured Bartholomew he would return within the hour.

Bartholomew was alone. He ordered eggs and a roll and some cheese. And a cup of bitter, chicory-flavored coffee. And three refills.

He was relieved. Doyle had removed himself from the scene without him having to say anything that might have hurt his feelings. All he had to do now was figure out how to get to Portugal.

Bartholomew did not much care for the literary device known as *Deus ex Machina*. Though he was all for divine intervention, especially when it came in response to heartfelt prayer. Now it was about to be applied to his own life, in the form of the two women who had been observing this tableau since he and Doyle had come into the café.

47 | m&m redux

"It's him, I tell you," whispered the stocky woman with the pencil-thin cigar. "It's Brother Barnabas!"

"Ridiculous!" hissed her slender companion, peering at him through steel-rimmed glasses. "And his name was Bartholomew, not Barnabas. What would a monk from Cape Cod be doing in Madrid?"

"Having breakfast, from the look of it. And it's no more ridiculous than his being in Bermuda last year and getting involved in a murder investigation." She had a conspiratorial glint in her eye. "C'mon, don't you want to find out what he's up to?"

"Maudie, you're incorrigible!"

"That's *unsinkable*—though I sank a bit last year." The speaker was Maud Brown, a semiretired investment counselor from Anaheim, in her indeterminate seventies. Until the summer of '99 she'd been known as "the Unsinkable Maudie Brown," having ridden out every bear market for the past thirty years. Then she got caught in the dot-com, telcom meltdown and saw her hard-earned millions melt away like so many others.

She was still an outspoken embarrassment to Margaret Chalmers, her cousin and long-suffering traveling companion. But much of it was now bravado.

Margaret ("Oh, call me Mags, everyone does") came from Philadelphia and had rowed at Wellesley, as had her daughter. As would her granddaughter. Also in her indeterminate seventies (these days, good nutrition and exercise made it hard to tell how old anyone was), Margaret was a food nut. She was never without her L.L. Bean tote with its emergency rations, in the event they were served a totally inedible meal (as happened once in Bucharest).

Her cousin might tease her about her portable stash of "nuts and berries and twigs, oh my!" But she took quiet pride in the fact that she actually weighed one pound less than when she pulled the #3 oar on the varsity eight more than half a century ago. Back then she'd been likened to Katherine Hepburn in *The Philadelphia Story*, and ever since, she'd worn tailored slacks of the sort Kate made famous.

She could hardly have been more opposite her brash West Coast cousin—which explained why they got on so well on their peripatetic globetrotting. Their travels had taken them to Bermuda the previous fall, to Henley in the spring for strawberries and clotted cream—and all those scrumptious boys in their seersucker jackets and straw boaters. And now they were in Madrid.

"All right, Maud, it *is* Brother Bartholomew. That doesn't mean we're supposed to get involved with him. What if he's here on monastic business?"

"Well, it wouldn't do any harm to find out."

Margaret scowled. "You always do this, and I always hate it!"

"And you're always glad later."

"Not in Cairo."

"Which you never let me forget!"

They watched the monk eat his eggs.

"Look," said Maud breaking the ice that had crusted between them, "all we're going to do is go over and say hello."

And without waiting for an answer, she got up and started across the café. After a moment Margaret trailed after her, disapproving all the way.

≈

Bartholomew was astounded when they came up to him. "What are *you* two doing here?"

"Funny," replied Maud with a chuckle, as she sat down in one of the unused chairs at his table, "that's what we were wondering about you."

Margaret was speechless with embarrassment at her cousin's presumption, but relieved when Bartholomew gestured for her to take the remaining chair. "It's good to see you guys!" he exclaimed, meaning it.

"You, too," they replied, also meaning it.

They reminisced about their shared escapade in Bermuda the year before, and the cousins M&M revealed they were on their way to Pamplona for the festival.

Bartholomew stared at them. "That's where *I'm* going! But not right away. I've business in Portugal first."

"Monastic business?"

"Of a sort."

Maud gave him a discerning look. "*Confidential* monastic business."

He nodded again.

"Portugal," mused Margaret. "Lisbon? Estoril?"

"Both."

"And then Pamplona?"

He nodded, smiling. "You wouldn't be looking for a driver, would you, ma'am? One who can carry bags and deal with concierges and change money and fix cars? And who speaks a modicum of Spanish?"

"You see, Mags?" cried her cousin. "I *told* you we were supposed to come over here!"

Margaret just shook her head in wonder.

"You're a godsend!" exclaimed Maud happily, and Bartholomew chuckled. He'd been thinking the same thing about them, with a capital G.

"What about your friend?" asked Margaret. "The one you came in here with?"

"Oh, he's just someone I met on the plane," Bartholomew answered, which was partially true.

"We thought you were traveling together."

"So did he. But we're not."

"Louie," said Margaret, recalling a line from her favorite movie, "I think this is the beginning of a beautiful friendship."

Catching sight of the time, he realized Doyle would be back soon. "Have you rented your car yet?"

"We were about to," said Margaret.

"Well, if you'll arrange for the car," suggested Bartholomew, "I'll see to the bags. I assume yours are in checked baggage?" They nodded. "I'll get a cart and the bags and meet you at the car rental."

In twelve minutes he had gathered the bags. In ten more, they were driving out of the rental car area in a stick-shift Peugeot 406.

Just as Doyle entered the terminal.

48 | a slight change in plans

Brother Bartholomew rose early to have his quiet time at approximately the same time as he would have gone to Lauds at home. Next he would clean and gas the car, get reliable directions to wherever they were going that day, and have the car in front of the hotel, ready for loading.

After that, he would drink coffee until they appeared. As soon as they did, while they ordered breakfast and perused the *International Herald Tribune*, he would bring down their bags, load them, and settle his bill. He insisted on paying his own way, but did not object when they insisted on augmenting what he would have spent, so they could all stay in a five-star.

Both of them liked to drive, so the only time Bartholomew got to was after lunch, while the ladies napped. There was never a question about who would do the navigating.

Being navigator did have its compensations, like suggesting their itinerary. He proposed they do the coast of Portugal first, from Oporto down to Estoril, then Lisbon and back to Madrid before heading up to Pamplona.

"You do have a place to stay when we get there?" Margaret asked him. "Because there aren't many hotels, and they're booked months in advance for the fiesta."

Bartholomew smiled. "Being a monk has some advantages. I'm sure they'll find a bed for me in their monastery."

In Oporto, after breakfast he waved them off sightseeing, shopping, and beaching, while he went about his "monastic business"—about which they had become increasingly curious, and he increasingly reticent.

Along the waterfront he inquired in every place of business if anyone knew a seafaring family, name of Silviera, who had relatives in America—specifically fishermen out of Provincetown, and who also might be related to a freighter captain.

Late in the afternoon, about the time he was ready to give up, in a ship chandler's shop he found someone who said he was describing the American relatives of Mario Bordalo, an Oporto sea captain whose freighter was home-ported in Lisbon.

Bingo.

In Lisbon he went to the Maritime Registry, where he found that the name of Captain Bordalo's ship was the *Estrela do Mar*, and her owner was Transport Borges. He called that organization and was eventually put through to a woman who could speak English and was familiar with their ship schedules.

"This is Bartholomew Doane speaking. I have urgent need of communicating with Captain M. Bordalo, aboard the *Estrela do Mar*. I believe she's one of yours."

"What is this in connection with?

"Church business."

"What sort of Church business?"

"That's confidential, I'm afraid."

"Who did you say you were?"

"Bartholomew Doane. *Brother* Bartholomew Doane, with Faith Abbey in Massachusetts."

That did it. Actually, he wasn't quite sure *what* did it, but she was more pleasant and forthcoming after that. The *Estrela do Mar* was due in Lisbon in six days (the 11th) but would be dropping off cargo in San Sebastian in three (the 8th).

San Sebastian was the closest Spanish port to Pamplona. The cargo could only be the statues. But they would have less than three days to get them over to Pamplona and ready to join the Procession.

That evening at dinner he casually suggested a slight change in plans. They were scheduled to leave for Madrid in the morning and go up to Pamplona the next day. Instead, why not go to San Sebastian on the coast for two days? The best beach in Spain. They could spend the nights of the 7th and 8th there and go straight to Pamplona on the 9th.

"That leaves us only four days at the fiesta!" cried Margaret. "And that was the whole reason for coming!"

Bartholomew said nothing.

Maud looked at her, a little impatient. "Which would you rather have, two days at the best beach in Spain, or two more days of dusty peasants drinking and singing all night?"

Margaret thought about it. "Well, when you put it like that. . . . But we're *not* leaving Pamplona till the festival's over on the twelfth!"

Maud threw up her hands in surrender. "Come on, you know you'll love San Sebastian! I hear they have marvelous vineyards that we can tour."

Margaret reluctantly agreed, but as they got up from the table, Bartholomew caught her giving him a dagger look. Tomorrow was not going to be a walk in the park.

49 | the canterbury game

The atmosphere was a bit frosty at breakfast, and a bit more by the time they were pulling away in the Peugeot.

Well, this was his fault, thought Bartholomew. He would have to do the icebreaking. "You know," he said, apropos of nothing, "in a way this is like being on a pilgrimage. In the Middle Ages people would make long journeys—to Canterbury, or Rome, or the Holy Land, for reasons of spiritual purification. Often whatever happened en route was as important as what happened when they reached their destination. For a pilgrim, getting there was at least half the fun."

"Yes," replied Margaret caustically, "we read Chaucer, too."

"Exactly!" declared Bartholomew, resolutely cheerful. "We haven't done the *Canterbury Tales* thing yet, each one telling their story. And we've still got five hundred forty kilometers to go."

Silence from the front seat.

"Margaret," he went on, undeterred, "you mentioned you once rowed. Why?"

She turned to wither him with her scorn. "Who appointed you activities director?"

That hurt. When they got to Madrid, he would leave them and find his own way to San Sebastian.

Maud, who was driving, turned and looked at her cousin. "Mags, what has gotten into you? For the last two days you've had your knickers in a twist, and now you're being downright snotty! Is this all because we're going to San Sebastian? Because if it is, it's not worth it! We'll go to Pamplona tomorrow!"

Margaret was speechless. And before she could respond, Maud added, "Yes, you should be shocked! You're always complaining about my embarrassing you. Well, you've embarrassed me! Was that the way they taught you to behave at Miss Porter's? Because if it was, I'm freaking glad I didn't go to finishing school! It's finished *you* off good!"

After that outburst another twenty kilometers passed without anyone speaking.

Then Margaret, as an act of contrition, broke the silence. "I guess I took up rowing because my father rowed. At Saint Paul's and Yale. My brother followed in his footsteps, and I was constantly trying to outdo my brother, if possible. I never could. After college he kept up his rowing at the Vesper Boat Club and eventually rowed double-scull with Kell."

"Kell?" Maud asked.

"Jack Kelly, Grace's brother."

"Oh."

"What's the romance in it?" Bartholomew asked, pursuing his original line of questioning.

"I guess it's—" she thought a moment, then mused, "the *cleanness* of it. When you're rowing well, the scull just glides over the water. You reach out, make a clean catch, lean back, putting your legs into it. Then you make a neat release, feather your blades, and come slowly forward, letting the boat run out underneath you. You reach out and roll up, ready for the next catch."

She smiled dreamily. "All you've left behind is a pair of vortices in the water, matching the pair behind them and the pair behind them."

"That's—*beautiful*," murmured Bartholomew. "Now I know."

"Me, too," exclaimed Maud. "I loved that."

"What's it like," he asked, "rowing with others?"

Margaret laughed, now thoroughly enjoying the Canterbury game. "The same, only different. Crew's been called the perfect team sport. In an eight-oared shell, if one person is a quarter-inch off dead center, or a fraction of a second late at the catch, or if one oar is skying on the return, it throws the whole boat off. If one person runs out of gas or catches a crab, it ruins it for everyone." She paused. "So you gut it out for the sake of the others, knowing that they are gutting it out for you."

"That's also beautiful," remarked Bartholomew.

"Builds character," Margaret replied.

After lunch and their siesta, he asked Maud how she became a broker.

"My father was part of the consortium that brought power over the Rockies from Boulder Dam and then Grand Coulee Dam in the Thirties. As a little girl, I used to go with him into the foothills, to watch them erecting those high-tension towers and stringing the lines. Tower after tower, they would stretch away, spanning valleys, crossing mountains, like the footsteps of a giant striding to the sea."

"Maud, that's beautiful," said Margaret. "I didn't know you—"

"Well, you never asked me," said Maud, a little embarrassed.

"And the stock market?" prompted Bartholomew.

"The market—the American economy—is a reflection of the nation's confidence. And I've always been bullish on America. The trick was to find companies that were trying a little harder—before everyone else found them. The way I got to be unsinkable was pretty much like Liza running over the ice floe in *Uncle Tom's Cabin*. You pick your next chunk of ice fast, confident that you picked right. The main thing was to keep moving; the hounds were right behind you!"

They laughed. And bantered all the way to Madrid.

The next morning on the way to San Sebastian, they resumed the Canterbury game. "All right, Brother Bart, your turn. Why did you become a monk?"

50 | let there be light

Why did he become a monk? He told them of his childhood on Cape Cod and of his fisherman father, of whom he thought the world. Of his mother who taught English and dreamed of his one day going to Dartmouth. He told of volunteering to become a corpsman with the Marines in Viet Nam. He skipped the horror of combat, of trying to save men who could not be saved, of trying not to make friends because so many died or were cruelly maimed. Of going so numb you just did the next thing that needed to be done and then the next.

He did not tell them of the medal for repeatedly returning to pull wounded men out of a mortared foxhole that the VC had zeroed in on. Six men who would have bled to death, were it not for him.

He did tell them, because they asked, of learning of the death of his father when his boat went down over the Grand Banks. And how that news did what all the horror couldn't: put him over the edge, into walking catatonia. How he wandered off into the bush and didn't emerge for more than a day.

And then, how the kindest human being he'd ever known, one with a silver cross on his collar, came to see him in the recovery ward each day and finally got him talking. And wanting to go on living. And then believing in a higher power, a God who loved him.

When he mustered out, he went to Dartmouth to please his mother, majored in forestry, became a park ranger assigned to the Cape's National Seashore, and finally accepted God's call to a life of service as a religious.

He told them about life at the abbey, and what it felt like to sing Gregorian Chant at midnight in a basilica lit only by candles. "I guess that's my romance," he concluded.

They drove on for a few K, thinking about that.

Then Margaret, behind the wheel, said, "I think the real question is not why you entered monastic life, but why you stayed in."

She turned to Maud in the passenger seat. "I mean, he's educated, capable, intelligent—he could be leading a normal life. Married, with children. And probably successful at anything he put his hand to. So why—this?"

"To me, God is real," he answered simply. "You have to start there. And if He's real—and He *cares*—then everything else follows."

"No," declared Margaret, "it does not. I have an intellect and, thanks to my parents and some fine institutions, it is a highly-trained intellect. I'm not going to set that aside for some—divine fantasy."

Bartholomew shrugged and smiled. "You asked—"

"I'm *not* going to waste my time indulging in some construct of corporate wishful thinking."

"In other words," Bartholomew responded, "man created God in his image, to fill some void in his world view. Some need to believe he was loved by an all-wise, all-powerful supreme being."

"Something like that."

"Well, I will never be able to persuade you otherwise. I do hope someday you find what I've found."

"I hope not," Margaret concluded. "It would be the first sign I was going soft in the head, the early stages of Alzheimer's."

The rest of the way to San Sebastian, they traveled in polite silence—no laughter, no banter. And they went to bed early.

૨**

The morning dawned hot and hazy, but not humid, and with no wind stirring the water, the pellucid sea slid ashore with the tiniest of splashes. Brother Bartholomew, in khaki shorts and a short-sleeved denim shirt with a small blue cross embroidered over his heart, sat on the hotel terrace, his sandaled feet up on the low wall. Gazing out at the calm ocean he sipped coffee and weighed the events of the day before.

Should he have avoided the subject? Made light of it? There was no question that he'd ruined the rest of the drive. Yet—was he going to deny his call? Pretend it didn't matter as much to him as it did? It might have saved unpleasantness, but there was a higher accountability.

"Is this seat taken?" It was Maud, down an hour earlier than usual.

"Morning," he said, smiling. "Can I get you some coffee?"

"I'll get it in a minute." She sat down, a grave expression on her face.

Oh, Lord, thought Bartholomew, it's worse than I thought. He braced himself.

"Margaret's still asleep," her cousin went on. "She doesn't know I'm down here." She lowered her voice. "I want to hear about God."

Bartholomew's cup stopped halfway to his mouth.

"I mean, He's obviously more to you than a wishful construct."

Bartholomew smiled. "He's—everything."

"Well, start at the beginning." She glanced at her watch. "Only hurry up. We don't have a lot of time before she comes down."

Bartholomew nodded. "God is—love," he began, searching for the right words. "He's a heart Person, so the intellect isn't much help here. But the intuition is. You'll know who He is in your heart, before your head even gets in the game. Don't worry about that. Trust your heart; your head will catch up soon enough."

Maud smiled. "I can do that. I did, for all those unsinkable years. But I'm sinking now, Brother Bart. You know the cardinal rule of old money: Never touch capital. That's how it stays old. Well, I'm not just touching it; I'm mauling it. I'm down to my last million."

She nodded in the direction of the stairs. "She doesn't know it, but this is likely to be my last trip. I've got one son who's just been downsized, and at age fifty-two he's not likely to be upsized. And my other son fancied himself a day-trader and lost his shirt—and would have lost mine, too, if I'd augmented his trust fund."

She sighed. "I could use a caring God just now."

"Okay, tell Him. Just start talking to Him. You can even say, 'I don't even know if you exist, or if I'm just talking to the air. But if you're real, I need to know you love me.'"

"That's all?"

"It's just the beginning. But it's enough for now."

"There *is* more, isn't there?"

"A lifetime more." He laughed. "An adventure you can't even imagine!"

"I think I'll go for a walk on the beach," she mused, getting up. Then she looked at him. "It's true, isn't it. He's real." It was a statement, not a question. She knew.

Bartholomew watched her walk down the beach, white slacks rolled up, head bent, hands stuffed in pockets. Father, he thought, I *loved* that! It's been a long time.

You're a little rusty, he heard in his heart. *But you got it done.*

It's the best thing that's happened on this trip!

Which you were about to abandon, because you got your feelings hurt.

Will she connect with you?

She already has.

Will it take?

That's between her and me. You planted the seed. Leave the watering to me.

What about her cousin?

Leave her alone. She does not think she needs me.

Will she ever?

That is not your concern.

I wish—

What did Francis tell his followers?

"Evangelize, evangelize! And if you must, use words."

Go thou, and do likewise.

Live it without talking about it, and she will want it one day.

Exactly.

You know the part I liked the most? Seeing the light come on in her eyes, when she knew in her heart you are real.

Mine was seeing the light come on in your eyes, when you saw the light in hers.

51 | five saucers

He had other business in San Sebastian that day, he reminded himself. Unpleasant business.

It was not too hard to find out where and when the *Estrela do Mar* was offloading: Dock #4, around noon. He went there two hours early and found a bistro far enough away that he could keep track of what was happening without being noticed. Sitting outside at a small, white café table, he had a coffee and read the *Tribune*—a tourist whiling away the morning.

About an hour later, an old olive-drab truck with an olive-drab canvas covering its bed drove past where he sat and pulled onto the dock. It was followed by a minivan, both driven by women. And now he recalled their name for the truck: Generalissimo Fiat. From its color and the canvas canopy in back, it must have been a military transport once.

So he was right. He'd figured it out, all of it. Then why was there no elation? Why was there only dread?

And what exactly was he supposed to do now? That, he hadn't figured out, not any of it. Should he call the police? The

Guardia Civil? Put a call in to Chief Burke and leave it in his hands?

He ordered another coffee. In a moment the waiter brought it, removing the old cup, but leaving its saucer on the stack accumulating on the little table. Four, and counting, thought Bartholomew. He smiled wryly at the quaint way they kept a customer apprised of how much he was consuming. Useful, if one happened to be drinking something stronger than coffee.

The *Estrela do Mar* appeared on stage left, delicately maneuvering in toward the dock. There were women standing amidships, five of them at the railing, waving to the two on the dock. He ordered another coffee.

The five now came down the gangway with their gear. Their friends on the dock greeted them warmly and stowed their baggage in the back of the minivan, whose rear seat had been removed (Europe's understanding of the minivan concept being a lot minier than America's). On the truck the canvas was removed from its frame, ready to receive its valuable cargo.

With great care, each angel was off-loaded by means of a boom and sling, and gently lowered onto the bed of the truck, where it was securely anchored. Then the canvas was spread over the frame, effectively concealing the cargo for the journey.

Bartholomew watched—and wondered if he should be doing something. Before he'd left the States, he and the Abbess had sensed God had some role for him to play before this drama's final curtain. But it didn't seem like intervening here and now was *it*. He ordered one more coffee.

When the canvas was secured, the stocky woman who'd been the first down the gangway and had overseen the loading of the angels, took over driving the truck. The tall one got in with her, as did the thin, medium one. The other four got in the minivan, and the two vehicles left the dock. And came his way.

It occurred to him to raise the newspaper, so they wouldn't see him. But he didn't. He looked right into the truck's cab as it passed. He saw Marias Constanza, Immaculata, and Esperanza.

The truck veered and nearly went over the curb. They had seen him.

52 | dom miguel

Bartholomew and the cousins reached Pamplona at noon on the 9th. The fiesta was now in its sixth day, and all but the heartiest celebrants were worn down. There were still hundreds of them, happily milling about the streets, eating lunch, having a siesta, killing time till the start of the bullfights.

Margaret, nervous that their reservations might not survive the crush of more than a million tourists arriving for the festival, had called ahead (twice) to make sure the Yoldi Hotel was holding their room. It was. Did Brother Bartholomew want to call the monastery? No, he would take his chances.

They got directions to the monastery and followed the road that wound up into the foothills.

At the monastery, the Brother on duty in the reception area came out to the car to greet them. "Brother Bartholomew? Welcome! We've been expecting you!"

Seeing he was in good hands, Maud and Margaret departed warmly, saying they'd see him around the fiesta.

In a moment the Abbot came up. Dom Miguel was about the same height and age as Bartholomew, but his hair was so short he looked almost bald. The dark eyes were deep-set, the cheeks hollow, the nose beaked. And he wore round steel-rimmed glasses. All of which caused him to bear a startling resemblance to Maximilian Kolbe, the martyr saint of Auschwitz.

"Good to see you, Bartholomew!" he said in excellent English. "Your Abbess wrote to tell me you would be coming. How wonderful you can be here for our millennial celebration! As soon as you get settled, I'll give you a tour."

The guestmaster showed him to his room—Spartan but clean. One bunk, one straight-backed chair, one desk, one reading light. A picture on the wall, of a beatific Daniel in the lions' den, looking up to heaven. And a window looking out over the valley. A monk's cell for visiting monks. He would be happy here.

Dom Miguel took delight in showing him around, and seemed to have an intriguing anecdote for each item of interest. He was most curious about Bartholomew's activities at Faith Abbey, and the more he shared, the more obvious became the similarities of their lives. They shared a love of Gregorian Chant and observed the same offices at the same times of day. And here, as at home, the creative arts were flourishing—stained glass, drawing, painting, weaving, and even a resident poet.

Bartholomew kept thinking, wait till Mother Michaela hears this! God was doing the same thing here as He was doing at home. An ocean might separate them, and many centuries; it didn't matter. In an epiphany he had a new understanding of the Renaissance—all the creative arts operating everywhere in harmony to glorify God. In Spain, in America—wherever God gathered a people to live together to His glory, blooms of creativity should be expected.

When the Abbot learned that Bartholomew led Faith Abbey's guild of calligraphers, he insisted on showing him their scriptorium, which was in the crypt beneath the ancient chapel.

The crypt? People were buried there? Some, centuries ago. Now they had a burial ground on the hill behind the monastery. As he followed Dom Miguel down the stone spiral staircase, Bartholomew prepared himself for something dank and grim. He couldn't have been more surprised. It was actually quite cozy, with iron sconces lining the stone walls, and a great hearth for warmth in the cold season.

Beside which, a gray cat was sleeping in a basket by the hearth, and all along the south wall, high slit windows admitted an abundance of daylight.

The copying tables with slightly tilted surfaces were of hard oak, darkened and worn smooth by centuries of unbroken use.

"A *real* scriptorium!" Bartholomew murmured, as he ran his hand along the wood with the deep patina. "Libraries were created here." He shook his head, speechless.

Dom Miguel beamed. "You're the first calligrapher from America to visit us. Let me show you some of our treasures." From cupboards and broad, flat drawers he produced them, each one astonishing Bartholomew till finally his receptors were burned out and he could barely respond with the appreciation they deserved. There were illuminations the likes of which he had not seen outside of Ireland, and calligraphy so clean and spare and elegant, it almost brought tears to his eyes.

And the more he appreciated them, the more Dom Miguel produced.

"I'm sensing this once was a great center of learning and the arts," Bartholomew observed.

"It was," replied the Abbot. "You've seen the caliber of the penmanship. We also had master artists training apprentices." He went to another set of drawers and produced sketches dating all the way back to the fifteenth century. He took his time—indeed, it was as if time stood still.

At first, Bartholomew had felt guilty by taking so much of his time. But gradually he realized that the Abbot was enjoying this as much as he was.

He had the distinct impression that the monastery was timeless. It was always here and would always be here. Monks passing through it left their mark, like pilgrims passing a huge boulder and leaving their initials and the date on it. The pilgrims passed away. The boulder remained for eternity.

Dom Miguel was about to put away one sheaf of drawings and bring out another, when Bartholomew raised a hand. Wait a moment. There were eight finished drawings—large charcoal figure studies of monks, or perhaps other students. They were breathtaking—considerably more accomplished than the other works they'd looked at. But Bartholomew was equally fascinated by six pages of exercises—a hand, an eye, an apple, a wall sconce, the light coming through a window—one of the windows above them. The practice sketches were done with a fine-pointed orange pencil, and the painstaking precision and effortless control were extraordinary.

He turned back to the larger ones. There was something vaguely familiar about them, though the date in the lower right hand corner, 1558, and the modest initials, D.K, meant nothing to him. Still—

"What can you tell me about these?" he asked his host.

"Funny you should ask," said Dom Miguel, smiling. "I asked the same question of Dom Peregrino, the Abbot who took me on a tour at the time of my first vows twenty-six years ago." He chuckled. "As he had asked the Abbot before him."

He turned to Bartholomew. "I can only tell you what I was told. A lad of seventeen or eighteen had come to the monastery to perfect his skill." He spread out the exercise sheets over the table next to them. "But as you can see, he was obviously advanced—he could have been teaching the teachers."

He pointed to different aspects. "Look at the highlights, the way he builds his shadows, the ease with which he captures the defining line. And look here, at this eyelid. The boy was a master already."

At that moment the gray cat, which had been sleeping by the hearth, came over and rubbed against the Abbot's leg. Dom Miguel reached down and petted him. "The monastery cat. Actually we have two, Perico and Miguel. This one's Miguel."

"Named for you?"

"Oh, no!" the monk laughed. "For our local hero."

"Miguel Indurain."

The Abbot looked at him with new appreciation. "You ride?"

"I used to. Not much anymore."

"We'll go out later. I think we can find a bike that will fit you."

Bartholomew shook his head. "I'd embarrass myself and slow you up. I've seen these hills; no wonder Indurain was such a good climber."

The Abbot put the drawings away carefully. "We'll go up now; I've saved the best for last."

Bartholomew took a last look around. "Hard to believe there could be anything better than this."

"You'll see."

He led his guest up the spiral staircase and out into the cloister.

"Your roses are breathtaking!" Bartholomew exclaimed. "What a lot of work someone has done!"

"Several, actually."

Then his guest noted the statues—ten, with two unoccupied pedestals. And realized the Abbot was watching him.

"These are almost as old as the monastery," explained Dom Miguel. "But I suspect you already know that."

Bartholomew kept smiling. "What happened to these two?"

"I suspect you know that, too."

"Tell me anyway."

The Abbot did. Including the part about that Abbot and the mayor disappearing—in what remained to this day one of the great mysteries of Navarre.

Then he persuaded Bartholomew to give up his reserve and come for a ride. Actually Bartholomew was not as unconfident as he had let on. Though he'd not ridden since he left home, he'd been in top form then. Of course, in one's indeterminate early fifties, whatever fitness level one attained dissipated quickly without daily reinforcement. And Cape Cod was pancake-flat, whereas here they were in foothills.

Dom Miguel found him a Bianchi in good condition that actually fit and was only a few years older than the one the Abbot himself was riding. His host took it easy on him, and together they enjoyed the long glide down into town. He showed Bartholomew all the prominent sites, including the bullring and the barricaded chute down which the bulls ran each morning.

They had an orange drink, and then it was time to head back up, brothers in spirit now, as well as in calling.

The climb was as hard as Bartholomew had feared. But he relaxed and stayed seated, content to pedal in the lowest gears at a high cadence. Spinning up the hills like Lance Armstrong. Who had learned that secret from Miguel Indurain.

53 | las tres bandidas

On a road that appeared on no map—that was no more than two parallel tracks over an obscure mountain pass, amidst breathtaking down slopes and jagged outcroppings in the Southern Pyrenees—the old Fiat truck gingerly felt its way. The secondary streets of Pamplona may have received their pavement a generation ago. This old smugglers' route would never know such luxury.

Other than the occasional logging truck—or smuggler—no one came this way. Which was exactly why Maria Constanza had picked it, after sending the minivan home by a more civilized route. When she was a girl, her uncle had once shown her this path, where his father and other men and women from their village had held the pass during the war.

The day was warm and sunny with a good breeze keeping it from getting sticky, as the old truck took its time, finding the best footing for its skinny tires. Actually it was doing surprisingly well on the rugged terrain. It had plenty of clearance, having been built half a century before when more than a few European mountain roads were not much better than this one.

Maria Constanza was concentrating on the driving, while the other two nattered on to keep their minds off the precipitous fall-off to their right, and their queasy stomachs.

"Can you get over Brother Bartholomew being there this morning?" Immaculata was saying. "I couldn't breathe for about a minute after we passed him."

"Me, neither," agreed Esperanza. "I don't think I've ever been so sick with fear. Somehow he'd figured it out, all of it. It was about half an hour before it dawned on me that he didn't do anything."

"And he was alone," Immaculata added. "There were no police with him. No *Guardia*. No media. Just him. Watching."

"He's a good man," Esperanza mused. "He has a good soul. I've seen it."

"What do you mean?"

"I've looked into his eyes. They're the windows of the soul, and sometimes you can see what's inside a person through their eyes."

Immaculata shivered. "Don't talk that way! You know I don't like it when you get mystical! But—I agree. I felt sorry when he started getting involved."

"It wasn't his fault; it was mine," remarked Esperanza. "If I'd not done those drawings—"

"If you'd not done those drawings," Immaculata interjected, "we never would have gotten the statues."

"But I took too long. He saw me. And remembered."

"Well, nothing can be done about it now."

Esperanza nodded. "Why did he come? And then not do anything?"

Immaculata had no answer for that.

And now Constanza spoke. "I hope you two are praying!" she grumbled, as she wrestled with the steering wheel to keep the left front wheel out of the too-deep rut it kept trying to dive into.

"We never stopped!" exclaimed Immaculata cheerfully.

"Amen, Sister!" seconded Esperanza, joining her enthusiasm. "Can you believe it was a *year* ago we began this operation?"

Immaculata shook her head. "Seems more like a month." She chuckled. "We were driving an old truck then, too. That old moving van, sneaking into Boston like a band of terrorists."

Esperanza laughed. "We were the only ones who were terrified!" "And now we're about to do it again," cried Immaculata, her voice gaining bravado. "*¡Vivan las tres bandidas!*"

Constanza scowled, refusing to enter into their high-spirited badinage. Her total concentration was given to keeping them from tipping and spilling down the mountainside.

"You know," Immaculata marveled, "I cannot believe we actually did it! I mean, whoever would have dreamed we could?"

"And the sad part is," said Esperanza wistfully, "we can never tell anyone. No one but Mother Pat will ever know. We will be the unsung heroes of the Great Saint Return of Navarre!"

"We can't even write it down and tuck it away, to be opened after we've gone home to Jesus," lamented Immaculata.

"We'll be going home to Jesus a lot sooner than you think," barked Constanza, "if you two don't stop congratulating yourselves and get back to praying!"

"Oh, come on, Con!" chided Esperanza. "Stop being such a sourpuss."

"You think God is pleased with your exulting?" demanded Constanza.

"I *do* think He's pleased!" declared Immaculata defiantly. "I think He's been helping us all along!"

"She's right," concurred Esperanza. "Look at all the close calls, the narrow escapes. Look at this morning! Brother Bartholomew, immobilized!"

"God did that!" agreed Immaculata. "I tell you, He's—"

Constanza took her eyes off the road to glare at the other two—and the truck gave a sudden lurch and went down into the rut she'd been struggling to avoid.

They were stuck. Really stuck. And the load in back was so heavy, the old jack was of no use. Nor did they dare untie and try to move the statues without a block and tackle.

It grew very silent in the cab.

Finally Constanza got out to assess the damage. The other two followed her, their heads hanging like contrite schoolgirls.

Constanza got down on her hands and knees to get a closer look, then down on her stomach.

When she got up and brushed herself off, the other two searched her face for a glimmer of hope. There was none.

She confirmed the worst: "We're not getting out of here without help. Massive help."

Immaculata checked her cell phone. "No signal. No way of telling Maria Pat what's happened to us."

"We have a bigger worry than that," said Constanza grimly. "No one knows we came this way. And no one lives anywhere around here for kilometers. We could be here a long time."

Now Esperanza murmured. "If someone does come, we'd better hope and pray it's someone we want to meet."

Constanza nodded. "I think all three of us had better start doing some serious praying."

They did.

And after an hour Esperanza looked up and said quietly, "It's in God's hands."

54 | fiesta

After supper, the Abbot had another surprise for Brother Bartholomew. "Come on, we're going down the hill." Seeing his guest's expression he chuckled and added, "by car."

They laughed.

"Wear your robe," Dom Miguel advised. "It will afford you a measure of protection."

"Will I need it?"

"It's fiesta," replied his host with a shrug, as if that explained everything.

It was dark by the time the white Volkswagen Golf made its way down to the town's car park. Leaving the car there, Dom Miguel led the way to the center of town, explaining that it had changed completely since Hemingway immortalized it eighty years before. In his day the streets were mostly unpaved, and only a handful of *locos* with more courage than brains dared to run in front of the bulls.

Bartholomew asked about the run—strictly from a specta-tor's point of view—and Dom Miguel took him over to where the barricades were waiting. Each morning at 8:00, the eight bulls that would face matadors in the afternoon would be released to thunder down the barricaded streets to the *corrida*. But such was the power of *The Sun Also Rises* that each generation sent its hardcore romantics to Pamplona. Papa would have to take much of the responsibility for turning the run into what it had become today—an "extreme sport" with several thousand in Nikes and Reeboks participating.

They went back to the main square, now filled with revelers, with more *peñas* snaking in from the side streets, each led by its own trumpeter.

All at once from the next side street came the hair-raising thunder of deep field drums, echoing and re-echoing off the walls of the narrow street. It was a shocking, arresting sound. Everyone froze.

Out of the side street came the local militia, sharp-columned and straight, led by flags, swinging their arms, caps low over their eyes. Suddenly it was 1936, and everything went eerily silent, except for the pounding, mesmerizing drumbeat.

Then the spirit of fiesta reasserted itself. A *peña* deliberately infiltrated the column, plying the soldiers with wine from their *botas*, linking arms with the bewildered young men in uniforms, and soon reducing the smart-looking column to a chaotic, happy muddle. To the dismay of no one but the sergeant in charge.

Bartholomew grinned. Fiesta wins! Dom Miguel was smiling broadly, too, for the moment shedding any resemblance to Maximilian Kolbe. And the *peña*, heady with its success, now wound around the two priests, one in a gray robe, the other in a beige one. Wine was offered, and attempts were made to link arms, both graciously declined.

Dom Miguel grabbed Bartholomew's arm and led him to the nearest sanctuary, which happened to be the Bar Txoco. All the tables were taken, indoors and out, but there were two extra chairs at a table to the left. Dom Miguel asked the two diners if he and his friend might join them, just for a moment.

And Margaret Chalmers, in her best Miss Porter's Spanish, assured him that he and his friend were welcome.

Then she saw that the friend was Brother Bartholomew, whom she had never seen in his formal habit. Well, they were still welcome.

Maud was thrilled! "Bart! How *are* you!" she exclaimed, clasping his hand with both of hers. "I've thought about you *so much* since San Sebastian!" Her eyes were dancing with delight (and perhaps a liter or two of *vino negro*). "You were right! What an adventure!"

Bartholomew tried to smile as he genteelly extracted his hand. What must the Abbot be thinking? Was that a look of bemusement? Or rapid reevaluation.

"Um, these ladies," he endeavored to explain, "were kind enough to give me a ride here—"

"Here and there and everywhere!" chimed in Maud.

Bartholomew persevered. "Maud, Margaret, this is Dom Miguel, the Abbot of the Monastery of San Fermín, the saint whose fiesta this is."

"We're honored, your grace," declared Maud, trying to be solemn. "If I were standing up, I'd curtsey."

"If you were standing up, which in itself would be a feat," observed Margaret acidly, "and you tried to curtsey, you'd fall over!"

Bartholomew pressed on, regardless. "Dom Miguel, these are my friends Maud Brown and Margaret Chalmers. From America," he added, needlessly.

"Welcome to Pamplona," said Dom Miguel warmly. "We're glad to have you here."

"I'll bet," murmured Margaret.

Dom Miguel ignored her sarcasm. "Have you been to a bullfight?"

"We're going tomorrow," said Maud. "Is it okay to cheer for the bull?"

Bartholomew wondered how far Benedictine hospitality could stretch before it snapped. He tried to think of something to help the situation and couldn't.

"If the bull wins," responded Dom Miguel patiently, "a horse goes down. Or a matador."

Now Margaret weighed in with her opinion, venting more than just disapproval. "I think it's barbaric and cruel, nothing more than a blood sport! No, it's not even that, because there's so little sport in it. What it is, is a throwback to the Coliseum!"

Appalled, Maud was about to reprimand her for her incredible rudeness, but Bartholomew caught her eye and gave the slightest shake of his head. She held her tongue.

Still smiling, though with difficulty, Dom Miguel said calmly, "The bullfight derives from a symbolic pageant of the early Church in this country, depicting the struggle between light and darkness, dating back more than a thousand years. It has always been a test of supreme courage."

They were listening now, even Margaret.

"The matador stands in proxy for each of us," the monk went on. "When one faces evil, it is often frightening and sometimes overwhelming. It takes a very brave man to stand his ground when evil suddenly bears down on him, intent on destroying him. He has no wall to hide behind, no army in front to protect him. All he has is his faith."

He paused. "If he will stand, unafraid, unflinching, it is enough. But if he falters, breaks and runs, he will only have to face evil again. And next time—evil will know he's afraid and can be broken."

The women were silent. So was Bartholomew, who felt goose bumps on his arm. He still had no desire to see a bull-fight, but now he could respect the tradition.

At that moment another *peña* line came weaving past, veering close to where they sat. At the end of the Congo line of happy revelers was a foreigner the *peña* had adopted. One who was learning their song and their dance, a brace of *botas* bouncing on his hips like six-shooters.

It was Doyle.

Bartholomew recognized him at the moment he recognized Bartholomew. Indeed, it was a moment of recognition all around. Maud pointed at him. "Isn't that your friend from the Madrid airport? I'm sure it is."

Bartholomew was also sure, and had no desire to act on the information. He didn't have to. Doyle did.

"Boyo!" he shouted, "ye abandoned me!" He tried to extricate himself from the *peña,* but they would have none of it, one grabbing him on each arm. He was theirs for the duration.

As they happily pulled him away, he looked back almost plaintively.

And Bartholomew could almost feel sorry for him.

Then he noted that Dom Miguel had recognized him, too. Which explained his host's subsequent abrupt decision to return up the hill. Fun's fun, but enough's enough, thought Bartholomew, as he joined the Abbot in bidding M&M *buenas noches.*

৯৯

The next morning, the day before the procession, Bartholomew took care of his last piece of monastic business. Asking if he could borrow again the Bianchi he had used the day before, he glided down the winding road to the convent they had passed. And pulled in. And asked if he could have a word with the Mother Superior.

He was shown into the reception area, where he found a chair and waited. And waited. Then got up and looked out the window, into what was apparently their garage area. The minivan he'd seen on the dock at San Sebastian was there. But not the truck.

Finally the Mother Superior appeared—short, indeterminate midforties, and to Bartholomew's discerning eye, carrying the weight of the world. He introduced himself, as did she. Like the Abbot's, her English was excellent.

The pleasantries about the town, the weather, the fiesta, the monastery up the hill where he was staying, took all of two minutes. Then she asked how they might be of service to him. As if she did not already know.

"We enjoyed so much having your Sisters with us," he said as pleasantly as he could, keeping it light. "We called them the Three Marias."

She smiled at that. "They enjoyed it, too. A wonderful experience." She, too, was keeping it light. And revealing nothing.

"I was one of the two abbey members who helped them with their English."

"Yes, they wrote me about you. Thank you for your kindness to them."

Bartholomew smiled. "Oh, the pleasure was mine, I assure you! Are they here now? It would be fun to see them. They left so quickly, I didn't have a chance to say goodbye."

"Oh." She paused. "They're—not back yet."

"I see." His excuse for the visit having now evaporated, he stood up to leave.

She walked out with him. As he got back on his bike, he said, "I hope they make it in time for the procession."

She looked at him, startled. And then tried to smile, and with difficulty said, "So do I, Brother Bartholomew. So do I."

"Are their chances—good?"

Her voice broke as she replied, "It's in God's hands."

55 | three-dream flight

That night Bartholomew tossed and dreamed, as he did when he was deeply troubled. It was a crazy dream. The old truck was in it, in a ditch beside a mountain track that he was coming down, towards the three Marias. But instead of riding a fat-tired mountain bike, he was on a skinny-tired road warrior. The old Bianchi.

He tried to stop, to see if they were all right. But the brakes wouldn't work, and he rolled right past them. And they silently watched him pass, sitting in their formal black habits at a small white café table on the grass beside the track. They were sipping coffee from little cups, each with a stack of saucers beside her cup.

The next dream was more disturbing. He was standing in what seemed to be a cathedral—vast and dimly lit, but not cold. He was alone. With time to drift—like out on the flats at home. There were prayer chapels off the main sanctuary. He went into the nearest. There was a large painting of the Madonna and Child. Light seemed to emanate from them, the brightest coming from the infant, whose right hand was upraised. He came closer, extended his hand up towards the canvas. Stretched. But it was out of reach.

The next chapel contained a life-sized, lifelike painted sculpture of Christ on the Cross. Gazing at it, his attention was drawn to the right hand. Blood was oozing from the nail wound. And dripping on the chapel floor. His heart pounded in his chest. He had to do something to relieve the suffering of the one being held by the nails. He started to reach toward the nailed bleeding hand, but stopped short, frozen by the realization that he had driven that nail through that flesh.

Shuddering, he left the chapel and went to the next. Here was a stone angel, larger than life, wings half spread, eyes looking into his own, right hand reaching out to him. Beckoning him. He went forward and reaching out, touched the tip of the outstretched hand.

And awoke.

He got up, went down the dimly lit corridor to use the facilities, and came back to bed. In his absence, a visitor had joined him. Cat-sized. Sitting on the end of his bunk, watching him.

"Come on, *amigo*," he said under his breath, as he went to the bed to lift the cat off it and put him out in the corridor. "We both need our sleep. At least I do."

He was about to pick up the cat, when he stopped. It had been nearly a year since Pangur Ban had died. It would be good to—

No, he interrupted himself. It would not be good. It would be painful. That scab's healed over. Leave it alone.

In the end, he compromised. He propped open the door to the corridor, so the cat—he didn't know whether it was Perico or Miguel—could leave if he wanted to, and wouldn't have to scratch to be let out.

The cat elected to stay for the moment. And his presence at the end of Bartholomew's bed had a sad but calming effect. His next dream—he had wondered if this would be a three-dream flight—was of the scriptorium down in the crypt.

At least, it seemed to be the scriptorium. But the iron sconces held real torches, not electric lights. And the tables were lighter colored. And in the hearth a fire was going, warming an iron pot of something that smelled awfully good. Drawn by the smell, he went over and admired the iron hook and swivel arrangement that suspended the pot, yet enabled it to be swung out into the room. Ingenious! Odd he hadn't noticed it before.

He reached down to pet the dozing cat—and was surprised to find it was black, not gray. Dreams—somehow he knew that he was having one—were weird that way. Almost whimsically changing minor details, as if they were having fun with the one having the dream.

Hearing something behind him, he turned from the black cat and noticed a young man in a leather jerkin and woolen pants open the drawer where the ancient drawings were kept and take out one of the exercise sheets that still had some unused white space on it. Putting it on the table closest to the flickering light from the wall sconce, he opened a small cupboard, extracted a pencil, freshened its orange point on a piece of roughened stone, and proceeded to draw—with his left hand.

That finished, he looked around for something else to render. On the mantel over the hearth was a four-inch figurine of a man standing, head bowed, hands down and open, praying. Carefully he took it over to the table and resumed his seat on the stool. He set the little figure before him, turning it this way and that. When he had an angle he liked, with a few quick strokes he caught the essence of the figure.

He's gotten it right, thought Bartholomew, watching over the lad's shoulder. In less than a minute.

Then the artist bent over the table and drew another sketch. The same figure, but different now. Elongated.

He woke up.

The cat was gone.

And he knew who D.K. was.

Las tres bandidas were beginning their third day of fasting and praying on the mountain. Fasting, not out of choice. Praying, very much out of choice. As Esperanza had said, it was in God's hands. But God was almost out of time. The procession was the next morning.

They had confessed and asked forgiveness for every sin they had ever committed, or contemplated, or even wished they could do. They had forgiven everyone who had ever consciously or subconsciously trespassed against them. They had vowed to do deeds of charity anonymously, and to bear only love in their hearts for those who had less than love in their hearts for them. To live lives of such purity that they would practically glow.

And nothing happened.

No one, good or evil, came up or down the track. They had located a little brook nearby—even in the wilderness God looked after His children—and caught water from it in a hubcap. So, while they were cold at night, hot in the daytime, and famished, they were not in physical jeopardy—yet.

Esperanza was getting on the nerves of the other two. Calm, smiling, she was content that this, too, was God's will. That they may have displeased Him initially, but He was not displeased with them now. In fact, she informed them, He was holding the three of them in the hollow of His hand. And at night, He sheltered them under His wings, like little chicks.

"That's all very good for you to say," Constanza retorted. "You already live more up there than down here. But—"

Before she could say any more, Esperanza raised a hand. "He wants us to praise Him. Right now."

"Well, I don't feel like praising Him right now!" announced Constanza. "And it might be a long time before I do."

Esperanza nodded. "He knows that. He wants us to, anyway."

Constanza scowled at her.

Esperanza started to sing. "Praise God, from whom all blessings flow. . . ."

Immaculata halfheartedly joined in. And finally Constanza, her heart not at all in it, added her voice to theirs.

Their song grew stronger, rising in the clear, early morning air.

They sang it again, louder. And again, louder still. All of them, wholeheartedly.

The hymn of praise pealed out over the mountain like church bells, echoing, reverberating, causing birds to sing, inviting the very heavens to join in.

"Praise Father, Son, and Holy Ghost!" The fifth time through, they were so full of joy, they were disappointed when Esperanza stopped them. Putting a finger to her lips, she cocked her head to listen.

Below them, around the bend, they could hear a motor. A big one, in a low gear. In a moment, a truck appeared—a great, empty, flatbed logging truck. With a crane and a boom behind its double cab, for picking up felled and stripped-out timber. In the cab was a crew of four of the biggest loggers they'd ever seen. Anxious to get up the mountain to retrieve the trees they'd cut the week before.

In fifteen minutes, they were waving back to them from their departing truck. And Generalissimo Fiat was upright again, and impatient to get underway.

So were the three Marias. Who prayed and sang hymns of praise all the way home.

è&

Someone else was having difficulty praising God that morning. Mother Maria Patientia was more than a little put out with her nephew.

Raul Baroja, ace field correspondent for Radio Madrid, had just come by the convent and vented his feelings. To his aunt, they were obviously coming out of fear, but that made them no easier to accept.

He had put his reputation on the line, he told her heatedly, for this "event"—whatever it turned out to be. And so had his boss; the managing director of the television news department was putting *his* reputation on the line, backing Raul.

"A lot is riding on this, Aunt Cristina," he'd concluded in her private office, less than an hour before. "I've got our best people with me—the best cameraman, the best soundman, the best producer-engineer. Plus, there are two other stories breaking just now. Last night in Barcelona, they cracked an Al Qaeda cell. Even bigger is what's happening just north of here. For the first time since Indurain a Spanish rider has a chance of taking the yellow jersey in the Tour de France! And they're in the Pyrenees right now! We're going there, as soon as we're done here. But the point is, they want us there *right now!*"

Maria Patientia did not know what to say. She could not tell him that her three dear friends and their parcels had gone missing. Had not been heard from in two days. That everything was about to blow up in her face. In all their faces. So she just stood there, looking at him.

Seeing what was in her eyes, he softened his tone. "Look, I know something's gone wrong. You don't have to tell me; it's written all over you. I'll tell you what: If you'll release me by sundown, everything'll be all right. I'm already here with the crew; it'll take us less than an hour to get there. We could do a Sunday highlight on Spain's return to glory in the Tour, and all will be forgotten."

She sighed and nodded assent. How could she do otherwise?

Now it really *was* in God's hands.

57 | at the bar txoco

After breakfast that morning, Brother Bartholomew asked the Abbot if he might have a word with him. The latter took him out on his private terrace, with its commanding view of the valley and the town below.

"Did you sleep well?" asked Dom Miguel.

His guest smiled. "Yes and no. That's what I wanted to talk to you about. You remember those sketches you showed me? The ones in orange pencil?"

"Of course."

"Well, I dreamed about him."

"Who?"

"D.K. In the dream I was watching him work." He turned to Dom Miguel. "Can you tell me anything else about him?" he pleaded. "Anything at all."

His host looked at the hazy sky and shook his head. "Nothing that I haven't already told you. I vaguely remember someone saying he was a vagabond, who'd drifted in from one of the islands in the eastern Mediterranean—Cyprus or Crete. Why?"

"Because I think—" He stopped. Don't go there. Not yet. Be sure.

The Abbot looked at him intently. "It's very difficult," he admitted, "to contain my curiosity."

Bartholomew smiled. "It's very difficult not to tell you what's coming to me. I would want to confirm it first, with a qualified expert. And by one of those coincidences—that you and I don't believe are coincidental—one happens to be in town right now. Maybe the only one in all of Navarre. The only problem is, he's drunk."

"And now my curiosity has become inordinate!" He was about to say more, when a look of realization crossed his face. "Could he not be brought to sobriety?"

"He could. But sober he might be more—of a problem."

Both monks looked out over the valley.

"What do you propose to do?" asked Dom Miguel.

"I don't know."

The Abbot sighed. "I guess we'll all know tomorrow. The procession begins at ten o'clock, which means it should reach us by noon. Then the Bishop will say Mass. The Sisters of Mary will be here. The mayor. The town dignitaries, the Cathedral congregation—in all, we're expecting more than a thousand celebrants. It is, after all, our millennial celebration."

"I'm looking forward to it."

Dom Miguel tapped his long fingers together. "So, what is next for you?"

"I wish I knew, Dom." He looked down at the town. "I guess I'll go down there this afternoon. It feels like everything's on hold for the moment."

❧

He caught a ride down into town with the Brother who was fetching what they would need to provide refreshments after Mass for the vast crowd that would be coming up to the monastery tomorrow.

Now in its seventh day, the fiesta had lost much of its steam. It would rev up again tonight, the next-to-last night, with the hardcore revelers looking for a final fling to tide them over till next year.

"Brother Bart! Over here!" It was Maud, calling to him from a table at the Bar Txoco, where she and Margaret and Sean Padraig Doyle—of course—were all lounging, somnolent in the noonday sun, sipping something that might be tea from tall frosty glasses, waiting for it to be time to go to the bullring.

Bartholomew headed over to join them. In the sun-drenched plaza, with groups of white-clad farmers passing by, he could almost imagine others sprawled with them at their table—Errol Flynn, Ava Gardner, Ty Power, Mel Ferrer. . . . He shook his head and rejoined the twenty-first century.

Everyone, even Margaret—even Dr. D—was glad to see him. Ordering iced tea, he caught up on all that they had seen and done.

"These dear ladies rescued me this morning, as I was about to make the worst judgment call of my life."

Bartholomew laughed. "Tell me you *weren't* thinking of running with the bulls!" He stared at him. "Oh, dear God, you *were!*"

Doyle nodded meekly. "I've been on the wagon ever since, drinking half the tea in Navarre."

"Well," said Bartholomew, pausing to survey him, "you do look a little better than you did at the end of that *peña* line last night."

"So Bart, tell us what you've been up to," asked Maud. Before he could answer, she added, "I have got to talk to you sometime—not here—about what's happened to me since you and I talked."

Margaret looked at her watch and stood up. "Maud, we need to leave right now if we're not going to miss the first bull." She left enough euros for their tea, then smiled at Bartholomew. "After what the Abbot told us last night, I don't want to miss a bit of it."

Maud sighed and got to her feet. "Maybe we can catch up later," she said to Bartholomew, before trailing after her cousin.

"Interesting ladies," Doyle commented, watching them leave. "The big one thinks the world of you. The thin one can't stand you."

"Bartholomew chuckled. "Well, at least I'm not luke-warm."

"They told me of your peregrinations up and down the Portuguese coast. That must have been fun."

"It was."

"I got the impression the itinerary was entirely your idea, and that you were preoccupied with highly confidential 'monastic business' during the daytime."

Bartholomew smiled. "They like to pump melodrama into everything; it's one of the ways they entertain themselves on their trips. They're making it far more mysterious than it was."

"Oh? What was it?"

"Confidential."

Doyle ordered another tea for both of them. "When I heard of the last-minute change of plans, to go to San Sebastian instead of coming right here, I knew you'd found what you were looking for."

"And what would that be?"

"Where the statues were coming ashore."

Bartholomew said nothing.

"So—are they here?"

"I don't know," he said honestly.

Angry that his monk friend was still being uncooperative, Doyle declared, "I'll tell you what, boyo! They're *not* here! Because I've had a long chat with the officer in charge of the local *Guardia Civil* detachment. And another with the mayor. And another with the local chief of police. It's amazing how cooperative they all are once they heard the amount of compensation that might be in the offing, as it were. Even split several ways, it would mean new houses and new cars and college educations for grandchildren all around."

"I thought the ILE had cut the cord."

Some of the wind went out of Doyle's sails. "They have. But the local laddies don't know that. And the truth is, I'm sure it would all be back on the table if the whereabouts of the statues were known."

Bartholomew looked at him. "You really don't know where they are, do you."

"I know they're not in Pamplona, or anywhere in the outskirts. But they're in Navarre. From what the ladies told me, I figure they must have come ashore in San Sebastian on the eighth. That's forty-eight hours ago. In that time we've had details looking in every barn, every grove, every garage, and talking to anyone who could tell us anything."

He pounded the table with his fist. "They're not here! And nobody has seen anything!"

Bartholomew shrugged. "Then you must be wrong."

"I'm not wrong! And you know it! They're just a whole lot smarter than I ever gave them credit for! Staying away, as if they knew we were watching every road into town! Just waiting for them! I tell you, these aren't nuns! They're the Great Train Robbers!"

Bartholomew laughed in spite of himself. And felt immensely relieved. And for the first time since he arrived—for the first time since he learned that the Sisters had left Eastport—he felt happy.

58 | the eve of battle

Raul Baroja knocked on the door of his aunt's private office. She looked up from her computer and smiled. Not a tired, defeated smile. A real one. Looking at her, he grinned. "You've heard something, haven't you?"

"I have," she admitted, and taking him by the arm she led him out onto her terrace. In the early evening, the sun was a copper orb on the horizon, and the dust suspended in the air was transformed into a golden haze.

"Breathtaking," she said, looking up at him, "don't you think?"

"I do. The crew is out right now, capturing it—footage we can also add to our stock library."

She smiled. "You have enough confidence in my 'event' that you weren't packing up to leave."

"I figured you must have gotten good news, or you'd have sent us on our way by now."

She nodded and put a hand on his arm. "I can now guarantee what I could only promise before."

"Wonderful! I'm glad for you! And for all of us. And since it's actually going to happen, and we're here, can you give me some kind of heads up?"

She looked down the valley, and there, faithful as the sun, was her hawk ascending through the haze, spiraling slowly upward. She pointed her out to her nephew.

"Does she do that every evening?"

"Pretty much."

He whipped out his cell phone, and flipping it open, punched a sequence of keys. "Roberto? Raul. I'm at the convent. Look, there's a hawk climbing a thermal here. Terrific shot, with the city and the setting sun in the background. You anywhere near here? The monastery? Great! Take a look down the valley; you'll see her coming."

He listened and turned to his aunt. "They've got her."

"And by the way," he said to the engineer, "we're on for tomorrow. Yeah, it's definite. So get the fireworks tonight, and the bull run in the morning. But I want you locked and loaded by—" he turned to his aunt and raised his eyebrows.

"Ten," she whispered, "for the start of the Procession."

"Nine-thirty," Raul said, "central square. Bring the extra battery packs and both sound booms. Tell everyone. See you there."

He snapped the phone shut, stuck it in his shirt pocket, and turned to his aunt. "Okay, out with it."

"Before I tell you, you must promise me—before God—that you will never reveal what I am about to tell you."

He looked at her quizzically. "Aunt Cristina, you haven't robbed a bank or anything?" He meant it as a joke, but she was startled by it, nonetheless.

"I'm going to tell you the whole thing, since it's certain to come out tomorrow anyway. I want you to hear *my* version of it first. Then you can report it any way you like."

He looked at her shrewdly. "It *is* big, isn't it?"

She nodded.

"Bigger than an Al Qaeda cell in Barcelona."

She nodded again.

"Bigger than a Spaniard taking the *maillot jaune.*"

Another nod.

He relaxed and, beaming, said, "Let's have it."

Taking her eyes off the hawk, which was up to the monastery and was undoubtedly being filmed, she told him the whole story, leaving nothing out.

When she finished, he was speechless. Finally, he managed, "Aunt Cristina, this isn't big. It's *huge!* But I'm worried. You could go to jail!"

"*You're* worried? How do you think *I* feel?" But she was laughing. "Anyway, that's why you're here. How you present the story is the only thing that will keep me—us—from spending a good deal of the rest of our lives as guests of the government, and I hear they're not really into Benedictine hospitality."

He shook his head in awe. "You're an amazing woman, you know that? You've thought this whole thing through."

She laughed. "To borrow from Samuel Johnson, the prospect of one's imminent incarceration wonderfully concentrates the mind."

He looked up at the last of the crimson orb, and the sky darkening above it. Its clarity promised a perfect shooting day tomorrow. "You're right, you know," he mused. "How it's presented tomorrow will make all the difference."

He took her hand. "You're going to be throwing yourselves on the mercy of the court."

"I'm not sure I like the sound of that."

"You will, before that sun goes down tomorrow."

"Are you sure?"

He looked her in the eye. "Aunt Cristina, you asked me to trust you. And I did. And I'm glad." He paused. "Now I'm asking you to trust me."

❧

Other preparations were being made that evening. In the mayor's office—not the new one, the old one with the balcony and the ancient bullfight posters going back to 1917—were gathered the chief of police, the lieutenant in charge of the *Guardia Civil,* and the mayor himself. On the massive mahogany desk a street map of Pamplona was laid out.

Behind the desk with a pointer was Sean Padraig Doyle. "With the monastery under constant surveillance, they have not dared smuggle them in. And they know we're not going to let up. So the only way they can get the statues back on their pedestals is to use the procession as cover. So, check out any long flatbed truck with a raised platform. If all goes well, we should have the statues—and the guilty Sisters—in custody before the procession even begins."

"What about the people?" asked the mayor. "I know them. They're going to be more than a little upset when they realize we've arrested three Sisters of Mary and their Mother Superior, for trying to return the monastery's cloister statues."

Doyle slammed the pointer down on the desk, startling everyone. "That's wrong thinking! They are not the monastery's statues! They are the property of the Isabel Langford Eldredge Museum, bought and paid for legally nearly ninety years ago. You are merely returning stolen property to its rightful owner."

"I don't know," said the police chief. "There are going to be a lot of people. We even issued a permit to Radio Madrid this morning. They're going to have a television crew there. Besides— everyone loves the Sisters of Mary. And the monks at the monastery. You'll be leaving with your statues," he said to Doyle. "But this is our town, our people. We've got to go on living here."

"Well, I don't," said the *Guardia Civil* lieutenant. "I'm not from here. I'm not even Basque. And none of my men are. So let us make the actual arrest."

"A perfect solution!" exclaimed the mayor happily. "We'll find the statues," he nodded to the police chief, "but the Guard will do the actual arresting and taking custody."

Doyle nodded. "Sounds like a plan. But now we need to consider all contingencies. Like, what do we do," he turned to the chief, "if your people don't locate the statues? We need to have a last line of defense, as it were."

On the map he tapped the front courtyard outside the monastery's main entrance. "The reviewing stand will be here, and the speakers' platform next to it, here. Everyone will be going inside for the Bishop's open-air Mass as soon as the procession is completed."

Doyle looked at the Guard lieutenant. "In the unlikely event that the statues are not apprehended before the procession arrives, your men can perform a discreet physical inspection of each truck, each float, each giant figure that goes through those gates."

The lieutenant frowned, and Doyle anticipated his objection. "If anyone asks, you received a terrorist warning, maybe linked to that Al Qaeda cell they just found over in Barcelona, and you're just double-checking everything going into the monastery, that's all."

He tapped the reviewing stand on the map. "Station the rest of your men out of sight behind the stand. They'll be right there, if needed."

He looked up from the map. "Gentlemen, I need not remind you how much depends on your successful execution of this plan."

The mayor, as always, had the last word. "Just remember," he said to the other two (and himself), "all we're doing is our civic duty. Returning stolen property to its rightful owner. Taking the perpetrators into custody. Their fate is not on your hands—I mean, in your hands. It will be decided by a jury. And if they're convicted, their sentence will be decided by a judge. Your responsibility ends tomorrow."

59 | return to darkness

Bartholomew knew he would not sleep well that night, even if the gray cat returned. So there was no point in going to bed early. He went out to the cloister and, hands clasped behind him, strolled along the covered slate walkway. Other than his footfalls, the only sound was the soothing plash of the fountain in the center of the cloister. Surrounded by the rose garden and illuminated by the half moon, it made for a scene of complete serenity.

Bartholomew sat down on the low wall bordering the cloister. He gazed at one statue and then the next, imagining what they might say to one another after the monks had gone to sleep.

They're not a bad batch, these.

Not like the previous generation. Did you ever hear such controlling prayers? Telling Him that He must do this! He really needed to do that! They seemed to have it reversed, about who was supposed to be serving whom.

But they did get it straightened out eventually. Because at bottom, they loved Him.

No. At bottom, they remembered He loved them.

Gradually Bartholomew realized he was not alone. Someone else was sitting on the wall, across from him. Should he—no, he thought, he's coming over.

The silhouette walked across the cloister courtyard. It was Dom Miguel. "I come out here when I can't sleep," he explained.

"I can't, either," said his guest. "I have the feeling everything's going to be resolved tomorrow."

Dom Miguel nodded.

"Shakespeare understood a night like this," Bartholomew went on. "In *Henry V,* he wrote of the Eve of St. Crispin's Day— the great battle when the English, vastly outnumbered, defeated the French. The king couldn't sleep. Neither could anyone else, at least on the English side."

Dom Miguel waited.

"The point was, everyone accepted there wasn't going to be any sleep that night. So the king made the best possible use of it, visiting campfire after campfire. Knowing that each one he visited would tell of it to those he didn't visit. By morning they would all know he cared. And they would be ready to die for him."

"Is that in the play?"

"No. I just thought of it."

His host nodded. "Would you like to spend this evening profitably?"

Bartholomew looked at him, a little surprised.

"From what you've told me about what you do at home, I gather you have a sideline. Helping solve crimes?"

Bartholomew smiled. "It's something that seems to have come to me in my late middle age."

"Well, we have one. The one I told you about."

Dom Miguel recapped the unexplained disappearance of the Abbot and the mayor in 1917. "It's so old!" he said apologetically. "Yet it does endure."

Bartholomew smiled in the moonlight. "I must confess I'm intrigued. But how can I help?"

"Oh, there's a clue," reported his host, smiling. "It's made no sense to anyone. But—I will give it to you. You can contemplate it, while I finally settle into the arms of Morpheus."

The clue was a poem that the then-Abbot had written and left behind. It was neatly lettered on a now-yellowed sheet of good stationery, with a sketch of a waterfall underneath it, in the same ink, presumably by the same hand.

Bartholomew took it to his cell, lay down on the bed, and studied it.

RETURN TO DARKNESS

Life is a journey
from darkness to light.
One comes from light everlasting
entering as a tiny spark
into perfect darkness.

Embarking on one's shadow voyage
The great light is forgotten
But not entirely;
The heart ever seeks to return
To that light without source or end.

One may gather light
as one gathers years,
for everything in life
is either a lesson,
a reward, or a test.

Each choice one makes
either attracts light
or rejects it
and each influences the next.

Choices towards darkness
believe they are
choices towards light—
right choices
made for all the right reasons.

Thus one born to seek the light
and return to it
may become instead
unaware
a seeker of darkness.

Too late now—
as one entered
so shall one return—
perfect darkness to
perfect darkness.

60 | sanctuary

As the procession wound its way up the hill toward the monastery, the sun took no prisoners. The giant masks were heavy and hot. The corps of militia, which had started out crisp and cool behind its deep field drums, was wilting and disheveled. The carriers of the Cathedral's religious statuary were sweating profusely and staggering under their heavy loads. The band, having run through their repertoire four times, were marching in silence to the cadence of their snare drums, saving their breath for their final run-through in front of the reviewing stand in the monastery's courtyard. The people on the pageant floats were still smiling, still throwing candy—and wishing for something cool to drink.

But the people of Pamplona were a people who knew how to endure. Life in the hills was never soft, never easy. They had come through drought, unreliable markets for their produce, and, two generations ago, a bitter civil war that no one won. Their iron had been through the refiner's fire. They would climb on. And they would celebrate Mass with the Bishop on the grounds of the monastery that had stood for a thousand years.

And just when they stumbled and were assailed by doubt, Veronica came to wipe their brow. In front of the convent, which was two-thirds of the way up the hill, the Sisters of Mary had turned their courtyard into a respite station. There were tables with water, tea, and orange juice dispensers, others with orange slices and bananas, cakes and cookies.

But knowing that the procession must keep moving, there were teams of Sisters moving among the processioners. Each team had a Sister with a water dispenser on her back, another carrying paper cups, another with a towel to wipe away sweat, and another to offer chocolate or an orange slice. Their goal was to reach every pilgrim who needed succor, and they did. And never were the many who received so grateful to the few who gave.

At the reviewing stand in front of the monastery, a great cheer went up as the flags leading the procession hove into view. The cheers rolled down the hill in waves, and the processioners smiled. It was all worth it now. The militia covered down and sharpened up its lines. The band decided maybe they'd play one more set now, and still have breath for another when it was their turn in front of the reviewing stand.

Everyone in the reviewing stand was grinning, laughing, happy. Save one. In the section reserved for the Most Important of the Very Important People, Dr. S. P. Doyle was in a quiet rage. On one side of him was the chief of police; on the other, the mayor. The *Guardia* lieutenant was down with his men. He would have been seated with the other MI-VIPs, except that his superior, the Commandant of the *Guardia Civil* for all of Navarre, was sitting with the Bishop. So the lieutenant was down with his men, who thus far had turned up nothing. Nor had the police in their pre-procession sweep of all the pageant vehicles.

In frustration, Doyle asked the police chief to have them check the ambulance and fire trucks as well, and the maintenance vehicles that would be the cow's tail of the procession.

Nothing.

Arriving in the courtyard and lining up to go through the portals, the front ranks of the Procession soon caused a back-up, as Doyle had anticipated. The Guard did their investigating swiftly and unobtrusively, also as anticipated. In fact, everything was going according to plan. Except there was no sign of the statues.

The flags went in, the militia went in, the first floats went in, the giant heads went in. The band paused to run through its repertoire, then it went in. And more floats started going in.

"Have the lieutenant check them," whispered Doyle to the chief of police.

"We've already checked them," the chief whispered back.

"Check them again!"

Word was relayed to the lieutenant, and the Guard double-checked under the platforms of the remaining trucks before they went in.

Nothing.

And then Doyle saw one truck, smaller than the rest, with no raised platform but with two floral angels on the back, wings semi-spread, one beckoning, the other reading from a scroll. He stared at it. Glanced at the list of entries the chief had given him, and the list of floats that had been checked in the pre-procession sweep. This truck with three women in the cab was on neither. It must have entered the procession en route.

As it drew closer, he recognized the beckoning angel. From the drawing of Sister Maria Esperanza at Faith Abbey.

"There it is!" he shouted down to the lieutenant. "Stop that one!"

But the lieutenant, aware that his superior had no knowledge of what was going on and was watching, hesitated.

"Hurry, man!" cried Doyle. "If they get through those gates, they'll claim sanctuary!"

The lieutenant started to order his men toward the old Fiat, whose canvas canopy had been removed to display the beautiful, flower-bedecked angels.

But as he did, Maria Esperanza alighted from the cab and hurried toward the reviewing stand, while Maria Constanza lined the truck up with the gates.

At that moment, the float ahead of them passed through the gates, leaving no one in front. With only twenty meters of open ground to cover, Constanza accelerated as much as she dared, for fear of toppling their precious cargo.

The lieutenant leaped in front of the truck, both arms outstretched.

Constanza, carefully applying the brakes, managed to bring Generalissimo Fiat to a halt inches from the lieutenant's brave chest.

In the Radio Madrid mobile unit, Raul Baroja, alerted to which truck would be carrying the statues, directed Camera 1 to stay on that truck at all times, no matter what. And Camera 2 was to focus on the procession, the reviewing stand, the gates, and the action in the MI-VIP section.

Camera 2 was the result of an emergency call he had put in the night before to the head of the news department. Without revealing exactly what the story was, because he had promised his aunt he wouldn't, he convinced his boss that it was important enough to switch the backup crew from the Tour de France to Pamplona. It was not huge. It was global. They had driven half the night to get here.

Grabbing a mic, Raul left the mobile unit to start giving the voiceover, while behind him Roberto was calling the camera. "Camera #2: Zoom in on that nun talking to the *Guardia* Commandant. That's key! She was in the truck. Camera #1: Give me a close-up of the nun behind the wheel. Good! Now see if you can get one of the angels with the reviewing stand in the background. Camera #2: Pan to the truck. . . ."

Esperanza was having a quiet but intense exchange with the Commandant of the Guard, whom years before, when he was only a captain, she had persuaded to give the Fiat to the convent. She was smiling. He was smiling. He called down to his lieutenant, who reluctantly but obediently stepped aside.

The truck started forward.

Doyle shouted something to the police captain on his left, who shook his head. No further action would be taken. He turned to the mayor on his right and whispered something to him—probably doubling the amount he could expect, if he intervened right now.

The mayor started down the steps.

At that moment, less than five meters from the gates, the tire on the left front wheel of the old Fiat—the wheel that had been so abused by the rut on the mountain track—gave up the ghost. In a grotesque act of fealty, the truck sank down on its left front rim.

Time stood still. Everyone was frozen in place.

Then slowly and with great tenderness, Constanza engaged the clutch. And the Generalissimo, on bended knee, moved slowly, painfully forward.

Everyone watched, transfixed. No sound was heard but the grinding of the rim on the courtyard stones. The gallant old soldier was almost there.

And then—it was through!

A tremendous cheer went up from all who observed this gallant *paseo*, though none but a handful knew the magnitude of what had just been accomplished.

Sanctuary!

61 | the moment of truth

Commander Doyle may have lost a battle, but he was determined to win the war. Rallying his defeated forces, the mayor and the police chief, he led them through the gates and over to the sagging truck around which admirers had gathered.

Sometimes inspired command required the example of personal valor. Doyle himself climbed up on the back of the truck and started tearing off the flower-covered wire mesh in the form of a beckoning angel.

The onlookers were shocked and murmured disapprovingly, but did nothing to stop him. The police chief and mayor were right there, and they were letting him do it.

As the wire mesh began to come away, to everyone's astonishment, instead of a wooden frame being underneath, there was a stone statue—a very old stone statue. Camera 1 was catching it all. Camera 2 was now focused on the mayor, who had signaled Raul Baroja that he wanted to say something. Baroja introduced him, and the mayor addressed the camera—and all around him within earshot.

"What you are seeing," he announced, "is the result of a long, careful, and thorough investigation. A fine example of police work at its best." He turned to the police chief (as did Camera 2), and smiling, nodded his appreciation.

Turning back to the camera, he went on, "A year ago these two statues were stolen from a prominent museum in Boston, Massachusetts, where they had resided for nearly ninety years. An extensive manhunt, or should I say statue-hunt, was launched, to no avail. Because the perpetrators had hidden them until they could smuggle them and sneak them back to this monastery, whose Abbot in 1917 had sold them perfectly legitimately to the museum."

He paused, and allowed more bystanders to get closer. "But their plan was foiled by your elected and appointed officials." He and the police chief both nodded to the cameras.

Doyle had finished removing the wire mesh from the second statue, and Camera 2 now turned to them.

The mayor still had Camera 1 on him, for his concluding remarks. "The stolen property will now be taken into custody, as will the perpetrators, who will await arraignment as our guests."

And that would have seemed to be that.

Except Raul Baroja retrieved the microphone and stepped in front of Camera 1. Walking around to where the sun was on him, and the statues were directly behind him, over his right shoulder—and the mayor, the police chief, and Doyle completely out of the picture. He greeted the viewers as he would old comrades, for his commentaries were a popular feature of the Sunday video magazine.

Then he looked squarely at Camera 1 and said, "There's another story here, friends. Another way of looking at what you've just witnessed."

He started walking toward the cloister, Cameras 1 and 2 accompanying him. "Come with me now, into the cloister—the most sacred space—of one of our great national treasures. The Monastery of San Fermín, which this year is celebrating its thousandth anniversary. Here's some of the footage we shot yesterday."

He watched the portable monitor that the assistant sound-man was carrying—a distant establishing shot of the hills at sunset, the town, the monastery in the foreground.

"Last evening that hawk climbed up here, just as she has, and her ancestors have, for centuries. And this morning, for the last time of this fiesta honoring the patron saint of this monastery, the bulls ran in the streets."

He gave them ten seconds of the bull run.

"Hopefully this monastery will last another thousand years. Hopefully these cloistered walls will always grow roses, under the watchful eyes of these ancient saints." He gestured to the statues, and Camera 1 stayed on him, as Camera 2 slowly panned from the face of one statue to the next.

"But in 1917, two of these old friends, San Fermín and Santa Benedicta, were sold to an American museum. Oh, it was all very legal, very proper." He paused. "Of course, the monks who lived here had no say in the matter. It was done without their knowledge, while they were down in the Cathedral for Good Friday. But it *was* legal. We have been repeatedly assured of that."

He pointed to the empty pedestals, which Camera 2 picked up. "But two priceless antiquities disappeared on that day. And do you know what, friends? The monks of this monastery," he paused, while on the portable monitor, an interior shot showed the monks at Vespers yesterday evening, sun streaming in the windows, their heads bowed in prayer, "have prayed for the return of those statues"—cut to empty pedestals, cut to statues on the truck outside—"*every day since!*"

The engineer frantically hand-signaled Raul Baroja to stretch it, expand. The feed was going national! *Live!* Now! Keep going!

"There's a mystery involved in all of this, friends. Two mysteries. The first was that the mayor back then and the Abbot, the two men who arranged the sale, disappeared. Nothing was ever seen of them again. We know where the money went, however. Into a new, very expensive Hispano-Suiza motorcar for the mayor—that lies wrecked in ruins at the bottom of a cliff near here."

The portable showed an old archival news photo of a close-up of the wreck.

"The other mystery was where the statues went. No one knew. And ironically, because of a fire that destroyed their records, no one at the museum in Boston knew where they had come from."

He signaled the engineer, who relayed something to the mobile unit. Camera 2 located the three Sisters who were standing with the police chief—not exactly under arrest, but not exactly free, either.

"Last year, that second mystery was solved. Three Sisters of Mary of Navarre, from this monastery's sister convent just down the hill," cut to this morning's Veronica station, "saw the statues in the museum and recognized them—where they came from, and where they belonged—and went about effecting their return."

The engineer was excitedly hand signaling Raul Baroja again. Gesturing a ball—other networks had picked up the feed. The story was going global.

"If they had followed conventional means, negotiations for the return of the statues might well have dragged on for another millennium. Instead, with the approval of their Mother Superior, they followed a highly unconventional but time-honored Basque tradition. They took matters into their own hands!"

Onlookers cheered, and Raul Baroja looked into the camera solemnly, preparing to deliver his closing remarks. "Friends," he said, as if he were addressing a jury—which he was—"you will have to decide if these Sisters—these simple, holy women who have never done anything wrong in their lives—are common criminals. Or are they responding to a felt need, as they have all their lives, selflessly and at great risk? Are they thieves? Or are they patriots! Avenging angels! Innocent but brave commandos, returning to Pamplona, to Navarre—to all of Spain—what belongs here, and what was always intended to remain here!"

He smiled and beneath the camera's view, signaled to cut.

The producer jumped down from the mobile unit and came running over to Baroja, holding out his cell phone.

"It's the boss in Madrid! Wants to talk to you! Says it's the best thing you've ever done!"

Baroja took the phone and received the accolade.

Another call came in, also from Madrid, on a phone that was handed to the mayor. It was from the Presidential Palace, where the broadcast was being watched. Nothing was to be done with the statues. Or to the Sisters. Everything was on hold.

62 | d.k.

Doyle had murder in his eye when he found Brother Bartholomew on his knees in the chapel.

"Well, you've ruined me, boyo!" he shouted, not caring that he was shattering sacred silence. "Not only will I never be able to work in Art again or teach again; I'll be lucky to get a job bagging groceries!"

"Shh, Dr. D," whispered Bartholomew, smiling. "This is a house of prayer."

"'Tis a house of hypocrites, if it houses the likes of you!" He declared and went on in that vein at full volume, until the Abbot came in to see what all the shouting was about.

Bartholomew was still smiling. "Dom Miguel, this is the art expert I told you about. My former History of Art professor, and a very good one, regardless of what you might assume from his present behavior."

"Oh, come down off your high horse, you two faced, sanctimonious snot!" exclaimed Doyle, in no mood to be ameliorated.

Unperturbed, Bartholomew turned to the Abbot. "I think there may be a way to resolve this—dilemma, on whose horns we seem to be impaled. Would you take us down to the crypt?"

The Abbot led the way down the stone spiral stairs. When they had arrived, he said, "I presume you want to show him the drawings."

"I do."

The Abbot spread the eight large drawings over the calligraphy tables, then the six pages of exercise sketches.

"Take a look at these," invited Bartholomew.

Still simmering, Doyle bent over the drawings. Bartholomew watched his face, as the anger, frustration, fear—melted away. In its place came appreciation. Then profound appreciation. Then staggering awe. "Oh . . . my . . . God!"

Bartholomew pointed to the initials in the lower right-hand corner of the finished drawings: D.K. "I think these stand for Domenikos Theotocopoulos. What do you think?"

Doyle was speechless. Slowly he raised his eyes to Bartholomew's. They were full of tears. "My God!" he gasped. "My God!"

Bartholomew turned to the Abbot. "After Domenikos left here, he went to Rome to study under Titian, then to Venice to paint with Tintoretto. Then he came back to Spain and settled in Toledo. But he never forgot his heritage, and always signed his work, "The Greek."

"El Greco," said Dom Miguel.

Doyle was weeping. "This is the summit of my life, boyo. As long as I live, there will never be another moment like this."

Bartholomew put an arm around his shoulder. "We've still got a situation to resolve upstairs." He glanced down at the drawings. "But there may be a way to satisfy everyone."

The Abbot looked at him. He was not smiling. "I was listening when Raul Baroja made his moving speech. Mark Antony over the body of Caesar. I can tell you this: This monastery—this *Abbot*—is never going to permit the loss of *another* national treasure! So if you were even thinking. . . ." His voice trailed off.

Bartholomew smiled. "I could not agree more! What I had in mind is something that happens all the time. A traveling exhibition. The monastery would retain ownership of the drawings and sketches," he was thinking on his feet, "or the monastery and the Church would. But the first people to see them should be the people of Pamplona. In the Cathedral. You mentioned your Bishop's enthusiasm for the arts. After here, they could go to Madrid. I'm sure the Prado would love to have them."

Dom Miguel nodded and smiled, catching the vision.

"After that," Bartholomew continued, "a world tour. The American part of which would be arranged and orchestrated by the ILE Museum, where the drawings and sketches would make their first appearance. They would pay you a licensing fee, of course—I would think in the realm of a million dollars. Which you, Dom, would then graciously return to them, in exchange for their gift back to you of the two lost statues."

Doyle chuckled. "You're good, boyo. Too bad you're a monk. I could use a partner like you."

Bartholomew turned to the Abbot. "Do you see any reason why all the credit for this discovery shouldn't go to our friend here? After all, he did bring the museum into the picture, as it were."

Dom Miguel smiled. "No reason at all."

Bartholomew grinned and turned to Doyle. "The cameras are still up there, working on the scoop of the summer. You can go up there and give them the scoop of the year! The first televised coverage of the Lost El Grecos! You'll be on the front page of every paper in the world!"

Doyle was overwhelmed. "Give me a moment, laddie. I could not talk to me own mother in this condition."

"Take your time. But before you go up there, we need to work out your story, so we're all on the same page." He paused. "Oh, and one other thing: If I were you, I'd call the museum immediately. They're undoubtedly watching CNN."

He laughed. "You can let them in on the El Greco discovery—that *you* have just made—and suggest an amicable settlement that would put the ILE in the forefront of all American museums, and keep it there. Imagine how much they will enjoy telling the Met that they can't have the drawings until Christmas, because the National Gallery is ahead of them!"

Doyle chuckled, imagining just that.

Bartholomew turned back to Dom Miguel. "You'll need a representative to travel with the exhibition. You'll also need a scholar to provide the commentary for the art book, which will present the Lost El Grecos to the world. And an agent to license each country for the tour and negotiate appropriate royalties for the translated edition." He paused. "They might all be the same person."

Dom Miguel turned to the Irishman. "Dr. Doyle?"

Doyle bowed deeply. "Honored. Let's talk, then I'll make that call."

He turned to Bartholomew. "I will never, *ever* be able to—"

Bartholomew shook his head. "Never mind. I'm just glad we're friends again."

63 | moonlight sonata

Unable to sleep, Mother Maria Patientia stood out on her terrace, still numb from the day's events. She looked up at the half moon, not bright enough to obliterate the stars.

You did it, she thought, looking up at them. I never thought you would. I didn't see how you possibly could. In a million years I could not have plotted it to work out this well. . . . But you did it.

I am so grateful! Not for myself, but for them. You are so wonderfully kind. What can I do to thank you?

You know.

What we agreed on.

Yes.

It will be hard.

Yes.

You'll help me?

Of course.

When?

You've already begun.

And she realized that she had. Her mind was so taken up with assignment the Bishop had given her—to arrange and mount the El Greco Exhibition—that she'd not thought of Miguel once.

You *are* helping me, aren't you!

My child, you and I will be so busy planning realities to come, you will have no time for fantasies of the past.

Amen, Father! I believe it! And we can start with the El Greco. Now I think—

My child, I have called you to be my servant, not my manager. Relax. Wait on me. Let us do this together.

Yes, Father. Maria Patientia, at your service.

୧ᴥ

Up the hill that night, someone else could not sleep. Bartholomew again sought the serenity of the cloister. There were no empty pedestals now. He sat on the low wall and let the Moonlight Sonata of roses, fountain, and old saints sink in.

He heard someone come up behind him. It was Dom Miguel. "There will be many other nights for sleeping," he mused happily, addressing their joint problem. "A most extraordinary day!"

Bartholomew nodded. "I'll be leaving in the morning."

"Must you? I was hoping you could stay on a few days, see the fruit of your—of Dr. Doyle's—discovery."

"I need to get back. By the way, I've been thinking about that poem you showed me. I think it's a womb poem."

"How?"

"The spark of light is the soul, sent by God from eternal light into perfect darkness, to begin its life on earth," Bartholomew went on, half thinking to himself. "The womb. And he returns to perfect darkness—at least, complete darkness—death."

Bartholomew looked up at San Fermín. "But as I was reading it, it occurred to me that there's another perfect darkness. An earth womb. A cave."

He looked at his host. "Are there any cave systems around here?"

"Yes, as a matter of fact. But they've all been well explored. Every year cave crawlers come here."

Bartholomew frowned. "What about the waterfall? Is there a falls around here?"

Dom Miguel nodded. "It's probably the falls up above us—not far from where they found the wreck of the mayor's car."

Bartholomew nodded. "Sometimes there's a cave behind a falls. You might want to check that out. The poem was written by someone in despair, who could see no other way for him but to return to perfect darkness. If you do find a cave, I suspect you'll also find the answer."

Dom Miguel smiled. "We have two young monks who would love that challenge."

Just then the gray cat came and rubbed against Dom Miguel's leg.

"He's saying goodbye," the Abbot said, a trace of sadness in his tone.

"Are you going on a trip?"

"No, he is."

"Where's he going?"

"With you."

"*What?*"

"A gift, from our house to yours. To replace the friend you told me about, Pangur Ban—though I'm sure no cat could ever do that."

"I couldn't accept, Dom. He belongs here."

"No, his brother Perico belongs here. Miguel belongs in your friary. Besides, he will give me an excuse to come over next year and see how he's doing."

Bartholomew nodded, too moved to speak.